ACCESS DENIED
(and other eighth grade error messages)

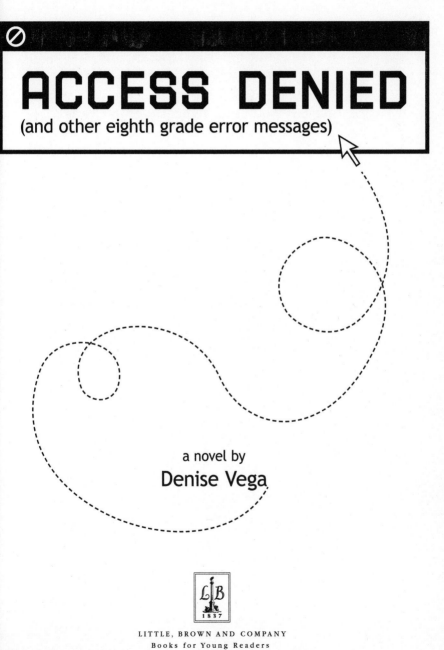

⊘ ACCESS DENIED

(and other eighth grade error messages)

a novel by
Denise Vega

LITTLE, BROWN AND COMPANY
Books for Young Readers
New York Boston

Also by Denise Vega:

Click Here
[to find out how i survived seventh grade]

Little, Brown and Company
Hachette Book Group USA
237 Park Avenue, New York, NY 10017
Visit our Web site at www.lb-kids.com

Little, Brown and Company is a division of Hachette Book Group, Inc.
The Little, Brown name and logo are trademarks of Hachette Book Group, Inc.

First Edition: July 2009

The characters and events portrayed in this book are fictitious. Any similarity to real persons,
living or dead, is coincidental and not intended by the author.

Library of Congress Cataloging-in-Publication Data
Vega, Denise.
Access denied : (and other eighth grade error messages) / by Denise Vega. —1st ed.
p. cm.
Summary: In eighth grade, computer whiz Erin Swift learns a lot about friendship,
relationships with boys, maturity, guilt, and forgiveness.
ISBN 978-0-316-03448-7
[1. Interpersonal relations—Fiction. 2. Friendship—Fiction. 3. Blogs—Fiction. 4. Middle
schools—Fiction. 5. Schools—Fiction.] I. Title.
PZ7.V4865Ac 2009
[Fic]—dc22
2008045296

10 9 8 7 6 5 4 3 2 1

RRD-C

Printed in the United States of America

To my niece, Jordan Rae Applehans,
who shared not only her eighth grade experiences with me,
but also her wisdom.
Keep doing great things, J!

This is the new and improved, totally secret & private home page of ERIN PENELOPE SWIFT. Thanks 2 computer camp, I added way cool stuff like video & podcasts. I'm using more "lingo" now that I can finally IM and I know more of that stuff. I rock.

THINGS YOU SHOULD KNOW ABOUT ME 😊

* I am totally over the Year of Humiliating Events (YOHE), aka seventh grade, when this personal, private, no-one-will-see-but-me blog was blasted over the school Intranet (that would be Molly Brown Middle School, aka MBMS) & every1 hated me 4 awhile.

* Jillian Gail Hennessey—aka Jilly—was my BFF . . . then wasn't cuz of YOHE . . . now is again—goes out w/ Bus Boy (Jon Lanner). I call him Bus Boy cuz he 1st noticed her on the bus last year. Now he's at Wash Hi w/ Chris, my big bro. Jilly & I were not on the same track at MBMS last year but they switch it around every year so maybe this year we'll be 2gether.

* Mark, Rosie, Carla & Tyler r also buds . . . went 2 computer camp w/ all except Carla, who isn't really into computers the way we r . . . Carla was my locker partner last year & is hanging out w/ us more . . . I had crush on Tyler during camp . . . he liked Rosie . . . Rosie liked some guy from another school . . . we're done w/ all that now.

* I used 2 have a major crush on Mark but no1 knew until the BN (Blog Nightmare) . . . then he liked Jilly . . . then didn't . . . we actually had a lame kiss & decided friends better—he started going out w/ Kara Simmons in July.

* Serena Worthington has always been mean 2 me but last year we came 2 a truce. We're not *friend* friends but she did come 2 my bday party & we can @ least talk & joke around a little now. I deleted the SW Hate-o-Rama/Dislike-o-Rama page cuz of that & also cuz she doesn't need 2 be taking up space on my website (except 4 here where I explain—2 WHO???—why her page is history).

THINGS THAT BOTHER ME 🏴‍☠️

✱ My parents seem 2 be on my case more l8ly.

✱ I can't seem 2 talk 2 my mom like I used 2.

THINGS THAT JUST ARE 🌀

✱ This year my parents made me choose b/t bball & soccer so I picked bball.

✱ Chris still wears orange boxers w/ green frogs on them, even tho that info got out during the YOHE . . . dating Bethany since May.
DISGUSTING FACT #1: Bethany picks her nose.
DISGUSTING FACT #2: She has touched Chris w/ those booger fingers.
2 bad cuz she's really nice.

INFO ABOUT THE LINKS

MY LIFE is still where I spill my guts. I tried not writing in a blog at all but couldn't do it.

MUG SHOTS has a few pix of me & my buds.

HOT—⊙—METER is where I'll list all the hot guys in my life (please let me have some). Right now it's just Mark cuz even tho we r just friends, he is still very hot & he's the only 1 I can think of. & yes, the text scrolls—thank u computer camp & JavaScript.

LOOK AND LISTEN is where I have videos & podcasts. Jilly & I made some goofy videos @ her house & Mark & I did a podcast about the history of soccer 4 English last year. He was the interviewer & I was the soccer ball.

SNICKERS is just there cuz I love Snickers almost as much as I love cherry Tootsie Pops & when I click it, it reminds me where my stash of Snickers is.

THE PED STOPS HERE

CHAPTER 1

PARENTAL MISGUIDANCE SUGGESTED

"WHY CAN'T I GO?" I stood on one side of the island in the kitchen, my mom on the other. She was chopping onions for dinner with a chopper that made a loud thwacking sound when she pressed down on the handle.

"Because —" *Thwack!* "— you're too young to go to a rock concert." She paused to look up at me. "I know Carla's dad will be there but it's not about parental supervision. It's about being in an environment that you don't need to be exposed to right now." She paused, itching her nose with the back of her hand. "Maybe if it was a different band. But that one . . ."

Her voice trailed off as my insides curled up, hardening into stone. Every time I turned around lately there was a new rule and each one began with NO. No staying out past ten on a weekend night (the city curfew was eleven!), no short skirts (which I don't wear anyway), no unsupervised parties, no cell until high school, no web presence (meaning no MySpace, no live blog, no nothing, even though I totally know about being safe online) — and on and on until we got to the latest NO — no rock concert. They did say yes to IM *finally* but way late — most of my friends had been IMing since 5th or 6th grade.

"Why do you always do this?" I asked. "Everyone else gets to go."

Which technically wasn't true. Rosie wasn't going either. But Jilly, Mark, Tyler, and all of my other friends were.

"You know better than to use the 'everyone else is doing it' argument. That doesn't fly in this house." Mom scraped the chopped onions into a bowl and placed another half onion in the chopper. Her lips pursed as she concentrated on another *thwack*. A few gray strands curled out of her brown hair and her eyelids seemed to droop. She suddenly looked like someone I didn't know—or maybe just someone who didn't know *me*—and I had no idea when that had happened. After the BN we'd gotten close but then summer came and I was doing a lot more with my friends and things felt different. We never used to fight—well, almost never. But now we do.

"But it's true," I said. "And it's embarrassing to always have to say my parents won't let me." They wouldn't even let me go to just any PG-13 movie. Hello? PG-*13*? *I'm* thirteen? But no, my mom had to see the movie first or go to one of those online parental movie guides that rated the amount of "bad stuff" in the movie and described various scenes. She practically had to write a research paper on it. And sometimes she'd do all that and wouldn't let me go and I'd have to lie and tell my friends I had a family thing so I wouldn't be completely humiliated. But I had a feeling they knew anyway, which made it even worse.

"Well, I'm sorry if we embarrass you, Erin, but that's the way it is." *Thwack!* She dumped the rest of the onions in the bowl. "I didn't go to a rock concert until I was sixteen."

"Things are different now," I said. "Kids grow up faster."

My mom shook her head. "No, they don't. You're just getting exposed to things at an earlier age. That doesn't mean you can handle them." She picked at some stray bits of onion stuck on the chopper blade. "It's about safety and well-being and whether your mind and emotions can process all of it in an effective manner." She turned to the sink and washed her hands, scrubbing each finger.

I groaned. I hated when she talked like some parenting magazine article. "But you were so proud of how I handled things last year. Don't you think I can handle this?"

"We *are* proud of how you handled last year. But this is different." My mom put her hands on the counter and looked at me, her face softening. "I know how important this is to you, Erin. Really. But you have to understand that it's my job to do what's best for you, regardless of what you want or what other parents are allowing their kids to do." She crossed to the sink and rinsed out the chopper. "I know this seems like the end of the world right now, but there will be lots of concerts in your life, Erin. And lots of other things when you're ready for them. I don't know why you all have to rush out and do everything right now."

"I'm not rushing out to do everything right now," I said. "I just want to go to this one concert with my friends right before we start *eighth grade.*"

"You're not going, Erin," my mom said, placing the chopper on the rack to dry, "and that's final."

The stone inside me cracked.

"I'm not a baby!" I shouted. "And I wish you'd stop treating me like one!" Tears pricked my eyes. Why did that always happen? Why did I feel like crying when I was mad? I ran upstairs and slammed my door, enjoying the satisfying *bang* that reverberated through the house. I didn't care if my "behavior" wasn't showing my maturity. It felt good to slam a door.

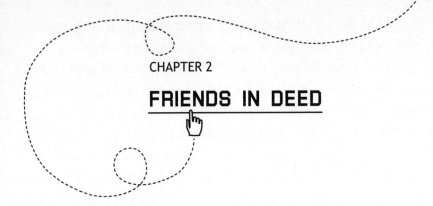

CHAPTER 2

FRIENDS IN DEED

I STAYED IN MY ROOM the rest of the night, refusing to come down for dinner. I wouldn't even talk to my dad, who tried to get me to come out with a lame joke about a rock star walking into a bar. How could he make fun of my situation when he was one of the two Parental Paranoids keeping me from having a good time?

I turned up the volume on my speakers in reply.

"If you get hungry, you can warm up some food later," he said loudly through the door.

"I won't get hungry," I replied, trusting the music to drown out my grumbling stomach.

"Okay," he said, "But if you or your stomach changes your mind . . ." He tapped twice on the door before shuffling away.

"Never!" I shouted after him, flopping down on my bed. Maybe I should go on a hunger strike until they let me go to the concert. They would find me wasting away in my room, barely able to raise my head off my pillow, but with Jilly's help I'd have just enough strength to put on my new probably-too-short shorts with the to-die-for layered tank tops, dab on some makeup, fix my hair, and slip into a car that would whisk me away to the concert. There I would finally eat and regain my full strength so I could dance and clap my hands to the beat.

The stomach grumbles were becoming unbearable. I rolled over on my side and tried to think of something besides the roast chicken that was cooking in the oven, its aroma wafting up the stairs and under my door.

I glanced at the clock. Barely ten minutes had passed since my dad had come up. Why did I say never? Never was a long, long time.

An hour later, there was a sharp knock on the door. I sat up straight, grateful for getting lost in my book. I was still hungry, but I didn't feel like I might start eating the bedpost anymore.

"Yeah?" I said cautiously.

"It's me." My brother's voice was low outside the door.

"Come in."

Chris stepped inside, carrying a plate of food and a glass of water. It was all I could do not to leap off my bed and gobble it down with my fingers.

"I figured you were lying about being hungry." He held the plate out and I immediately shoveled a mound of mashed potatoes and gravy into my mouth. He pulled out the chair and flipped it around so he was sitting with his arms resting on the back. "I know you're mad that you can't go to the concert but you've got to suck it up or they're never going to let you do anything."

"I can't help it," I said, between bites. "It's totally unfair." When he started to speak, I held up my hand. "And don't tell me you didn't get to go to a concert until you were in high school. This isn't about you."

Chris laughed. "No, it's about you messing up your future. And mine. They're talking about having a family night the night of the concert so you won't feel left out. There goes my Friday night."

"Sorry," I muttered.

Chris brushed his fingers through his hair, making it stand up at odd angles. "Just be cool, Erin. That's all I'm saying. Take it from someone who's been there."

That night Mark sent me an IM.

> **Slamdunk12:** Bummer about the concert. We'll miss u.
> **Webqueen429:** Thx. Maybe they'll change their minds.
> **Slamdunk12:** Hope so.

I watched the cursor blinking on my screen. Then Mark started typing again.

> **Slamdunk12:** Confession: My mom screens PG-13 movies b4 she'll let me c them.
> **Webqueen429:** WHAT??? Serious?
> **Slamdunk12:** Dead

Mark had to be one of the coolest people on the planet. I knew he was telling me because of the whole concert thing. How many guys would admit something like that?

> **Webqueen429:** ur just saying that.
> **Slamdunk12:** No. Truth.
> **Webqueen429:** Mine 2. But u knew that already, right?
> **Slamdunk12:** ☺
> **Webqueen429:** So they screen PG-13 movies but u can go 2 a rock concert?
> **Slamdunk12:** Strange but true.

I smiled.

> **Webqueen429:** Thx
> **Slamdunk12:** 4 what?

I wanted to say for our friendship. For knowing I felt bad and trying to make me feel better. For just being you. But I knew if I said all that he'd either barf on his keyboard or run screaming from the room.

So I didn't.

A second IM window popped up on my screen.

Jillrox713: EPS, u there?

Webqueen429: Yep.

Jillrox713: Just wanted 2 say it totally stinks abt concert.

Webqueen429: u could stay home w/ me 2 show yr support.

Jillrox713: <VBG> u no I luv u but —

Webqueen429: u really want 2 go.

Jillrox713: Is that ok?

It would have been great if she was willing to stay with me but bad too because I would have felt guilty for making her miss it.

Webqueen429: Sure. I was just kidding. What r u doing right now?

Jillrox713: Texting Jon. U?

Webqueen429: IMing Mark.

Jillrox713: Ooh la la. Does Kara know?

Webqueen429: ha ha.

Jillrox713: Say hey for me.

Ding.

Slamdunk12: E, u there?

Webqueen429: Sorry. Jilly was IMing. She says hey.

Slamdunk12: Hey 2 Jilly.

I wanted to keep talking but Chris was breathing down my neck to use the computer.

Webqueen429: Chris needs the computer. Gtg cu

Slamdunk12: Hey 2 Chris. cu

That night I lay in my bed, smiling up at the ceiling. It totally stunk that I couldn't go to the concert but it made me feel good that Mark cared enough to tell me about the movie thing and Jilly had checked in. It was good to have friends who understood when your parents were driving you crazy.

Sunday, August 17

THINGS THAT ROCK 🎸

* School starts on Tues . . . Jilly & I r on the same track!

* Rosie, Tyler, & Mark r also on my track—clearly a sign that 8th grade will be the BEST. Serena is 2.

* Mark & Jilly have been super nice since the concert . . . said it was fun but not as fun w/o me which I know was a big fat lie but nice of them 2 say, esp Mark cuz Kara was there 2.

THINGS THAT STINK 🌪

* School starts on Tues—summer is almost over.

* A pimple is getting ready 2 burst on my chin. I'm trying everything 2 make it go away by Tues.

5 THINGS I PLAN TO DO THIS YEAR ★

* Make the best MBMS website EVER.

* Have my first period in an unembarrassing place @ an unembarrassing time (no idea how 2 do this but will think of something)—*see TOP 5 FIRST PERIOD NIGHTMARES chart*

* Not obsess about boys (except 2 judge them 4 Hot-o-Meter).

* Strut my 8th grade stuff cuz any1 who can survive the YOHE can DO & BE ANYTHING (even if my parents don't think so).

Will Erin P. Swift meet her goals? Will she find love among the wireless networks? (Finding love is different from obsessing about boys, isn't it?) . . . Stay tuned.

HOT—✪—METER

💚 #1 Mark Sacks—the hair, the butt in shorts—need I say more?
Other cute guys will go here as I spot them . . .

TOP 5 FIRST PERIOD NIGHTMARES
(not in any particular order)

1. In school, wearing white pants, unprepared.

2. In school, wearing white pants, in front of people I don't know, unprepared.

3. In school, wearing white pants, in front of the boy I used 2 like who is now a good friend, unprepared.

   (Even tho I don't own a pair of white pants, these r all still scary.)

4. In school, ANYWHERE, w/ ANYONE, wearing ANYTHING.

5. At home w/ only my brother, who won't even look at clean female undergarments, let alone toss me a pad.

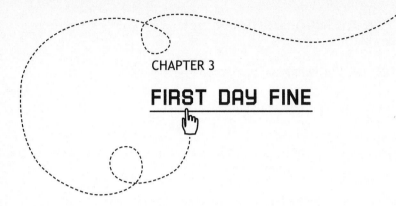

CHAPTER 3

FIRST DAY FINE

JILLY AND I SAT ON the bus together on Tuesday, taking one of the seats in the back. There wasn't a sign, there wasn't an official rule—everyone just knew the eighth graders had dibs on the last four rows. I noticed the seventh graders sunk low in their seats, eyes shifting back and forth, never looking back at us—the eighth graders.

"Your hair looks great," Jilly said as the bus lurched down the street.

"No thanks to you," I laughed. Back in July she'd tried to put red highlights in my hair and turned parts of it orange. Not attractive. Now it was back to plain brown. But the sun had brought out some natural red and I'd gotten it cut so it fell softly around my face.

"Yeah, well, I *thought* I knew what I was doing." She laughed and brushed her own blondish-brown hair over her shoulder. She had it pulled back in a barrette with two tiny braids hanging beneath it, tied off with beads. Her light eyeshadow brought out the gold flecks in her eyes and her blush and mascara were just right. Of course, she started wearing makeup at the beginning of seventh grade so she had lots of practice, plus two older sisters who gave her tips. I was pretty new at the makeup game and didn't wear much. Jilly tried to get me to wear more, but it felt weird, so I didn't. And I never wore any when I played sports, though lots of girls did. I mean, it was *sports*. Get a grip.

"So," Jilly said, bringing me back to the bus. "Is Mark in any of your classes?"

Oh, here we go. She thought I still *like* liked him.

The bus screeched to a stop and Kara got on, sitting two rows ahead of us with some of her friends. She hadn't ridden our bus last year because her mom drove her. But now her mom was working so she had to take the bus.

Jilly watched Kara. "It's very rare that girls and boys can just be friends, you know. There has to be the exact right mix of things."

I sighed. I knew she wouldn't give it up.

"I guess Mark and I have the right mix," I said.

Tapping a polished nail on the seat in front of her, Jilly shook her head. "There has to be absolutely no physical attraction, you should have things in common but not things that might bring you together romantically, and it helps if you're both involved with someone else."

"We're friends," I said.

"Because he has a girlfriend." She applied lip gloss using a small mirror.

"We'd be friends even if he didn't have a girlfriend."

"Not for long," Jilly said. "It's the *When Harry Met Sally* syndrome."

"The what?"

"It's an old movie my mom told me about." Jilly pulled out a mirror and lip gloss. "It's about how men and women can't ever really be just friends."

"That's crazy," I said.

Jilly raised an eyebrow. "If you try to be real friends with a boy, friends like you and I are, it won't stay just friends. It will always turn into something more."

"Do you have proof of this?" I asked. "In real life?"

"Well, no," Jilly admitted. "But I bet if we thought about it, we could come up with some." She rubbed her lips together before shoving the tube and mirror into her makeup bag.

"You can look me right in the eye and tell me you have absolutely no feelings at all for Mark 'Cute Boy' Sacks?"

I cringed at the nickname I had used for him in my blog last year. "Don't call him that," I whispered.

"No one's listening," she said, leaning closer. "So?"

"He's my friend, Jilly. Geez. Not everything is about romance, you know."

She sighed. "Okay, so I'm a little bit jealous." She grinned her look-at-my-mouth grin. "Do I have anything in my braces?" She'd gotten them right after the spring dance last year.

"All clear," I said. Then, "Jealous?"

Jilly ran her tongue over her teeth. "I wish Mark and I could have stayed friends. He's really nice and he was easy to talk to." She sighed. "But it just felt weird afterward, though it's easier now that so much time has passed and we're both going out with other people."

I nodded, grateful to see Rosie getting on the bus. Even though Rosie had her share of crushes, she wasn't into talking about it all the time so I could count on her to change the subject.

"Rosie!" I waved her down.

She pushed her way to the back of the bus and sat down in the seat behind us. No braids this year—just a short cut that curled nicely around her ears and made her look sophisticated.

"Hey, guys," she said as we exchanged high fives.

"I was just telling Erin there's no way girls and boys can stay friends," Jilly said to Rosie. I groaned. "There will always be one or the other or both who will start to like the other one more than a friend. Right?"

Before Rosie could answer, I fired my own question at her. "You and Mark have been friends since kindergarten or something. No attraction, right?"

Rosie furrowed her brow. "I think I kind of liked him in third grade and he liked me in fourth but he's more like my brother now, you know?"

"Exactly!" Jilly said triumphantly. "They totally don't count, Erin. My theory still holds."

"No it doesn't," I said, shaking my head. "They've been just friends for years."

"You two should just agree to disagree on this one," Rosie said before turning to Jilly. "So, how's Mr. Lanner?"

"Don't get her started on Bus Boy," I said, though I was grateful for the change of topic.

Jilly stuck her tongue out at me before looking at Rosie. "I miss him a lot. And this," she said, waving her hand around the bus, "is so—what's that word we learned in English last year? *Anticlimactic.*" She turned to me. "Remember how nervous and excited we were last year? How it was all a big adventure?"

I remembered the nervous part, all right, but it wasn't a big adventure—more like a nightmare. I was thrilled to be sitting on the bus right now with no one calling me names or asking about my totally secret, private blog.

"I'm sure you'll find an adventure somewhere, Hennessey." Rosie smiled. Then she turned to talk to a girl who had been trying to get her attention.

"I don't want adventure," Jilly said. "I just want Jon." She sat up suddenly and looked at me. "Do you think he'll meet someone in high school?"

"Well, I —"

"Maybe he already has," she said, gripping my arm. "Maybe he met a girl on the bus, just like he met me last year, and he's teasing her right now and she's giving him big eyes and he's asking her to sit with him and she's saying yes and then they're comparing class schedules and they find out they have lunch together and three other classes and then they run into each other in the hall and —" She covered her face with her hands. "I can't stand it! He's cheating on me already."

I sighed. "He isn't cheating on you, Jilly." Sticking my hand in the front pocket of my backpack, I felt around to make sure I'd packed a stash of Snickers. "He doesn't even take the bus, remember? He's in a carpool."

Jilly pulled her hands away from her face. "Oh, right. I forgot." She bit her lip and looked out the window again. "And there weren't any girls in the carpool."

"There, you see? No girls in the carpool. You're safe."

Jilly moaned. "Hardly. What about all the girls in his classes? And at lunch?" She shook her head. "I'm doomed."

"Jilly," I said, "don't worry about it until there's something to worry about."

She turned to me, eyes wide. "Do you think there's going to be something to worry about? Did he say something to you?"

"Oh, yeah. I forgot. He told me he was planning to do something evil behind your back while he was in high school. And of course he wanted to share it with me because I would never say anything to his girlfriend who happens to be my best friend."

Jilly relaxed against the seat. "Okay, so I'm being stupid."

I nodded. "That's the first smart thing you've said."

CHAPTER 4

HILLS AND VALLEYS

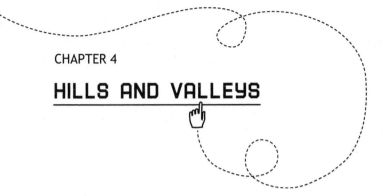

LOCKER COMBINATION? CHECK. OPENED ON first try? Check. Locker partner? Unknown, but I was in eighth grade now; I didn't worry about locker partners or who I sat with at lunch.

After putting my backpack away, I hung up two photos; one was of Jilly and me and the other was of the I-Club gang—me, Mark, Rosie, Tyler, and Steve. I closed the door, leaning against it as I looked down the familiar hall. Jilly's locker was down at the other end so she was making her way there. We weren't in the same homeroom but we had language arts and Spanish together.

I could see Mark down the hall too, talking to some guys. After cutting his hair last year, I was glad to see he'd grown it long again so it covered one eye. Kara stood next to him, her hand in his back pocket. She looked only at Mark, even when he wasn't talking, as if he was the only person in the hall.

Mark Sacks had a way of doing that to you.

I turned away before memories of old feelings came up, because sometimes the memory of a feeling could feel like a real feeling and I didn't need that. Surveying the hall in the other direction, I noticed the freshly painted walls, how the floors gleamed and the smell of disinfectant wafted through the air. The custodian, Mr. Foslowski, had been busy this summer.

"What trouble are you planning to start this year, young lady?"

Speaking of —

"Hi, Mr. F," I said as we knocked fists. He looked older this year, thinner, and he seemed to have even less of his gray hair, if that was possible. But he still had his goatee, and that same mischievous look in his eyes, the same broad smile. "The school looks great." I raised my eyebrows at him. "And to answer your question: none. I will be starting no trouble this year. And I won't be getting into any that I didn't start either."

"Never say never, Erin Swift." Mr. F winked at me. "Got your supply?"

I tapped the locker where my backpack hung on its hook. "Snickers and Tootsie Pops accounted for." Last year Mr. F and I found we shared a love of Tootsie Pops after I spilled my guts to him about Mark and Jilly liking each other and some other stuff. Over the summer I'd done some yard work for him and his wife and helped them with a garage sale to earn some extra money. And when our water heater flooded the basement, Mr. F had come to the rescue with a wet vac and lots of fans. We'd had them over for dinner a few times and they'd had us over too. We were now officially friends.

"Excellent," he said. "You know where to find me if you run out." He nodded again. "It's good to see you, Erin."

"You too, Mr. F."

We knocked fists again, then he tipped his spray bottle at me and walked away.

"Excuse me," a voice behind me said. "I think this is my locker."

I turned around and nearly collided with the biggest pair of breasts I'd ever seen. Not that I've encountered that many, especially up close and personal, but I'd seen a few.

"Uh, sorry." I was frozen to my spot, still a bit shocked.

"Can you quit staring at my chest and move so I can open the locker?"

My face shot through with heat and I raised my eyes to her face. Her eyeliner dramatically outlined her eyes and her eyeshadow was a deep bronze, capped with a darker brown. She looked about sixteen. She was a couple of inches shorter than me, even in her black boots, and wore a tight black skirt and a yellow t-shirt with sleeves as short as you could get without calling it a tank top, which was against the school dress code. A black belt with metal studs and metal bracelets jangling from her wrists completed the outfit. I'd bet my Nano she got to go to any concert she wanted to and didn't have to get permission for a PG-13 movie.

"I'm sorry," I said, stepping back.

She didn't say anything, just flipped her long, curly blond hair over her shoulder. It was clearly out of a bottle because I could see dark roots and her eyebrows were brown. She also had two pretty serious zits on her chin and one on her cheek, not very well hidden underneath her base makeup. I touched my own chin, feeling the pimple that had erupted, despite my best efforts to destroy it.

"I'm Erin," I said. "Erin Swift. I guess we're locker partners."

"Lucky me." She spun the lock without checking the combination, swinging the door open on the first try. She frowned as she surveyed my things.

"Do you need more room?" I said. "Or would you prefer the top shelf? It's just that I'm on the tall side and —"

"It's fine," she said, shoving a large black shoulder bag into the locker and sliding her books onto the bottom shelf. Then she pulled out a mirror with a magnetic back.

"Mind?" she said, pointing to the inside of the door.

"No." I didn't really want to look at myself every day but I also didn't want to start off the year with an annoyed locker partner.

She slapped it up and pulled a makeup case out of the black bag. Quickly and expertly, she applied more eyeliner, mascara, and lip gloss. She rubbed her full lips together, then flicked off a stray bit of mascara stuck to her eyelid. Now she looked about eighteen.

"So who do you have for homeroom?" I asked.

Pulling a wrinkled piece of paper from a pocket in her skirt, she squinted. "Brown."

"I've got Rochester but they're both this way," I said, motioning down the hall. She nodded and started walking quickly. I fell into step beside her, though I couldn't tell if she really wanted to walk with me or not. "Which track were you on last year?"

"None," she said. "I just moved here from Silicon Valley." I lifted my eyebrows. The computer mecca? "Near San Jose, California."

"I know where Silicon Valley is," I said.

"My bad," she said. "You into computers?"

"Pretty much." I told her about the Intranet Club—which would now be the Internet/Intranet Club, I guess—and how my mom was a webmaster. I didn't tell her about my totally secret private website and blog because, well, it was totally secret and private and besides, I'd just met her.

"I'm not usually a joiner," she said, "but that sounds pretty cool. And my dad's a real techie, an innovator in some of the Internet technology. It's kind of in my blood, you know?"

Great. She probably knew *way* more than I did.

The first bell rang.

"Got to get to homeroom," I said, turning down the hall.

"Right," she said. "Thanks for the chat, Erin Swift."

It wasn't until I was settled in my seat that I realized she'd never told me her name.

Tuesday, August 19

Reede Harper. That's her name . . . didn't even have 2 ask cuz people were already talking abt her. Apparently, she's famous & she's only been here 1 day.

"Reede w/ an e on the end" — that's what she told me l8r.

Reede w/ an e on the end is way cooler than Erin. Why did my parents have 2 name me after some great-aunt I'd never met? Why couldn't I have a cool name like Reede?

THINGS WE KNOW ABOUT REEDE HARPER ☀

* She has big 1s.

* She knows famous computer people.

* All the guys love her.

* Most of the girls already h8 her. The 1s that don't r only pretending 2 like her so they can get in on some of the boy attn she's getting.

* She is way cool w/o even trying. How does that work?

THINGS WE KNOW ABOUT ERIN SWIFT 🐌

* She has normal-sized 1s 4 a 13-year-old (so why do I feel bad? Some girls r still flat. As in ironing board, table, door. Jilly's still barely got anything but she looks amazing, like a model, so she doesn't have 2 worry).

* She knows no1 famous except the guy who used 2 do local stinky cheese commercials cuz he went 2 college w/ her mom.

* No guys love her, most don't even know her, tho some might like her as a friend.

* Most girls don't know her either & of those who do, some like her, some don't.

THINGS THAT ANNOY ME & I'M NOT SURE WHY ⚕

* Tyler said something abt Reede . . . heard him talking @ lunch . . . didn't think he noticed girls like her.

* Reede is definitely going 2 join I-Club. I should be happy we'll have someone who knows a lot of cool stuff 2 make our site really awesome.

So why am I not happy?

CHAPTER 5

MAKING HISTORY

I SAT BETWEEN ROSIE AND Tyler in U.S. history the next day, with Mark behind me. Serena sat on the other side of the room. We waved at each other before she turned to chat with friends. Jilly told me Serena was going out with someone from another track. "And he's cute," she had said, as if only someone ugly would like Serena, who was actually pretty and could be nice when she wanted to, which I hoped would be a little more often this year.

"You're not going to blow us off now that Jilly's on our track too, are you?" Mark snapped a pencil at me and I caught it with one hand.

"No way," I said, tossing it back. "Besides, we've got I-Club."

"I-Club's going to be great this year," Tyler said. "Let's do streaming video." He still wore baggy pants and spiked his hair with the same gel that smelled slightly of pine. It was good to know some things didn't change.

I pulled out my notebook as our teacher stepped in. Mr. Perkins was tall and thin, with a cute goatee that matched his brown hair. Rosie and I looked at each other and grinned. History just got a lot more interesting.

The bell rang and Mr. Perkins called us to attention, then started taking attendance. A minute later, Reede Harper arrived, stopping just inside the door. She smiled and ducked her head, her long hair falling over her face like she was embarrassed, but it seemed like an act. Everyone's eyes shifted towards her and I knew if I looked around, tongues would be hanging out of mouths.

"Stop drooling," I said to Tyler. He scowled at me.

"And you are . . . ?" Mr. Perkins asked.

"Reede Harper," she said. "I'm new. Sorry I'm late." She didn't look sorry and didn't offer an explanation or a tardy pass. Mr. Perkins didn't ask for either but I wondered. Her hair was messed up around her face like she'd tried to fix it without a brush or mirror. Maybe she was already making out with someone in one of the custodian closets. Maybe Mr. F had already caught her. The thought gave me a ripple of satisfaction.

"Welcome, Reede," Mr. Perkins said, making a mark in his attendance book. "Since you're late, you'll have to take a seat in the dreaded front row." He motioned to an empty desk right in front of his, next to two other empty desks. Then he continued with attendance. "Michael Royston?"

"Here."

"Erin Swift?"

"Here." I raised my hand and Mr. Perkins nodded. Reede swung around in her seat and stared at me for a moment, then turned back around.

Tyler leaned over, whispering. "You know her?"

"She's my locker partner." I suddenly felt important, then stupid for feeling that way.

"Cool," Tyler said. "Maybe you could introduce me."

I rolled my eyes. "Introduce yourself."

"Fine," Tyler said. He turned and faced front, tapping his pencil on top of his textbook.

I sighed. "Tyler, if you want to meet her, you should just —"

"I said it was fine."

"But you're mad, and you shouldn't be. I think —"

"Miss Swift, is it?" My head shot up. Mr. Perkins was looking right at me, along with the rest of the class. "I know the first few days back are exciting and you want to catch up with your friends, but we've got a lot to accomplish as we travel back in time through U.S. history. Let's save the chitchat for your breaks."

"Sorry." I glanced at Tyler, who was looking straight ahead as if Mr. Perkins and his class were the most interesting thing in the world and he hadn't just been whispering to me so I had to whisper back.

"Okay, class," Mr. Perkins said, "I'm going to go over our course schedule."

Papers shuffled as we listened. Reede was nodding her head. And nodding her head some more. Ah ha. She was listening to her iPod. No wonder she was wearing her hair down around her face—it was hiding the cord that was no doubt snaking up the back of her shirt, the earbuds tucked inside her ears. We weren't allowed to have any kind of "listening or electronic device" in the classroom, and I couldn't believe she'd risk that right in front of Mr. Perkins, who stood just a few feet away.

I had a feeling Reede Harper did a lot of things against the rules.

After class, Reede walked out the door, surrounded by several boys. Mark, Rosie, and I weren't far behind.

"Gotta go," Mark said as we reached the hall intersection.

"Say hi to Kara for us," I said. Too bad Jilly wasn't here to see Mature Erin as she showed she no longer had feelings for Mark and wished him well with his little girlfriend.

"Right," Mark said, turning down the other hall without looking back.

"Are they all good?" Rosie asked when he left.

"Why are you asking me?" I said. "You're the one who's known him forever."

"But you're the one he talks to," Rosie said. Most girls would sound jealous. Rosie was just stating a fact.

"He hasn't said anything to me," I said. "They seem fine."

"Okay," Rosie said as she dropped me off at my locker, "see you on the bus later."

Reede showed up a minute later, smiling at her followers and waving them on. Then she turned to our locker. "Infants," she muttered as she pulled a pack of gum from her backpack. "Like I would ever go out with any of them."

"Yeah," I said, "a lot of them are really immature."

Reede leaned against the locker next to ours, blowing a bubble. It grew large in front of her face before she sucked in, popping it with a satisfying smack. "This school blows."

I stiffened. "It's not all bad," I said. "There are some pretty cool people here." I exchanged my history notebook for language arts and Spanish.

"I've just got to get through this year." She blew another bubble as her eyes roamed my body like some kind of airport scanning device. "You know, you're really cute but you don't know how to take it to hot."

I scowled at her. I hardly registered that she'd said I was "really cute." Where did she get off dissing my appearance the second day of school? "I'm an athlete," I said. Brilliant. I was basically agreeing that I wasn't hot and this was why.

"Athletes can be hot," Reede said, her eyes still skimming me. It felt like she was trying to mentally transform Erin the Ugly into Erin the Gorgeous. "What sports?"

"Mostly basketball but some soccer." Why was I talking to her? "So, did you get everything you needed out of the locker or what?"

"Don't need anything the first week. You just have to show up." She pulled her schedule out of her back pocket. "Where's Room 248?"

"I'm going that way," I said. "I could —"

"Never mind," she said, "I'll find it." She strode down the hall, her hips moving in a way I didn't think mine ever could, even with a lot of practice.

What was *her* problem? Was she too cool to be seen with me? It wasn't like I was a total loser at MBMS. At least, not anymore.

I slammed the locker door and a few people jumped. I didn't know what bothered me more — that she didn't want to walk with me or that I cared so much that she didn't.

Wednesday, August 20

THINGS THAT ARE REALLY ANNOYING 💀

> 💚 **#1 Mark Sacks** — the hair, the butt in shorts — need I say more?
> **#2 Mr. Perkins**
> *Other cute guys will go here as I spot them . . .*

✳ Reede Harper is totally stuck up.

✳ Even though RH is totally stuck up, people still like her.

✳ I survived the YOHE, helped create cool effects 4 the spring play last year, people know who I am & not in a bad way anymore & NONE OF IT MATTERS. Reede Harper is IT.

✳ I want Reede 2 like me even after she dissed my looks. WHY???

THINGS THAT MAKE ME WONDER ☯

✳ Why haven't Jilly & her sisters taken me 2 hot?

✳ Could Reede Harper take me 2 hot?

✳ Do I want 2 go 2 hot & have people notice me 4 that?

✳ What would it be like 2 get attn 4 something besides complete & utter humiliation?

Mark just IM'd about I-Club. He knows some 7th graders who might be good. So glad he isn't worshipping Reede. Thank God 4 Kara.

I know it's lame that the only guy besides Mark on my Hot-o-Meter list so far is my history teacher. But he *is* very cute. Rosie thinks so 2 . . . & I want 2 have more than 1 on the 'Meter so there.

Also, it takes my mind off RH.

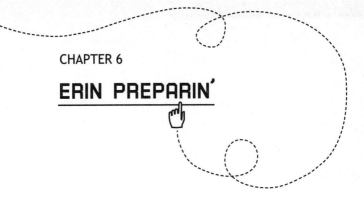

REEDE WAS STANDING AT OUR locker the next morning, applying mascara.

"No adoring fans?" I asked as she stepped aside to make room for me.

"No, thank God." She straightened up and did another eye-scan over my body.

"Would you mind not staring at me?" I said as I opened my backpack.

"Sorry." She shrugged and looked back at the mirror. "I kind of have this ability to make someone over in my mind and sometimes I do it without realizing it. You don't need much of a makeover, I just see you with —"

"Not interested," I interrupted, grabbing the books I'd need for my next few classes. "It's not all about looks, you know." Even as I said it, I was hearing her words echo in my head: *You don't need much of a makeover.*

Reede raised an eyebrow. "No. But they help."

I closed the locker just as Mark and Kara walked towards us down the hall.

"Hi, Erin." Kara's voice was bright, but she didn't look at me.

"Swift," Mark said, pointing at me. "Get ready to die at the Y."

I shook my head, smiling. That was his new phrase whenever we played basketball, which we were supposed to do this weekend. "You're the one who's going down," I said.

Kara's smile flipped to a frown.

A familiar twinge of guilt-annoyance pinched me. Kara claimed it was fine that Mark and I played basketball together, that she knew we were only friends and "totally trusted" us. But here she was looking pissed at the mention of Mark and me going to shoot hoops.

When I had asked Jilly about it, she had said of course it was fine because Mark and I had been playing together before he went out with anyone. And he always invited her.

"You're lucky because there aren't too many girls who have a friend who's a boy — that they do stuff with outside of school," she had said. Then she had said something really cool: "You shouldn't have to give up a good friendship for anyone." The way she had looked at me, I knew she was thinking of last year, when she told me I had to pick between my friendship with her and my friendship with Mark. Thankfully, we had worked it out after a big fight. But it was cool that she could bring it up.

"Who's the hottie with the hair?" Reede's voice brought me back to the hallway.

I frowned. I really didn't want Mark on Reede's radar. He seemed like the only guy who was immune to her. "Just another infant," I said, using her word.

"That one's an exception," she said, looking at me. "So, who's he to you?"

None of your business, I wanted to say but instead I said, "a friend."

She snorted. "Does he know that?"

"What do you mean?"

She glanced down the hall. "You didn't catch that little energy surge he sent your way?"

"Energy surge?"

Reede tucked her books against her hip. "He likes you, girl."

I furrowed my brow. "Um, hello? He had his arm around his girlfriend?"

"Who, by the way, is totally and completely jealous of you," Reede said. "And she's history."

I glanced down the hall where I could just make them out in the crowd.

"I give them another week, tops," Reede said.

"What?" I said. "You don't even know them."

"I don't have to know them to know how they feel," Reede said, with an authority that made me believe her. "He likes you, she can feel it, and she's totally jealous and trying not to show it. Didn't you hear how fake her 'hi' was?"

I didn't know how to answer that. If I said I had noticed, then it would be like I knew she was jealous of me and that sounded self-centered. But if I said I didn't notice, it would seem like I was a totally unobservant dork who couldn't read anyone's body language.

"Play the innocent bystander if you want, Erin," Reede said. "But that guy is totally into you and his little girlfriend is going to be solo very soon."

I looked at her.

"I think I just made your day," she said, walking backward down the hall. "You can thank me later." She turned around and picked up her pace, leaving me shaking my head. How could one person be so complicated? One minute Reede's dissing my look, the next she's saying Mark is sending me "energy surges" and is going to break up with Kara. I was so confused as I looked for Mr. F that I nearly barreled into Puppet Porter—I mean Mrs. Porter—our principal.

"Watch where you're going, Miss Swift," she said, as she placed a hand on my shoulder to steer me out of oncoming traffic. "Staying out of trouble so far, I hope?"

"Yes, Mrs. Porter," I said. "That's my plan."

"Excellent, excellent," she said. "And how are your puppets?"

"I don't have any puppets, Mrs. Porter." I sighed. Ever since I'd hit Serena last year for calling me a puppet and had to talk to Mrs. Porter, who had a whole collection of puppets, she thought I had a collection, too. "But how is *your* collection?"

"I added another marionette from Germany," she said. "You should stop by."

"Maybe I will," I said. "Right now I need to go." I ducked down the hall toward the gym where I spotted Mr. F outside one of the larger custodian closets.

"Running from trouble?" Mr. F said when I arrived, out of breath.

"Just my past," I said. I glanced at the open door, noticing several photos taped to it. "Were these up last year?"

"Same kids, different photos," Mr. F said.

"I can't believe I never noticed," I said. "Who are they?"

Mr. F emptied a box of paper towels and looked up. "Some of the best kids around."

"Better than us?" I joked, placing a roll of paper towels on the shelf next to the others.

He chuckled, then pointed to a young girl, whose toothless smile filled her face. "That's Olivia. She's seven." He shook his head. "Sweetest smile you'll ever see and the best hugger I've ever met." He picked up the empty box and set it in the hall. "They're kids at a place I visit."

"They're cute," I said. "I'd like to meet the best hugger."

"Maybe you will someday," Mr. F said. He offered me a Tootsie Pop from his jar on the shelf. "But I bet you didn't come here to talk about pictures. What's on your mind?"

I unwrapped the Tootsie and settled on top of a step ladder near the door. "There's this new girl."

"Reede Harper," Mr. F said. Now he was cleaning scrub brushes in the big sink, rubbing them together so the soap squished and squirted.

"How did you know?" I asked. "Aren't there a lot of new people every year?"

"Just a hunch," Mr. F said. "Go on."

"Well," I said, "at first she seemed really stuck up, like she was too cool for everyone, but then she says things that are the total opposite of that."

"Sounds pretty normal," Mr. F said, raising an eyebrow. "Is that all?"

I concentrated on peeling the wrapper off my Tootsie Pop. "Reede thinks this one guy is going to break up with his girlfriend and that he likes someone else."

Mr. F smiled. "I don't know if Mark will break up with Kara but I do think he likes you."

I almost fell over backward off the step ladder. "Would you stop that?"

Mr. F laughed, rinsing one of the brushes. "So, what's the problem with this situation?"

I put the Tootsie Pop in my mouth. "I don't know," I said, the round sucker pushing my cheek out. "I guess it's just, well, weird."

"Because of last year?" he said. "How you liked Mark and he liked Jilly but you stopped liking him and didn't think you liked him that way anymore. Only now that you've found out he might be interested in you, you may be taking a second look?"

I shook my head in amazement. "Are you sure you aren't a middle school girl under that gray hair?"

Mr. F chuckled. "I listen and observe, that's all."

Sighing, I folded the wrapper into a tiny square and tossed it into the garbage can next to the door. "So, I don't know what to do."

"Why do you need to do anything?" Setting the brushes carefully on the shelf above the sink, Mr F adjusted them in a neat row. "Nothing's happened yet. Why don't you let things go the way they will and then decide what to do."

I frowned. "But I want to be prepared."

"For what?"

"If they break up," I said. "If Mark likes me and asks me out. If Kara hates my guts."

Mr. F laughed. "That's a lot of ifs. I think you're much better off living right here, right now, and not preparing for things that may never happen."

"But what if they do?"

Mr. F put some cleaning supplies in the bucket. "Then you'll handle them with your usual good sense, Erin P. Swift." He lifted the bucket and turned to face me. "Lunch is almost over so if you want to eat, you'd better get going. And I've got to get to work."

"Thanks for nothing, Mr. F," I said as we knocked fists.

He laughed. "You're welcome."

Thursday, August 21

QUESTIONS TO PONDER

HOT—✪—METER

❤ **#1 Mark Sacks**—
the hair, the butt
in shorts—need I
say more?
#2 Mr. Perkins
*Other cute guys
will go here as I
spot them . . .*

✴ If Mark sent me an energy surge w/o me
knowing, did I accidentally send 1 back 2
him? Does he think I like him?

✴ Why is it that when u find out someone
might like u, u start paying more attn 2
them?

✴ Mr. F doesn't think we should be prepared
for what-ifs. Why not? Isn't it good 2 be prepared? I don't get that @
all.

✴ Is Kara really jealous of me? Her "Hi, Erin" did seem kind of fake.

THINGS THAT MAKE ME WONDER

✴ Why do I wish I'd let Reede finish telling me about her Erin Makeover?

✴ Why did I try dark eyeliner & more eyeshadow when I got home from
school?

✴ Why did I scrub it off the minute Mom called me down 2 help w/
dinner?

✴ Why am I looking @ myself in practically every reflective surface I
pass 2 c what Reede meant by "really cute"?

I'm starting 2 wonder if this athlete could really be hot. Is that ok?

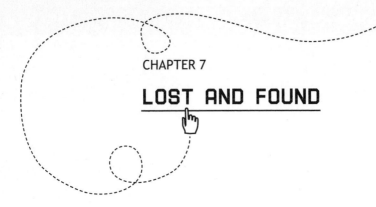

CHAPTER 7

LOST AND FOUND

WHEN ROSIE AND I WALKED into the computer lab for our computers and technology elective the next day, Reede was talking to our teacher, Ms. Moreno.

"My dad's a pretty big dude in the Internet world," Reede was saying. "I might be able to get the class some free software and stuff."

"That would be very nice," Ms. Moreno said. "Maybe he'd like to speak to the class, too?"

Reede shifted. "He travels a lot but I can ask him."

As I passed by, Reede smiled at me and I smiled back. But I felt a little twinge. *I* was the web expert here. Couldn't Reede just stay in her popular zone and let me be here?

When the bell rang, we all settled down. "Before we get started with class," Ms. Moreno said, "I wanted to mention the Intranet/Internet after-school club." She explained how we were going to work on both the MBMS Intranet and the website. "There are only twenty-five spots available for the club. Those of you who were in it last year will have priority. If there are more people who want to join than there are spots, I'll use a lottery system."

She smiled at Reede. "I hope you'll consider joining us. We could use someone with your experience." I frowned. What experience? For all we knew, she didn't know a plug-in from a light socket. What about *my* experience? What about all the great stuff I did last year? I knew more than anyone about web design, even most of the eighth graders. What about that?

"Erin was one of the leaders in the club last year," Ms. Moreno said, as if reading my mind. "If you want to know everything there is to know about it, ask her."

"And everything there is to know about Erin herself," Serena said, laughing. "Whether you want to or not."

A few people chuckled and I laughed, too, before giving Serena a look. I didn't really want Reede to know about the YOHE.

"Can we have video clips on the website?" Steve asked.

"We'll see," Ms. Moreno said. "We'll need to concentrate on getting the basic structure and pages up first." She walked around to the side of her desk. "I'll have sign-up sheets for the club posted outside the lab next Wednesday. Now, let's talk about what we're planning to cover in this elective."

Even though Reede was honing in a little on my turf, I couldn't help feeling a ripple of excitement as I thought about I-Club and everything I wanted to do this year.

"The website's gonna rock," Tyler said to me after class. "See you at the Y on Saturday."

I smiled. Yes, the website would definitely rock. And Tyler had definitely improved his basketball skills since last year. Saturday would be a fun time.

That night I was doing the dishes. As I rinsed a pot, Chris dropped something on the counter next to me.

"I think this is yours," he said.

I looked down. It was my PEK (Period Emergency Kit)! My mom had given it to me in fifth grade. It was a small black cosmetic bag with three appliqués she had stitched on it—a basketball, a soccer ball, and a cute little computer mouse. Inside were two sizes of pads, two tampons, a tiny notebook and pencil in case I wanted to "record the event for posterity," and an IOU for chocolate.

"What does chocolate have to do with having your period?" I had asked her.

"Nothing," she had said. "And everything. Just something to enjoy when you take this step in your life."

"I found it when I was cleaning out my car," Chris said, bringing me back to the kitchen.

"Since when do you clean your car?" I asked suspiciously.

He laughed. "Since Bethany said she won't ride in the 'trashmobile' anymore."

"Thanks." Stuffing the bag into the top of my shorts, I turned back to the sink. Chris started putting things back into the refrigerator.

"What do you keep in there, a lock of Cute Boy's hair?" He thought he was so funny. Not only had the entire school read my totally secret private blog but it had also made the rounds of the high school, courtesy of Serena, who'd given a copy to her older sister.

"Very funny," I said, turning to place a plate in the dishwasher. Chris snatched the PEK from my waist. "Hey!" I said. "Give that back!"

He held it above his head. "Must be something pretty special in here." He grinned and shook it in front of my face before holding it up high again.

I paused in mid-reach. "Yeah," I said, dropping my hands. "It *is* special. In fact, it's perfectly fine if you open it up and look inside." I smiled.

He eyed me suspiciously. "So all of a sudden it's okay for me to look?" He held the bag at eye level and frowned. Then the light dawned. "Yikes." He tossed the bag toward me and wiped his hands on his pants.

"It's not contaminated, you dork." I unzipped the bag and held out a tampon. "See, it's wrapped in hermetically sealed plastic. But even if it wasn't, it's just a bunch of cotton." I held it out to him. "You afraid of a little cotton?"

He stepped around the island so the counter separated us.

I grinned. "Catch!" I tossed the tampon at him. He jumped back as if it was on fire.

I busted out laughing.

"What's the joke?" My dad stood in the doorway, eyebrows raised.

"Look out, Dad," I said, taking a protective stance. "Dangerous tampon inches away."

"Oh, for heaven's sake." Dad leaned over and picked it up, holding it out to me. "Now, Erin, you know you aren't supposed to scare your brother with feminine hygiene products."

"Sorry," I said, wiping off the tampon before tucking it back in the bag. "It won't happen again."

Chris shook his head. "This is the kind of thing that keeps brothers from chauffeuring their sisters to the mall or the library," he said before lumbering down the hall.

Dad looked at me, eyebrows raised. "Does this mean . . . ?"

I shook my head. "Not yet. Just making sure I'm prepared."

"Good. Well, I'm sure I'll find out when it happens."

"You'll be the sixth, seventh, or eighth one to know," I said.

He smiled. "At least I'm in the top ten." Squeezing my shoulder, he continued on his way.

Friday, August 22

THINGS THAT MAKE ME WONDER ◉

> ♡ **#1 Mark Sacks**—
> the hair, the butt
> in shorts—need I
> say more?
> **#2 Mr. Perkins**
> *Other cute guys*
> *will go here as I*
> *spot them . . .*

* Why haven't I had my period yet? I know my
  mom was 14 when she started but maybe
  something's wrong w/ me.

* Now that I've got the PEK back, I feel like IT
  may come anytime. I know that makes no
  sense but that's how I feel.

JOURNEY OF THE PEK

9:00 a.m. PEK in gym bag—I might have IT while I'm @ the Y w/ Mark
& Tyler tomorrow.

9:01 a.m. Out of bag—might fall out & they would c it.

9:05 a.m. In bag—IT could happen & I want 2 be prepared.

9:06 a.m. Out of bag—I'll just bring money.

9:07 a.m. In bag—what if they only have tampons, no pads? I don't
think I could put a tampon in, even tho Mom explained it . . . freaks me
out. & what if the machine is broken?

9:08 a.m. Out of bag—knowing it's in there will distract me & I'll miss
my shots.

9:09 a.m. In bag, zipped in a secret inside pocket that I forgot
about . . . stupid not 2 bring it. I'm sure Reede has had hers & she
wouldn't think twice about tossing supplies in2 her bag, not caring who
saw them.

Geez. When did something like going 2 the Y 2 shoot hoops become so
complicated?

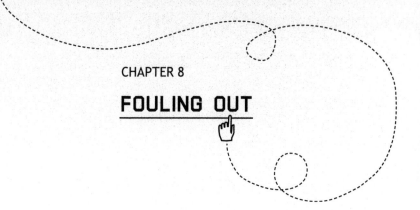

CHAPTER 8

FOULING OUT

THE NEXT MORNING I SHOWED up at the Y with Rosie. Tyler and Mark were already there, shooting baskets. We warmed up a little with Around the World, then played a few games of two-on-two—first boys against girls, then Tyler and me against Mark and Rosie, and finally we switched again, with Mark and me against Tyler and Rosie.

Mark and I won the first game pretty easily. We took a break after that so Rosie and I could get some water. As I started back on the court, Mark froze in mid-shot.

"Hey," he said. "What are you doing here?"

Kara stood at the door with Cindy, one of her friends. "Tyler invited us."

"You're just in time to watch us cream them," Tyler said. "Unless you want to play? You could be on my team."

Kara hesitated, then looked at Cindy, who shook her head. "We'll just watch." They sat down next to our duffel bags.

"Hey, guys." I waved to them as I took my position in front of Rosie to defend the basket. I suddenly felt nervous around the girl who might be jealous of me. Mark seemed uncomfortable, too. He missed an easy lay-up and later passed the ball to Rosie instead of me.

"In case you didn't realize," I said, punching him in the arm as he ran by, "Rosie's on the other team."

"Sorry," he muttered, not returning the punch like he usually did.

When I made a sweet swish from the right side, he seemed to loosen up, giving me a high five, before positioning himself in front of Tyler.

The game ended fifteen minutes later, with Tyler and Rosie beating us by six.

"You should come more often," Tyler said to Kara as the girls joined us on the court. "You're good luck."

Kara smiled but her eyes were on Mark. She started to put her arm around his waist.

"I'm all sweaty," he said, pulling away.

"I don't mind." She held on, shifting so she stood between Mark and me. "Cindy and I were going to grab a sandwich at Subway. Want to come?"

"All of us?" Tyler asked.

Kara glanced at me, then back at Tyler. "Sure."

"I only have a dollar," I said.

"I'll pay for you," Mark said. Kara frowned but he didn't seem to notice.

"I've got you," Rosie said. "I did a bunch of babysitting last week so I'm loaded."

"I'll pay you back." I walked over to pick up my duffel bag. I wanted to make sure Kara knew I wasn't interested in Mark. *See? I'm just hanging out with Rosie and Tyler. I won't take Mark's money and I don't need to stand right next to him.*

At Subway, there wasn't a big enough booth for all of us so Rosie and I sat in one booth while Kara, Mark, Tyler, and Cindy sat in the one next to us. I even sat on the side farthest away from them. There was no way she could think I liked Mark after all that effort.

When we were finished, Kara, Cindy, and Rosie got picked up first. Kara squeezed Mark's arm. "Call me," she said. She glanced at me before hurrying to the car.

The rest of us sat on the brick wall outside the Y, waiting for our rides.

"So that was cool that Kara and Cindy came," Tyler said.

"Yeah," Mark said. But he didn't sound like he thought it was very cool.

Tyler tossed a pinecone into the street. "Why haven't you invited her before?"

"I have," Mark said, picking up three pinecones. "Every time—except for today because she always says no and I decided to stop asking." Mark tossed one cone toward the V in a nearby tree. It hit the trunk and dropped to the ground.

"I guess she changed her mind," Tyler said.

We threw pinecones at the tree until our parents came to pick us up.

I made eight out of ten through the V.

Mark only made two.

Our whole family went over to Mr. and Mrs. F's house for dinner that night and afterward we set up Family Cranium, a game Mrs. F had bought to play with the grandkids when they came to visit. It was me, Mr. F, and my mom against my dad, Mrs. F, and Chris. At one point Mr. F had to hum a song and my mom and I were supposed to guess it.

"Is that supposed to be a song we know?" I asked him. "It sounds like the garbage disposal."

Everyone cracked up and Mr. F gave me a mock glare. "I was going for vacuum cleaner."

That made us laugh all over again.

We ended up losing the game by just a few spaces on the board but we had a lot of fun.

"You all go out on the back patio and I'll bring the dessert," Mrs. F said, shooing us toward the door. My parents sat down with Chris at the table, but Mr. F wanted to show me his vegetable garden.

"Look at those tomatoes, Erin," he said, pointing to a fat red one that seemed to groan under its own weight, nearly touching the ground. He proceeded to give me the entire tour before pulling a few choice tomatoes and green peppers off for us to take home. I lifted them up to my face and breathed in deeply, enjoying the rich dirt smell mixed with green pepper.

"How are things with Reede and the gang?" Mr. F asked, pinching off some dead leaves from the plants.

"Pretty good," I said. "I guess Reede's this big computer expert and Ms. Moreno thinks she'll add a lot to the website."

"What do *you* think?"

I shrugged. "She was kind of bragging about stuff but I guess if she has good ideas, we should use them."

Mr. F continued his plucking, his eyes on the dead leaves. "I think it's good that you have an open mind about her, Erin."

I smiled. "I don't know how open it is, but I'm trying." I kneeled next to him and picked a dead leaf off a tomato plant. "It's kind of hard."

Mr. F dropped another dead leaf on the pile between us, nodding. "Even with everything that happened last year, you were still the go-to girl for the Intranet Club. It's hard to think that someone who's just shown up, who hasn't been around and worked hard to get there, might know more or do more than you."

"Exactly," I said, marveling once again at Mr. F's ability to get it. I glanced over at my family, who was helping Mrs. F set out plates for dessert. "Mr. F?"

"Um hm?"

"Why do you think it's easier to talk to some people than to other people?"

Mr. F leaned back, rubbing his nose with the back of his hand, pieces of dirt dropping from his fingers. "Well, now, that's a good question. What do you think?"

"I think some people understand better than other people."

Mr. F nodded. "Could be. Could also be that we don't give people a chance."

"What if they've used up all their chances?"

Mr. F looked at me, a slight smile on his face. "I sure hope there aren't a limited amount of chances when it comes to people we love."

"The whipped cream is melting, you two!" Mrs. F shouted from the patio. "Come and get it."

"How about some strawberry shortcake?" Mr. F asked, groaning as he pushed himself up and onto his feet.

"As long as you're not humming it," I said.

"For you, I'll remain silent." Mr. F put his arm around my shoulder and squeezed. I wrapped my arm around his waist and squeezed back.

Saturday, August 23

RANDOM THOUGHTS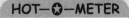

✱ Not sure what's up w/ Mark & Kara.

✱ I freaked over bringing the PEK 4 nothing — no period. Not even a hint of a cramp.

✱ We had a lot of fun @ Mr. F's house. Sometimes I wish he was my grandfather. My
dad's parents are both gone & my mom's
parents live in Idaho. I love them but we only see them sometimes @
Christmas or in the summer. They do a lot of traveling so I've never
been close 2 them.

COOL HAPPENIN'

Jilly's having an "unparty" on Sept 6! Just some people hanging
out . . . Bus Boy, me, a friend of BB's named Blake, & Dylan & Lauren
from J's track last year. I remember Dylan was cute. I wonder what
Blake looks like. Maybe I can add them 2 the Hot-o-Meter. I'm kinda
nervous but more excited 2 c what happens. I don't need RH 4 a
makeover — I can do this myself (and consult w/ Jilly's fashion queen
sis, Becca).

HOT—✪—METER

❤ #1 Mark Sacks —
the hair, the butt
in shorts — need I
say more?
#2 Mr. Perkins
*Other cute guys
will go here as I
spot them . . .*

CHAPTER 9

LIFE OF THE UNPARTY

WHEN I ARRIVED AT JILLY'S the Saturday of the unparty, she was vacuuming the carpet in the basement. She waved when she saw me, then did a double-take and turned off the vacuum.

"Wow, you look great!" she said. "I love that top. Where did you get it?"

"My dad gave it to me last year but I never wore it," I said, looking down at the white button-down blouse with just a hint of lace down the front, the short sleeves tied up on either side. I had unbuttoned the top two buttons and added a string of fake pearls and matching earrings. I'd also worn more eyeliner, per Becca's suggestion a few days ago. I wasn't sure I had gotten to hot . . . but I thought I was pretty warm. "You don't think it's too girlie for me?"

Jilly shook her head. "It really flatters your shape. Blake's going to go wild for you."

I grinned. Maybe I'd go wild for him, too.

Bus Boy and Blake arrived first, just after five. Bus Boy made polite conversation with Jilly's parents and then introduced Blake to all of us. He was *definitely* someone I could go wild for with his streaked blond hair, blue eyes, and an earring. He looked like a California surfer without the surf (I found out later he snowboarded — the mountain equivalent of surfing). He had a few zits on his chin but who didn't? (Well, actually I didn't at the moment, which was pretty sweet). Even with the zits, Blake was definitely Hot-o-Meter material.

As soon as we were downstairs and out of sight of the adults, Bus Boy grabbed Jilly and kissed her. She wrapped her arms around his neck and kissed him back — long and slow. Blake rolled his eyes at me. I smiled. He was *so* cute. *Don't make a fool of yourself, Erin.*

"Want something to drink?" I asked, walking over to the cooler.

Blake helped himself to a Coke and started munching on the chips. Then he eyed the foosball table. "You play?"

I tried to hide my grin. Jilly and I had been playing foosball since we were tall enough to reach the handles. "A little," I said casually. "You up for a game?"

We faced off while Jilly and Bus Boy grabbed some drinks and turned on the music. I dropped the ball and scored five points right off the bat.

"Man, you're good," Blake said, laughing. "I'm not used to playing singles. I keep forgetting to switch over to block your shot."

I liked that he could laugh about it. "It takes practice," I said. "You'll get the hang of it."

I beat him soundly three times before he fell to his knees, prostrate. "You are the Foosball Master, Erin Swift. I bow to your amazing skills."

I liked hearing him say my name. I placed my hand on his head, a jolt going through me as I touched his hair. Now *that* was an energy surge. "It is good you recognize my superior powers, young one."

He grabbed my hand and looked up at me. "Can you teach me, oh master?"

"It will be a long, hard journey but yes, I think I can."

He stood up, still gripping my hand, then let go as we both laughed. When Lauren and Dylan arrived, we played more foosball, with

Blake and me on the same team. We won against Lauren and Dylan but lost against Jilly and Bus Boy.

"We'll get 'em next time," Blake said as we leaned against the wall, watching Jilly and Bus Boy quickly rack up points against Lauren and Dylan.

"I'm plotting our strategy as we speak," I said, glad that he thought there'd be a next time.

Blake grinned at me and I grinned back, just as Jilly's mom came down.

"Need any more snacks or drinks?" Mrs. Hennessey said, checking the cooler.

"Maybe some more chips," Jilly said.

Jilly rolled her eyes after her mom left, muttering "spy" as she pulled the coffee table away from the couch. I smiled. Mrs. Hennessey had given Jilly strict rules for the unparty—daylight only, lights on at all times, no "messing around." It sounded like my mom; it was nice to know I wasn't the only one.

Bus Boy pulled out a deck of cards and we sat on the floor around the coffee table, playing Texas hold 'em until the pizza arrived. After we ate, the boys played foosball and Jilly, Lauren, and I sat on the couch and talked.

"Blake keeps looking over at you," Lauren whispered to me. "I think he likes you."

"It's only because I'm the only available girl here," I said modestly. But I'd noticed him looking, too, and it gave me a tingly feeling all over.

Lauren and Dylan's ride showed up at 7:45. Bus Boy and Jilly went for a walk so Blake and I were left by ourselves on the front porch while he waited for his dad to pick him and Bus Boy up. We talked about MBMS and how he liked high school okay but it was hard starting over, especially with sports.

"Yeah, I'm not looking forward to being at the bottom again," I said.

"I'll make sure you're taken care of," Blake said, rapping my knee with his knuckle. Man, he was *hot*. He might make my Hot-o-Meter explode. I couldn't believe I was sitting outside on a cool August evening chatting easily with this freshman in high school who actually seemed to like being with me and would make sure I was taken care of.

Bus Boy and Jilly came back just as a car pulled up in front of the house.

"There's our ride," Blake said, standing up. He said good-bye to Jilly, then motioned me to follow him down the sidewalk. "So," he said, his gaze faltering, "you want to hang out sometime?"

Was he asking me out? My heart did a little skip. "Um, sure."

"You got a cell?"

I shook my head.

"I'll get your e-mail from Hennessey." He punched my arm. "I'll beat you next time."

"In your dreams," I said, poking him back.

"Maybe," he said, looking at me briefly before heading down the walk, Bus Boy following behind.

I watched him go, my eyes drawn to the way his jeans hung loose on his butt, his shirt hanging out, untucked. What did he mean? Was he planning on dreaming about me? Or was he admitting that I actually would beat him again at foosball?

The thought of Blake Thornton or any other boy dreaming about me was so bizarre that I shook my head to get rid of the idea. Of course that's not what he meant. People like Blake Thornton didn't daydream about girls like me.

Did they?

Sunday, September 7

THINGS THAT ROCK

* I have a double d8 on Fri!!! We're going bowling, which should be a blast if I don't become the Amazing Gutter Ball Girl.

* A 9th grader wants 2 go out w/ ME, Erin Penelope Swift!

THINGS THAT ARE FREAKING ME OUT

* A 9th grader wants 2 go out w/ me. Hello? What universe is this happening in? What if he changes his mind after he's been back @ his school 4 a week & c's all those cute h.s. girls?

* He might try 2 kiss me. What if my breath stinks? What if I'm a horrible kisser & he's totally turned off? Have not kissed 4 real EVER. That kiss w/ Mark didn't count . . . basically missed lips cuz he faked left & cut right & I did the opposite. Our lips touched, barely, & then we both got all embarrassed & laughed & never talked about it again.

* My mom is driving us so she can meet Blake. I can already imagine the humiliation. I won't have 2 worry about embarrassing myself when we bowl — my mom will take care of that b4 we even start.

HOT—✪—METER

♥ **#1 Blake Thornton** — totally gorgeous 9th grade mountain surfer

#2 Dylan Beaumont — taken, but cute

#3 Mark Sacks — the hair, the butt in shorts — need I say more?

#4 Mr. Perkins (drops to #4 because of age gap)

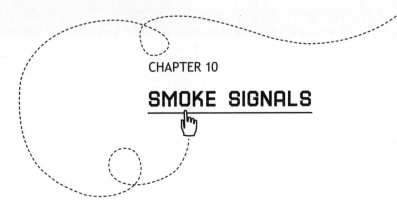

CHAPTER 10

SMOKE SIGNALS

"WE'RE ACTUALLY DOUBLE-DATING!" JILLY SQUEALED and grabbed my arm as she met me at the bus stop the next morning. "This is going to be so fun!"

"If my mom doesn't ruin it," I said. "And what about my clothes? My zits? My potential bad breath and lack of kissing skills?" And what would we talk about? It didn't matter that Blake and I had had a perfectly normal and fun conversation on Saturday. This was a DATE with a capital D and I'd never been on one.

Jilly laughed. "You'll look fantastic and be fantastic and charm him just like you did at my house." She sighed as the bus pulled up. "As for the kissing part, there aren't going to be a lot of opportunities at the bowling alley. Unfortunately."

Of course. A bright crowded bowling alley. A decent spin on the ball. No kissing so no chance of failing miserably. Perfect.

By the time we got to school, I was totally excited with just a touch of nervousness around the edges. I found myself holding my head higher, walking with a little swing to my hips. Could people tell I was going out with a ninth grader?

As I made my way down the hall, I saw Reede talking to Mr. F. He laughed and handed her a Tootsie Pop before pushing his trash can away. Stupid, but I felt a little jealous.

I stayed after school to talk to Ms. Fehrmann, my language arts teacher, about an assignment so I had time to kill while I waited for the activities bus. The halls were nearly empty as I headed for my locker. When I rounded the corner, I saw Reede putting on makeup. Did she ever do anything else?

"So, you were totally into the Hottie with the Hair last year," she said, opening her mouth wide as she brushed on mascara. "And you really pissed off some people."

So Serena had told her about the YOHE. I waited for my big reaction. Anger. Embarrassment. Fear. But nothing came.

"It was last winter," I said. "I don't know why Serena still cares. I don't."

"She was kidding about it," Reede said, then cocked her head. "Did you really wear a sandwich board? Man, you've got *guts,* girl."

I smiled. "Guts or stupidity, we're still not sure."

Reede smiled and turned to check her face and hair one more time before moving aside so I could get my books. "And I'm glad I'm not the only one who kissed her pillow before kissing the real thing."

My eyes bugged out. *"You?"*

Reede laughed. "Yes, me."

I couldn't believe it. Sophisticated Reede Harper kissing her pillow? Let's put *that* out on the MBMS website.

She pulled out her black bag and her other makeup case slipped out and hit the floor, spilling a lipstick and two cigarettes.

My heart stuttered. Having cigarettes was a huge rule breaker. And smoking them on school grounds could get you suspended. I felt my breath come faster, as if I was the one who had the cigarettes.

"Whoops," Reede said, snatching them up. "Wouldn't want anyone seeing those babies." She zipped the bag halfway, then stopped. "Want one?"

Huh? Did I look like I smoked? "No, thanks."

She shrugged. "See you tomorrow."

I watched her go, my mind racing. Reede Harper smoked. Reede Harper kissed her pillow. Reede Harper didn't think I was a dork, even though she now knew about my blog—knew I had called Mark a Hot Tamale and that I was a corn cob in the Thanksgiving play last year.

Huh.

Taking a deep breath, I turned and looked at myself in her mirror. *Did* I look like someone who smoked? I put my pencil between my fingers and held it near my mouth.

"What are you doing?"

Mark's voice startled me and I dropped the pencil.

"I didn't know you stayed after school today," I said, picking up the pencil.

"I had to talk to my algebra teacher." He wrinkled his brow. "It looked like you were pretending to smoke."

I snorted, hoping it sounded more convincing to him than it did to me. "Yeah, right. I was pretending to smoke."

"Well, you have been known to kiss your pillow."

"Shut up." I smacked him. "Why are you so annoying?"

Mark laughed and made a face, just as a set of arms wrapped around his waist from behind.

"I've been looking for you," Kara said. She leaned around him, frowning before forcing herself to smile. "Hey, Erin."

"Hey, Kara." I pulled the rest of my books out of my locker and shut the door. "Gotta go or I'll miss the bus."

"See ya," Mark called. I lifted my hand in a wave but didn't look back. No doubt they were lip-locked together, no pillows necessary. But hey, maybe that would be me with Blake Thornton, ninth grade cutie. I smiled. It was weird how a part of me was terrified to kiss him and part of me really wanted to.

The thought made me tingle all over.

Wednesday, September 10

MORE THINGS WE KNOW ABOUT REEDE HARPER 𝑈𝐼𝐸

* She smokes.

* She doesn't deny she smokes.

* She didn't dis me abt the YOHE.

MORE THINGS WE KNOW ABOUT ERIN SWIFT ❋

* She doesn't smoke.

* She would never smoke on or off campus not only cuz it's gross but cuz she's a rule follower.

* She is just going 2 wing the kissing thing — a pillow isn't even close anyway.

THINGS THAT MAKE ME WONDER ☯

* What would it feel like 2 break a rule? Maybe not a big 1 that got me expelled or anything, but a little 1, outside of school, just 2 test it out . . . test ME out.

* What would it feel like not 2 be 2 chicken 2 find out? Bawk.

* Will I get 2 kiss Blake on Fri? I think I want 2 but will I be 2 scared? Bawk, part 2.

HOT—✪—METER

♡ **#1 Blake Thornton** — totally gorgeous 9th grade mountain surfer

#2 Dylan Beaumont — taken, but cute

#3 Mark Sacks — the hair, the butt in shorts — need I say more?

#4 Mr. Perkins (drops to #4 because of age gap)

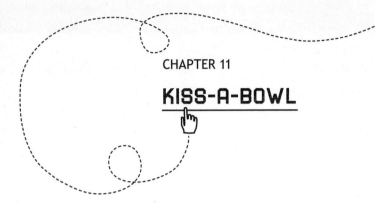

CHAPTER 11

KISS-A-BOWL

"EVERYONE WEARS THE UGLY BOWLING shoes, Erin. It's part of the fun and nobody cares." Jilly pulled open the doors to Donna's Bowl & Billiards on Friday afternoon. My mom was parking the car and the boys hadn't arrived yet so we had a little reprieve before the Let's Embarrass Erin show.

"*You* don't care?" This seemed strange coming from Jilly the Fashionista.

"It's bowling," Jilly said, "No one's looking at your feet because they're too busy seeing how bad you play." As we stepped inside the bowling alley, she gave me the once over. "I've never seen you so obsessed about your appearance before. How many outfits did you try on?"

"Six," I confessed, glancing toward the counter where the dreaded bowling shoes were lined up in cubbies.

"Erin Swift tried on *six* outfits? I can't believe it." Jilly shook her head. "Let me guess. This one was the first you tried on."

"Second," I said, tugging my double tank tops down over my jeans.

Jilly's eyes dropped briefly to my chest before returning to my face. "You look hot," she said. "Blake will be so distracted, he'll throw gutter balls."

I laughed. "I doubt that. He's pretty competitive." But it made me feel good anyway. I turned to the counter. "Come on, let's get the shoes on and find a lane before they get here."

When the boys showed up, my mom was sitting in one of the seats in our lane, looking a little too comfortable. I introduced her to Blake and she shook his hand warmly.

"It's very nice to meet you," she said. "Have you and Jon been friends a long time?"

Blake shook his head. "We met at a soccer camp over the summer and found out we were both going to Washington High School."

"Okay, mom," I said, tugging at her shirt. "Mrs. Hennessey will pick us up later. Thanks for the ride."

"I can take a hint," my mom said, winking at Blake. Oh, *please. Could you be any more embarrassing in front of a hottie I'm just getting to know and would like to get to know better if you don't ruin it by being a dork*?

"Did you have to wink?" I asked when we were out of earshot. "Nobody winks anymore, Mom. It's really stupid."

Her face fell. "I'm sorry," she said, then pushed out the door without saying good-bye.

I flicked away a niggle of guilt and hurried back to the group. The three of them were sitting in the chairs while the boys put their shoes on. "Sorry about that," I said. "She's a little—well, I'm not sure what she is exactly."

Everyone laughed, which made me feel better.

"Don't worry about it," Blake said. "Moms are supposed to be a little strange."

I smiled as I set up our game on the overhead board.

Bus Boy looked around before leaning over and kissing Jilly. They kept kissing so I turned away.

"Are you two going to bowl or get a room?" Blake asked, unzipping a bag I hadn't noticed before.

"You brought your own ball?" I put my hands on my hips.

"And his own shoes," Jilly said, pointing to Blake's feet. He had a nice pair of black shoes that looked like basic athletic shoes, not the ugly tan and red shoes we were wearing.

"No fair," I said.

Bus Boy turned to Jilly and me. "His mom bowls in a league and he bowls on Wii Sports so that makes him an expert."

"He has his own ball, Jon," Jilly said. "I think this goes beyond the Wii."

"It's probably his mom's," Bus Boy said, picking up several balls from the rack before settling on a green one with black specks.

"It's mine, bro," Blake said, pulling out a glossy blue ball. "See?" He held it out. Engraved near the holes in neat script was his name: *Blake Thornton*. He placed it on the ball return next to the standard black one I'd chosen. My ball looked slumped and weary next to his.

"I think we're in trouble," I said to Jilly, and she nodded.

"He's just trying to psyche us out," Bus Boy said, then turned to Blake. "I'm going to beat your sorry bowling butt."

"You bowl with your butt?" I asked Blake. "You must be very talented."

Blake laughed. I could get used to hearing that laugh. He caught my eye and my heart fluttered. Then he smiled mischievously.

I looked from him to his ball, then back at him. "Payback for foosball?"

"You know it, babe."

Blake dominated all of us, scoring over 200 every game. My high game was 125, Jilly's was 110 and Bus Boy's was 165.

"Want me to bowl with my butt?" Blake asked Bus Boy. "Make it a little more even?"

"You got lucky," Bus Boy said, unlacing his shoes. "Wait till next time."

We all laughed and decided to grab some burgers at a restaurant a few blocks away.

"I'll tell my mom to pick us up there," Jilly said, pulling out her cell phone. She and Bus Boy walked several feet ahead of us, each with a hand tucked into the other's back pocket. I marveled at how comfortable Jilly acted with Bus Boy. Sure she got jealous and insecure but she could touch him and kiss him in public no problem. I couldn't see myself ever doing that with anyone. I smiled as Bus Boy complained—loudly, over his shoulder—about Blake's win.

"Just admit you suck, Lanner," Blake called.

"I admit nothing," Bus Boy said. "Next time, you're going down."

"In bowling history, maybe," Blake said, and I cracked up.

"You really are good," I said. "I wish I could play like that."

"You could if you practiced," Blake said. "You've got a natural delivery; you just turn your wrist at the last second. That's why the ball goes off to the side." He reached for my wrist and held it in both of his hands, flicking it back and forth. "See, if you can keep it straight all the way through," he said, pulling my hand back, "you'll have a straighter aim at the pins." He carried my hand forward to demonstrate, then brought it down to his side.

"That makes sense," I said, waiting for him to let go. He didn't. He held onto my wrist as we walked and I wondered if it looked as weird as it felt to have someone holding your wrist instead of your hand. And then suddenly his hand was around mine, squeezing gently. I squeezed back, feeling the sweat between our palms—was it his or mine?

"Want some gum?" I asked.

"Sure." He looked relieved and I wondered if he was feeling as awkward as I was. But how could he? He was a hot blond high school boarder boy and I was just a middle school computer geek.

I handed him a stick of Doublemint before taking one for myself. He told me he had been bowling since he could hold a ball — "like you with foosball"—and I told him how I had to learn soccer and basket-ball to avoid being creamed by my brother.

Blake laughed. "I see your brother at school sometimes. He seems pretty cool."

"He can be," I said. "If you're not related to him."

We walked a little further, our pace slowing so that the distance be-tween us and Jilly and Bus Boy grew. As we passed a house with a lot of overgrown bushes and trees, Blake grabbed my arm and pulled me off the sidewalk and behind a hedge. My heart bounced wildly in my chest as he gripped my shoulders, his eyes peering into mine. We stared at each other, our noses and lips several inches apart, before Blake closed his eyes and leaned toward me.

I felt his lips—slightly rough and chapped—against my own. I kissed him back, hesitantly at first, unsure of what I was doing. But when he didn't pull away, and instead wrapped his arms around me, I relaxed. I reached my own arms around his neck and kept kissing him, moving my mouth with his. Then our mouths opened at the same time and I smelled his breath, Doublemint fresh with just a hint of the candy bar he'd gotten from the vending machine at the bowling alley.

Our mouths opened wider and I felt his tongue roam over mine. But before I could respond, I started gagging and choking.

Blake pulled away quickly. "My gum!"

I nodded, hitting my chest to release both wads from the back of my throat. They popped forward and I gasped, sucking in a few breaths and coughing.

"Are you okay?" Blake looked concerned as he patted my back awkwardly.

I nodded and pulled out the gum, holding it up between us. We both stared at the connected wads for a moment, then looked at each other and busted out laughing.

"Want your gum back?" I asked between gasps.

Blake shook his head. "You keep it," he said. "Consider it a gift."

"How thoughtful." I rolled the gum wad into a dirty ball and wrapped it in one of the gum wrappers I'd stuffed into my pocket.

"Are you two going to eat with us or get a room?" Bus Boy's voice startled me. He and Jilly stood on the sidewalk; Jilly had her hands on her hips, eyebrows raised.

Bus Boy glanced at the bush. "Oh, I see that instead of a room, you got a hedge."

My cheeks warmed and I pushed past them all to the sidewalk. "I'm hungry."

"Worked up a little appetite, Erin?" Jilly asked as she fell into step beside me. She grabbed my arm and leaned toward me so her lips were practically inside my ear. "Were you guys making out?"

"Jilly!" The boys were only a few feet behind. Couldn't we talk about this later? But she was looking at me with such eagerness, I had to give her something. "We kissed," I whispered.

She squealed and squeezed my arm. "I knew it!"

"But not for long," I said. "I practically choked on his gum."

Jilly looked at me. "What?" Then she laughed and shook her head.

"I know," I said. "Only *I* would choke on the guy's gum the first time we make out."

"At least you'll remember it," Jilly said, tucking her arm through mine.

Saturday , September 13

THINGS THAT ARE WEIRD 🌀

✱ Weird #1: My mom totally wanted me 2 dish about Blake . . . not since the BN have we talked abt boys.

✱ Weird #2: I don't want 2 talk 2 her about boys or anything . . . not sure why.

THINGS THAT ARE FREAKING ME OUT IN A GOOD WAY 📺

✱ Blake & I kissed again after we 8 burgers & b4 we got picked up. Right in front of Jilly & Bus Boy. It was AMAZING.

✱ Blake e-mailed me @ least 10 times since yesterday.

✱ Jilly can't stop talking about it & neither can I.

Mark called & asked where I was yesterday.

HOT—✪—METER

💘 **#1 Blake Thornton** — totally gorgeous 9th grade mountain surfer
#2 Dylan Beaumont — taken, but cute
#3 Mark Sacks — the hair, the butt in shorts — need I say more?
#4 Mr. Perkins (drops to #4 because of age gap)

· **Quiz** ·

1. If a guy who is 1 of yr best friends asks where u were, u tell him u:

   a. were kissing a hot boarder boy behind some bushes & in front of friends (don't think so).
   b. had 2 wash the dog (even if u don't have 1).
   c. had 2 practice your bowling stance (need 2 but didn't).
   d. had 2 help your mom pick out software (lame, but he bought it).

2. If a guy who is 1 of yr best friends asks where u were Fri & u LIED 2 him, u r:

   a. a very mature 8th grader waiting until u know 4 sure the BF status b4 making anything public.

b. a good friend protecting his feelings. (He likes Kara. What's 2 protect?)

c. a total loser who should be banned from the planet.

d. a very confused person who has no idea what she's doing.

Sigh. All I know is that Blake is cute & fun & I want 2 kiss him again & I don't want 2 have 2 explain it 2 Mark.

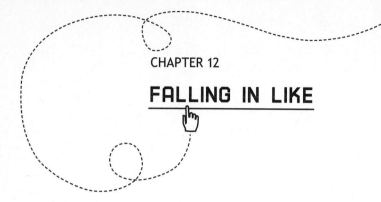

CHAPTER 12

FALLING IN LIKE

SO THIS WAS WHAT IT was like to have someone like you back. I loved knowing Blake was thinking about me and I could also see why Jilly was obsessed with texting. I grabbed her phone whenever I saw her because Blake had started texting me on it. Just little stuff like *wassup?* and *test in lit kicked my butt* because of course he couldn't say other stuff with Jilly able to read it. He saved that for IM and e-mail.

Can't wait 2 c u again he said in his last e-mail. *Let's do something this weekend. How about DQ? We can ride our bikes.*

I was pretty sure I was walking on air, even though my Chucks touched the floor.

When he called after school on Monday to ask about getting together on Saturday, I admitted my parents wouldn't let me *date* date until I was older.

"No worries," he said. "Jon and Jilly are in."

"Oh," I said, feeling a little disappointed. Even if I couldn't, didn't he want to be with me alone? "Great."

"We'll come to your house before we go so I can charm your mom again."

"You'd do that?"

"Sure."

Blake Thornton was beyond cool.

After we hung up, the phone rang immediately. Caller ID told me it was Mark.

"How about some hoops this weekend?"

"Sure," I said, then guilt pricked at me. Should I play basketball with Mark now that I was going out with Blake? *Were* we going out? No one had used the words "boyfriend" or "girlfriend" but we had kissed so that must mean something, right? I had no idea since this was the first time someone I liked liked me back. Maybe I should talk to Blake about it. But was it too soon to talk about that kind of stuff? We'd only been together twice, and one of those was at Jilly's when we met. Would he think I was pushing too hard with the relationship? Or would he be mad if I said nothing and he found out later I was with Mark. Maybe I should —

"Earth to E." Mark's voice jarred me back. "Come in, E."

"Sorry," I murmured. "I'm a little distracted."

"I noticed," Mark said. "Everything okay?"

No, it's not, I wanted to say. *I met this guy and he's really cute and we made out two times (but who's counting?) and I really like him and he likes me and it's amazing to have someone I like like me back and even though I don't like you that way anymore and you have a girlfriend, it still feels weird to tell you.*

"Just—some stuff," I said finally.

"Stuff," Mark said. "Anything to do with that guy you went bowling with on Friday?"

"What?" How did he find out? And why hadn't he said something sooner?

"Jilly mentioned it at school today," Mark said, as if reading my mind. "I thought you went shopping for software with your mom."

"Well, I was going to and then this came up and —" I stopped. I was digging a hole. "I'm sorry," I said. "I guess I just felt weird talking about it."

"Why? I talk to you about Kara."

"I know," I said, "but I don't really know what it is yet."

"You like this guy?" Mark asked. "What's his name—Blaze? Bronze?"

"Blake," I said, laughing. I couldn't tell if Mark was goofing up his name on purpose or not but it was nice to have it out there. "I don't know. I just met him."

"Are you going out with him again?"

"What's with the twenty questions?"

Mark laughed. "Just giving back some of what you do to me. 'How's Kara? Did you guys get together over the weekend? What color was her lip gloss?'"

I snorted. "I never asked you about her lip gloss," I said. "I'm surprised you even know what that is."

"It's that stuff you put on your eyelids, right?"

"You're hilarious, Sacks. Why don't you put some lip gloss on your big toe."

"I just might, Miss I-Have-a-Boyfriend."

"I don't," I said quickly. "At least, not yet."

"Kara's calling on the other line," Mark said. "I can let it go to voice mail."

"No, go ahead and talk to her. I need to get off anyway."

After I hung up, I headed downstairs to find my mom. I hated the way my stomach clenched every time I needed to ask her something now. It never used to be like this. But then again, *she* never used to be like this—worried, a little suspicious. I didn't know what her problem was but I wished she'd get over it so I could have some fun.

"You're riding your bikes?" She said it as if I'd told her we were going to skydive to get to DQ—without parachutes.

"Yeah," I said. "You know, those things with two wheels I've been riding since I was six?"

She gave me her don't-get-smart-with-me look.

I sighed. "They'll come here first so we can all ride together. Blake wants to say hello."

Finally, a smile. "Well, that's nice. I think it's fine but no stopping along the way. Straight there and straight back. All right?"

What did she think we were going to do, head to California? "All right."

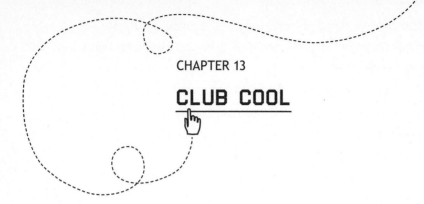

CHAPTER 13

CLUB COOL

JILLY WOULDN'T HAVE BELIEVED IT, but I was more excited about starting I-Club than I was about the DQ double-date on Saturday. As I stepped into the familiar computer lab that Thursday after school, I couldn't help grinning. The clusters of computers, the glowing monitors, the trackballs and mice neatly positioned beside each keyboard — it all gave me a jolt of excitement. Even though we had our computers and technology elective in here twice a week, the room looked different somehow. Soon we'd be creating web pages, links, and animated stuff, and all of it would go out on the Internet for everyone to see. I couldn't wait.

"Okay, people, settle down." Ms. Moreno stood in front of her desk, a stack of papers clutched in her hand. Mr. Arnett, who helped with I-Club, was flipping through software discs. I glanced around the room. Most of the old faces were back, including Serena. Reede sat near the back, Tyler on one side of her, Steve on the other. She raised her chin in greeting and I nodded.

Mark appeared in the doorway, talking to someone over his shoulder. A hand clutched his and I pictured Kara just outside the door. He said something to her and smiled. The hand released and he waved good-bye before coming inside, grinning at me as he dropped into a seat at one of the computer clusters.

There were about five or six seventh graders huddled in the corner beneath the Rules for Safe Surfing poster. Behind them was the familiar row of shelves holding books, manuals, and discs, all neatly stacked because I'd organized them myself last year.

"Find a seat, everyone," Ms. Moreno said. She rapped on the desktop and we quieted down. "We need to get our groups and get to work. We have a lot to do if we want to have a fully functioning website on the Internet by February or March."

"What about the Intranet?" someone asked. "Will that go away?"

"We'll have both," she said. "And we'll need to maintain both. Some of what we have for the Intranet can be used on our Internet website, which will help." Her eyes fell to the back of the room. I glanced over my shoulder. The seventh graders were still in a group, eying the empty seats, none of which were together. "You'll have to split up," Ms. Moreno said to them. "*Most* of the eighth graders don't bite, though I can't vouch for all of them."

The class chuckled and the seventh graders made their way to available seats.

"Okay, these are the group leaders." Ms. Moreno glanced down at her paper. "Erin Swift, Rosie Velarde, Mark Sacks, Jonathan Parker, and Zach Lucas. Could each of you make sure you're at a separate computer cluster and then —"

"Ms. Moreno." Steve waved his arm high in the air.

"— when I read off the groups, please —"

"Ms. Moreno!"

Ms. Moreno sighed. "What is it, Steven?" She was the only one who called him Steven. I thought it was because she was trying to make him sound older and more mature so he would act older and more mature. So far, it wasn't working.

"You forgot to call my name to be a group leader."

All the eighth graders broke out laughing.

"What?" Steve looked around at us, raising his hands in a question.

"Leader of what?" Rosie said. "Ways to get in trouble?"

We all laughed.

"Thank you, Steven," Ms. Moreno said, "but I've already chosen the leaders."

Steve pretended to pout while she had one of the seventh graders hand out the papers.

"I've divided up the categories for each group," she said. "Group leaders, when I call your name, raise your hand so people know who you are. Erin Swift, home page and look and feel of the site, and some miscellaneous pages. Erin's group will be Reede Harper, Scott Jensen, Joe Monahan, and Serena Worthington. Next leader is Mark Sacks, faculty and staff pages plus —"

I stopped listening. I had Reede "Silicon Valley Hot Makeover" Harper AND Serena in my group? I was feeling more comfortable around Reede, but what if she knew way more than I did and thought I was a total idiot? She grew up with a techno guru. She probably had a memory card embedded in her brain and wireless capabilities through her earlobe. And Serena? Well, even though things seemed okay between us, I still wasn't sure about her.

I scowled before turning back to my circle of computers where Reede, Scott, Joe, and Serena were gathering.

"So, Team Leader." Serena plopped down next to Reede, leaning her face around the monitor. "What will it be this year? Baring your butt instead of your soul?"

Scott shifted in his seat, staring down at his keyboard. He was an eighth grader and knew what Serena was talking about. Joe was a seventh grader so he just looked clueless. Reede smirked at me and I raised my eyebrows in response.

"Funny, Serena," I said, but she was looking at Reede and suddenly I got it. She wanted Reede to like her. She was using the YOHE to get in good with Reede. I had an odd wave of pity for her. "I don't think anyone wants to see my bare butt," I said, and everyone laughed. "And I'll try to keep my soul to myself this year."

"Except when you want to give it to a high school guy," Reede said, jiggling her shoulders in an ooh-la-la gesture.

Serena whipped her head in my direction. "What high school guy?"

"It's nothing," I mumbled, wondering how Reede had found out about Blake.

"That's not what I heard," Reede said.

Serena was about to say something else when Ms. Moreno called us to attention.

"Let's go over the handouts first," she said, holding up a copy of the stapled papers we all had in front of us. We spent the rest of the meeting discussing our game plan and making lists of the things we needed to do to get the website up and running.

After the meeting, Mark, Tyler, and Rosie hung back while I got my stuff together.

"Some group you've got, Swift," Mark said.

"Tell me about it." I said. "I need to talk to Ms. Moreno."

"Don't worry," Tyler said, "You're Erin Swift, Webmaster of the Universe."

I narrowed my eyes at him. "Is it Opposite Day?"

He smiled. "It's actually opposite of opposite day," Tyler said, pointing at me. "You rule, Erin P. Swift." He grinned wide.

Huh. Where did that cute dimple in his right cheek come from? How come I never noticed it when I had a crush on him at computer camp?

I smiled and pointed back at him. "Thanks, Ty. I'll catch you guys later."

The room emptied, leaving Ms. Moreno and I alone. "Before you say anything, may I say something first?" she asked. Obviously she knew why I'd stayed after everyone else was gone.

"I guess," I said.

"I put Serena in your group because I think she—well, I think you could be a positive influence on her."

I sighed. I just wanted to design the coolest school website ever. I didn't want to have to be a positive influence on anyone. It would be hard enough trying to be cool and competent in front of Reede.

And why do adults always do that anyway? Just when you're brave enough to say what you really feel, they force you to do what they want by giving you a compliment. It was some kind of twisted adult psychology and it was really annoying.

"And I put Reede in your group because she asked me to."

"What?"

Ms. Moreno smiled. "I think her exact words were, 'Erin Swift seems to be the computer and web expert around here. Can you put me in her group?'"

"She called me an expert?" I hated how eager my voice sounded, as if Reede's opinion was this big important thing. And yet, I had to admit it was.

"She did," Ms Moreno said. "I know you have a lot of ideas, too, but I think she'll bring a lot to the website."

I had more than a lot of ideas. I had an entire flowchart of the website, plus several mock-ups for the "look and feel," since Ms. Moreno hinted last year that I might be in charge of it. But I *did* feel a little better knowing Reede had told Ms. Moreno she wanted to work with me.

"I'm sure she will," I said. I hoped she'd really add something and not just want to use all of her ideas and tell me what to do.

CHAPTER 14

COMMUNICATION CONFUSIFICATION

MY PARENTS THOUGHT IT WAS wonderful that Ms. Moreno had "such confidence" in me to be a positive influence on Serena. I groaned and told them it was all just a big conspiracy by the adults to praise me into doing what they wanted. They gave each other the she's-thirteen-and-we-have-to-expect-this look and my dad said they knew I'd do the right thing.

Argh. Sometimes I'd like to do the wrong thing, just to shake people up.

"You've got to be kidding," Jilly said after I explained everything on the phone that night. "What does Ms. Moreno think? That you and Serena will suddenly be best friends?"

"I know." Finally someone who got it. I dropped down on my bed. "I can't believe I'm supposed to worry about Serena. I just want to make a good website."

"You'll be great," Jilly said. "Do you know what it's going to look like yet?"

"*I* do." I flipped through the flow charts I'd pulled out of my backpack. "But Ms. Moreno wants me to get Reede involved in the design, too."

"Ms. Moreno sure is asking you to do a lot of extra stuff."

"Tell me about it," I said. "But maybe Reede will have some good ideas." It was easier to be nice about Reede with Jilly so clearly on my side.

"Yeah, like how to wear too much makeup and still have all the guys drooling over you," Jilly said. I heard her bed squeak and then her cell ringtone. "Jon's texting. Can't wait for Saturday!"

After we'd hung up and I'd finished my homework, I went downstairs and got online. Mark sent me an IM right away.

> **Slamdunk12:** E, u there?
>
> **Webqueen429:** Yep.
>
> **Slamdunk12:** So r we hooping this wkend or what?
>
> **Webqueen429:** Sun @ 11?
>
> **Slamdunk12:** Be there or be a puppet.
>
> **Webqueen429:** ☺

My computer dinged.

> **BoardMan218:** Erin?
>
> **Webqueen429:** Hey, Blake.
>
> **BoardMan218:** Wassup?
>
> **Webqueen429:** Not much. U?
>
> **Slamdunk12:** E? E? U on w/ some1 else?
>
> **Webqueen429:** NOYB.
>
> **Slamdunk12:** ☺ Is it that Bloke? How's he doing?
>
> **Webqueen429:** How's Kara doing?
>
> **Slamdunk12:** Ok. Ok. So how'd it go w/ Moreno?
>
> **Webqueen429:** ☹ I'm still stuck w/ SW. My parents said that Ms. Moreno wouldn't have done it if she didn't think I was the right person, blah, blah, blah. But sometimes I don't want 2 be that person, u <no?>

I waited. I wondered what he was thinking as he stared at the screen, reading my words. Did he understand? Did he think I was stupid? Or maybe he was IMing Kara separately. Or watching ESPN.

Webqueen429: U there?

Slamdunk12: Yeah. Just—lotsa words 4 IM.

Webqueen429: ☺

Slamdunk12: What u said makes sense. I no what u mean. Did you do the history homework yet?

I smiled. Mark was still Mark, no matter what.

Webqueen429: Yep. U?

BoardMan218: Erin? Where'd you go? Wassup?

Webqueen429: Sorry. Not much. U?

BoardMan218: Same. You IM'ing some1 else?

Slamdunk12: E? Get off w/ Loverboy & talk 2 me. I need homewk help.

Webqueen429: Don't call him that.

Slamdunk12: Ah ha! u R talking 2 Bland.

Webqueen429: Shut up.

Slamdunk12: A little touchy, aren't u?

I furrowed my brow. I wasn't touchy. I just didn't want to talk about it.

Webqueen429: Is there a reason for this convo or what?

Slamdunk12: Fine. Yes. I'm wondering if u'll help a struggling student?

Webqueen429: Maybe u're not struggling, just lazy?

BoardMan218: Erin? What r u talking about?

Oops. How did Blake's window pop up over Mark's?

Webqueen429: Sorry. Someone needed homework help & I got mixed up.

BoardMan218: Who is it?

Slamdunk12: E? Come on. Quit leavin me hangin.

Webqueen429: Just a friend.

BoardMan218: That's wat they all say. What's his name?

Slamdunk12: I'm logging off. Call me when u r not so busy w/ your BF.

I waited but Mark didn't say anything else. I clicked on Blake's window.

Webqueen429: They logged off. Can't wait 4 Sat!

BoardMan218: Me either. & we need that foosball rematch.

Webqueen429: U like 2 suffer.

BoardMan218: U wish — Gtg

Webqueen429: c u

I was sweating and my breath was coming fast when I logged off. Whew. That was close.

Thursday, September 18

THINGS THAT MAKE ME WONDER ◉

✳ Why can't I tell BT about MS?

✳ Why can I tell MS about BT?

✳ Will my I-Club group be a total disaster?

✳ Why am I always asking questions that have no answers?

THINGS THAT ARE PRETTY COOL ☀

✳ Reede told Ms. Moreno I'm a web expert.

✳ Jilly understands my pain.

✳ Mark & I can joke about our BF/GF sitch.

THINGS THAT ROCK 🎸

✳ I'm going out w/ Blake on Sat!!!

HOT—✖—METER

💝 **#1 Blake Thornton** — totally gorgeous 9th grade mountain surfer

#2 Dylan Beaumont — taken, but cute

#3 Mark Sacks — the hair, the butt in shorts — need I say more?

#4 Tyler Galleon — well, not exactly hot but definitely on the Cute-o-Meter, mostly cuz of that dimple I never saw before

#5 Mr. Perkins

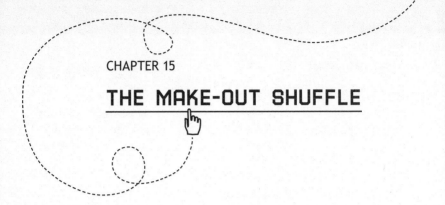

CHAPTER 15

THE MAKE-OUT SHUFFLE

JILLY, BUS BOY, AND BLAKE showed up at exactly three thirty-five Saturday afternoon. I know this because I was standing just inside the living room so I had a clear view of both the front walk through the window and the clock on the mantle above the fireplace. As Blake walked his bike up the driveway, I stepped back into the hallway and scurried back about halfway. When the doorbell rang, I stood there counting. I didn't want to look too eager.

"Do you want me to get it?" Chris said as he pounded down the stairs.

"No. Yes. No!" I shoved him away and strode down the hall, ignoring the kissy noises and laughter behind me. Talk about immature.

Blake stood on my front porch, looking ultra cute with his spiked blond hair and oversized T-shirt and baggy shorts. Jilly and Jon stayed on the sidewalk, their bikes leaning against them as they talked. Blake and I smiled at each other as he stepped inside. I had a brief flutter as he turned his face to me. Was he going to kiss me right here in the foyer, with my brother possibly spying?

Nope.

He had caught his reflection in the mirror hanging above the entry table and patted his hair with his hand.

"Can I get a glass of water?" Blake asked. "I forgot my water bottle at home."

My mom came in as Blake was sucking down the last drops.

"Good to see you again, Mrs. Swift," he said to her.

"You, too, Blake," my mom said.

"My dad said you designed the website for one of his clients. I checked it out and it's really cool."

"I appreciate that, Blake," she said, then patted his arm. "You don't need to butter me up. I know you're a nice boy."

Blake blushed, then grinned. "So, you've been listening to lies about me, then?"

My mom laughed. "You four have fun. Do you need any money?"

"I've got some," I said, backing away toward the door.

"Remember, straight there and straight back," my mom said to me. "No stopping."

"Don't worry about it, Mom." I hustled Blake out of there as fast as I could.

At Dairy Queen, Blake ordered a mint chocolate chip Blizzard and I had the Blizzard of the Month—something with bananas in it. I didn't really pay attention because Blake was gripping my elbow, standing so close behind me I could practically feel his breath in my hair.

The four of us ate at one of the tables, talking about whatever came to our minds; I was just happy to listen to Blake's voice and look into his amazing blue eyes. He was really into video games so he talked a lot about his Nintendo Wii and Xbox and I talked about our Playstation.

"You'll have to come over and play games sometime," he said.

Me? At Blake Thornton's house? I swallowed my freak-out and smiled. "That would be cool."

Jilly and Bus Boy talked about school and homework and whether or not Bus Boy would do well on the Wash High soccer team. When we were finished, we walked our bikes across the street toward the park. Blake gave me a smile before turning to Jilly and Bus Boy.

"We're under strict orders to go straight back," he said to them.

My cheeks warmed. Why was he announcing it?

"Straight means taking the inside path through the trees," Bus Boy said, pointing across the park. "We're staying on this path."

Blake looked at me and shrugged. "I guess it'll just be the two of us through the trees."

I smiled. So that's why he announced it.

After promising to meet up with Jilly and Bus Boy on the other side of the park, Blake motioned me to follow him. "Come on. I want to show you something."

Huh. I had thought this was a scheme to get us alone, but Blake looked all tour guide as we wound our way along the path, circling groves and benches along the way.

"What is it?" I asked. "A bird's nest?" What else could you show someone in a park?

"You'll see," was all he said.

He veered off the path near a grove of trees and leaned his bike against one of them. I did the same. He took my hand and we walked between two trees. "Look," he said, pointing up. I followed his finger, squinting into the branches as we kept walking.

The next thing I knew, he was kissing me. After I got over my surprise, I kissed him right back and we kept kissing, shuffling beneath the branches in an awkward dance. When we stopped kissing, we kept shuffling and I grinned.

"What do you call that?" I asked.

"The make-out shuffle," he said and we both laughed. "We're not stopping and we're going straight back—sort of."

I threw my arms around him and kissed him again. "You're the best."

We raced each other to the edge of the park, where we hooked up with Jilly and Bus Boy. Jilly raised her eyebrows, and I raised mine back. We both smiled before pushing off and riding toward home.

I was desperate to kiss Blake good-bye when we got back to my house but I didn't know who might be watching so I settled for a thanks and a wave.

"See you soon, Erin Swift," Blake said as he rode away.

"That was nice of all of them to ride back with you," my mom said when I stepped inside.

"Were you watching from the window?"

My mom laughed. "Yes, I was." She patted my arm. "Do you like him a lot?"

I shrugged. I did, but I didn't want to tell her for some reason.

Mom sighed. "Well, he seems very nice." She turned toward the kitchen. "It's funny, I always thought—well, it doesn't matter." She looked over her shoulder at me. "Dinner's almost ready. I hope you're hungry after ice cream."

I hardly registered food. I was focused on the other part. "What, Mom? You always thought what?"

She smiled. "It's nothing really, Erin. I just assumed that you and Mark —" She paused, then shook her head. "But I can see there aren't any sparks between you and I'd rather you were just friends with all these boys anyway. You know I was friends with your dad —"

"— for six years before you married him," I finished. "Yes, I know. You've told me a million times." I sighed. "Don't worry. Blake is really great and easy to talk to. I think we'll be good friends." Good friends with kissing benefits, but I wasn't going to tell her that.

"How was the big date?" Chris came into the kitchen, grabbing an apple.

"It wasn't a date," my mom and I said at the same time.

But with all the kissing that had gone on, I knew it kind of was.

Saturday, September 20

I think I'm officially in deep like. I really can't believe I'm kissing a boy . . . esp one like BT. & I'm trying not 2 think about how many other girls he might have brought 2 that spot between the trees.

Weird about my mom. Does she c something in Mark that I don't anymore? Or is it just cuz she knows him better than the other guys in my life that she thought we might get 2gether? (Or cuz he's been pretty much the only guy in my life until recently?) But she said she didn't see any sparks. Why is she even looking 4 them? And why do I care? I really don't want my mom thinking about my love life.

Blake e-mailed me five times 2nite & called 2 say g-nite. Beyond sweet.

Tomorrow I shoot hoops w/ Mark. I'm looking forward 2 it and feeling a little guilty 2.

HOT—✪—METER

💝 **#1 Blake Thornton** — totally gorgeous 9th grade mountain surfer

#2 Dylan Beaumont — taken, but cute

#3 Mark Sacks — the hair, the butt in shorts — need I say more?

#4 Tyler Galleon — well, not exactly hot but definitely on the Cute-o-Meter, mostly cuz of that dimple I never saw before

#5 Mr. Perkins

CHAPTER 16

THANK YOU FOR NOT SMOKING

SHOOTING HOOPS AT THE Y with Mark after making out with Blake the day before was, well, different. I felt more confident, like Mark and I were equals, which was weird. And I could flirt a little with him without it meaning anything since he knew about Blake.

"You're sure on your game today," Mark said when we took a water break after I beat him two out of three.

"I'd have been more on it if you hadn't fouled me on those two lay-ups," I said, nudging him with my elbow so he spilled his water.

"Hey," he said, elbowing me back. "And those were not fouls. They were totally legal." He flicked some water at me.

I flicked some back.

He held up his water bottle. "You want to start something?"

I held up mine. "Only if I can finish it."

We stood there, facing off with our water bottles, before we both laughed and drank.

"That was fun," I said as we stepped outside the Y to wait for our rides. It occurred to me that my mom never seemed bothered about me being alone with Mark. I guess it was because she'd never seen sparks. She knew it was safe.

"So, Reede's coming over to your house next weekend?" Mark asked as we sat down on the low brick walls, our basketballs resting on our laps.

"Yeah." She and I had been talking about getting together to plan the website. I had wanted to go to her house and meet her dad and see what kind of equipment and software they had but she said they were still disorganized from the move so we planned to meet at my lame house. She was all excited to hear I had an older brother but I warned her he was weird and taken.

"That just makes it more interesting," she had said.

Saturday morning Reede showed up at my house wearing tight jeans and a lace top. When she pulled off her jacket, her shirt hitched up and I saw her belly button ring glint in the light. She wore her usual amount of makeup and her hair was curled. She caught me checking her out and grinned.

"You never know who you might run into."

"He's asleep," I said, getting it.

"He'll wake up." She tossed her hair over her shoulder. "And I'll be ready."

"You haven't even seen him. You don't know him."

She smiled. "I've seen you. I know you. If he's anything close to a boy version of you, we're in business."

I shook my head, but couldn't help smiling at the compliment.

"How's *your* high school hunk?"

My cheeks warmed. "Fine," I said, walking to the kitchen table. "Let's brainstorm at the table, then we can get on the computer."

"Cool," Reede said. "I understand if you don't want to share the intimate details. Looks like you took it to hot without my help. Congratulations." As she scanned the room, I noticed she didn't have anything with her. No folders or notebooks or anything else. Maybe she had a flash drive in her pocket. "Your house is awesome," she said, then glanced out the kitchen window to the backyard. "Think I could sneak out back for a cig? I didn't get my morning drag and I don't think I'll be able to concentrate until I do."

Smoking? Here? My parents had gone to the hardware store but Chris might come down any minute. I glanced at the clock. Ten. He usually didn't get up until noon, but still . . .

"Hey, if you'd rather I didn't." She had an edge to her voice.

"It's, well —" *Speak up, Erin.* "My parents always seem to sniff things out, if you know what I mean. I don't want you to get in trouble."

"You mean *you* don't want to get in trouble," she said. "For having a smoker for a friend. Bad influence and all that." She slipped her jacket back on.

"You're leaving?"

"I'll walk down the block," she said. "That way no one gets in trouble." She paused, holding up the cigarette. "Want to share one?"

"No, thanks."

She looked at me for a second, then turned and headed out the front door. I'd spoken up. So why did I feel stupid? Like I was some wimp who couldn't even let someone smoke in the backyard when no one was around. Too scared of what my parents might say.

I sighed, getting out paper, rulers, and several pens and sharpened pencils. I brought out water and juice and some donuts, then wondered if I would look like some old lady serving tea or something. I took them back to the counter, then walked to the living room window where I could see the street. Reede was just a few houses down, sucking on her cigarette.

"Who's that?"

I started at Chris's voice, turning to look at him. He had on a ratty pair of sweats with rips in the knees, and a T-shirt with a huge hole in the back of the neck where he grabbed it to pull it over his head. His hair flew out to one side, like a diving platform.

"A girl from school," I said. "We're working on the new website together."

"She smokes."

"Duh." I looked back at Reede. She dropped her cigarette on the sidewalk, crushing it with the toe of her boot. I tugged at Chris's arm. "Get away from the window."

Chris followed me back into the kitchen. "I'd never go out with a girl who smokes." He hacked and spit into the sink.

"Gross," I said automatically. "I'd never go out with a guy who hacks loogies."

Chris snorted. "All guys hack loogies."

An image of Blake — then Mark — bringing up some big ol' booger spit flashed through my mind and I cringed. "Rinse it down," I said, pointing to the disgusting blob in the sink. Chris ignored me and pulled out a box of Cheerios from the cupboard. I turned on the sprayer at the sink and used about five gallons of water getting his loogie to finally slide down the drain.

A few seconds later the front door opened and Reede stepped in. "Should I have rung the doorbell again?" she called. "I never know about all that etiquette stuff." She stepped into the kitchen. "It's kind of chilly out. Do you have any —" She stopped talking when she saw Chris. "Crap." She ran her hand over her hair. "Hi."

"We actually do have crap but I'm not sure you'd be interested in it," Chris said.

Reede laughed. "I'm Reede."

"I'm Chris, the evil older brother."

She giggled, flipping her hair over her shoulder. I'd never heard Reede giggle before. It made her seem different, younger. "I don't always look like this. Saturday morning, you know."

I laughed. She must have spent at least two hours getting ready.

"He always looks like that," I said, pointing to Chris's hair.

Chris patted his hair down, but it sprang right back up. "And proud of it." He grabbed the milk from the fridge and carried everything into the family room.

Reede stared after him. Then she turned back to me. "God, he's hot."

I burst out laughing. "Are you kidding? He's a total slob. He's disgusting, trust me."

"He's your brother," Reede said. "He's supposed to be disgusting to you." She glanced around the kitchen. "Got any coffee?"

"Not made," I said. "And I don't know how to make it." I pulled a basket down from the top of the fridge. "How about hot chocolate?" I held up a packet.

"With or without marshmallows?"

I grimaced. Why didn't I just wear a sign that said, *Totally uncool*?

"I'm kidding, Erin," Reede said. "I like hot chocolate. I can get my big caffeine fix later."

We settled down at the kitchen table, mugs of hot chocolate in one hand, pencils in the other. I showed her my ideas and she liked them all.

"What were some of your ideas?" I asked. "Did you bring some stuff on a flash drive?"

Reede shook her head. "I feel like it's your show," she said. "I don't want to butt in."

"Ms. Moreno said you probably had some good ideas," I said. "I'm open."

"That's okay." Reede flipped through my pages. "I really like what you've got." We headed down to my mom's office and I got her laughing when I showed her how to throw virtual darts at Serena on the computer before bringing up some sample pages for the website.

"These are great, Swift. You really know what you're doing."

"Thanks," I said. "Do you think once we get going you could show some pages to your dad? I'm sure he's really busy and everything but it would be great to get his advice."

Reede's eyes shifted away from mine. "He doesn't really do web design," she said. "You know. Too busy with some of the bigger stuff." She stepped out of my mom's office.

"Right." Disappointed, I followed her. "So do you think we should do any animation on the home page? Or other fancy stuff? Do you know JavaScript?"

Reede didn't answer, just walked up the stairs. I followed her as she headed through the kitchen and stood near the entry to the family room. The TV blared as Chris sat on the couch, shoveling mounds of Cheerios into his mouth.

Reede turned around and walked back to the island where I was standing. "So, how serious are he and his little girlfriend?"

"They've been going out for a while," I said. "And no offense, but there's no way he'd go out with an eighth grader. He's a junior."

"Well, I'm not really —" She stopped and smiled. "A girl can dream, can't she?"

I frowned. Chris would totally dis her if she flirted with him. "So do you want to go over some color schemes?"

"Nah, I trust whatever you decide," she said. Huh. This wasn't how I had expected this to go at all. I thought I'd have to defend my lame ideas against her brilliant ones. But she either didn't have any or was being nice.

While she was using the guest bathroom, I helped my parents, who had stumbled in the back door with several bags.

"New doorknob and finally a lightbulb for the closet downstairs," my dad said.

Reede came in just then and I introduced her to my parents.

"It's nice to meet you," my mom said, her eyes taking in everything from Reede's bottled blond hair to the heavy eyeliner, to the tight shirt, to the belly ring.

"Erin said your dad has been a big force in the Internet," my dad said. "That's exciting."

"Yeah, it's pretty cool." Reede looked back down the hall. She seemed nervous and I wondered if she was worried about my parents smelling cigarette smoke on her. She turned to me. "Come on, Erin. We'd better get back to work before I have to go."

"Nice to meet you, Reede," my parents said at the same time. I saw them exchange a look before I turned to follow Reede back to my mom's basement office.

When it was time for her to leave, Reede wandered back toward the family room. "See you, Chris, the evil older brother."

Chris waved. "See you, Reede, Erin's interesting friend."

Reede grinned as we headed for the front door. "He thinks I'm interesting." She sighed. "Didn't I tell you high school boys are where it's at? The guys in middle school are so lame."

I wasn't sure how Chris calling her interesting and looking like a slob was proof that high school guys were a big thumbs up, but whatever. I did have some proof in Blake.

"Next time we can work at your house," I said.

"I don't mind coming here," Reede said, raising her eyebrows.

"He's got a —"

"— girlfriend," Reede finished. "I know."

My mom met us at the front door, holding Reede's jacket.

"Thanks, Mrs. Swift." Reede shrugged it on and was out the door before either of us could say anything else.

"Her jacket smells like smoke." My mom stared out the window toward the place where Reede had been smoking on the sidewalk.

"Maybe her parents smoke," I said. "Thanks for letting us use your computer. We got a lot done."

"Good," my mom said. She touched me lightly on the arm. "You know where we stand on smoking."

"Mom, I'm not smoking. God." I could hear Reede's voice: . . . *having a smoker for a friend. Bad influence and all that.*

"Watch your language." Mom's voice was sharp, then her face softened as she looked at me. "But I'm glad you're not."

"She's new this year," I said, reminding her of my Good Samaritan–like ways. "And she's nice."

"I'm sure she is," my mom said. "But that doesn't mean she isn't doing things she shouldn't be doing."

Sometimes my mom was fine and sometimes she seemed like one big lecture.

"I'm not going to do anything bad, Mom, if that's what you're worried about."

My mom stepped back and squeezed the back of my head. "I'm not worried," she said. "But it doesn't hurt to be aware."

"I'm aware, I'm aware," I said, ducking out from under her grasp. I hurried up to my room before she could say anything else.

Sunday, September 28

THINGS THAT ARE KIND OF ANNOYING

* My mom is on my case abt Reede.

* Reede smokes. If she didn't smoke, Mom would not be on my case abt her.

* Chris teased Reede so now she thinks she has a chance.

QUESTIONS TO PONDER

* Why didn't Reede bring any ideas 2 our meeting?

* Why didn't she answer my questions abt what she knew abt web stuff?

* Why was she so uncomfortable around my parents?

RANDOM STUFF

* Reede can switch from nice 2 kinda mean & back pretty fast. Makes me want 2 make sure I stay on her nice side.

* Blake, Mark, & Jilly IMed 2 find out how it went w/ Reede.

* Rosie called 2 find out.

* I wonder if anyone IMed or called Reede 2 find out how it went.

HOT—✪—METER

#1 Blake Thornton — totally gorgeous 9th grade mountain surfer

#2 Dylan Beaumont — taken, but cute

#3 Mark Sacks — the hair, the butt in shorts — need I say more?

#4 Tyler Galleon — well, not exactly hot but definitely on the Cute-o-Meter, mostly cuz of that dimple I never saw before

#5 Mr. Perkins

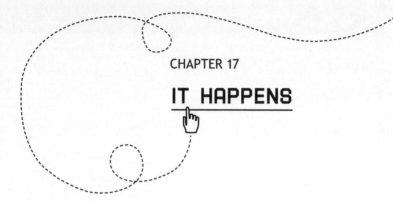

CHAPTER 17

IT HAPPENS

I CAME DOWNSTAIRS MONDAY MORNING just as my mom stepped out of the guest bathroom.

"Erin, have you seen my silver Celtic knot earrings?" My dad had given her the earrings for their tenth anniversary. They were her favorites. "I could have sworn I took them off in this bathroom on Saturday because I wanted to polish them. But they're not anywhere in there." She frowned. "I hope they didn't slip into the toilet and get flushed away."

"I'm sure they just fell behind something," I said. "Or maybe they're upstairs."

"I've checked everywhere." She rubbed her lips together. "Did Reede use that bathroom when she was here?"

I narrowed my eyes. "What? You think she took them?"

"Erin!" My mom's voice rose. "I just thought maybe she'd seen them."

"Well, I'm not going to ask her," I said.

"Why not?"

Was my mom really this dense? "Because she'd think we thought she took them."

"Oh, for heaven's sake, Erin." My mom shook her head and walked away, leaving me standing alone in the hall.

When we got to school, Jilly went to talk to a teacher and I headed for my locker. As I reached for my backpack, I felt something funny. Not funny, actually. Damp. In my underwear. Was I peeing my pants without even knowing it?

Oh. My. God.

Unzipping my backpack, I reached into the secret pocket where I had stashed my PEK.

It was empty.

Then I remembered I had taken everything out of my backpack when I was cleaning it. I must not have put the PEK back in.

I glanced around but didn't see anybody I really knew.

Bathroom. *Fast.*

I walked as quickly as you can when you are squeezing your thighs together and trying to squeeze other things together so nothing else comes out, even if you're not sure it will help because if they covered that in health class you sure don't remember it.

"You got something stuck up your butt?" Tyler asked as I passed him.

"Shut up," I said, and kept going. I pushed into the girls' bathroom and glanced at the machine—OUT OF ORDER. Surprise. I hurried to a stall, just as Serena came out of another one. She smiled at me and stepped to the sink.

I closed the stall door and sat on the toilet. My white underwear was stained a brownish-red. I checked the crotch of my jeans. There was a small stain on them. I looked at the outside of the jeans and breathed a sigh of relief. It hadn't leaked through.

Okay, now what? I knew the main office kept supplies but I couldn't risk going all the way down there without some kind of protection.

I glanced around, as if someone might have left an unused pad just for me. Nothing. My eyes fell to the toilet paper. Okay. I'd have to improvise. I pulled a bunch of toilet paper off the roll, folded it, and placed it in my underwear. As I pulled up my underwear, half the toilet paper unrolled and flopped out onto the floor. Great. I sat back down.

"So, Swift. Are you taking the biggest dump in the world, or what?"

I'd forgotten Serena was still out there.

"No!" The thought made me momentarily forget why I was in the bathroom in the first place. I would NEVER do that at school. What could be more embarrassing than stinking up the bathroom and having other people know it was you?

The door opened, but didn't close; someone was holding it open.

"Erin?" Rosie said. "I saw you rush down the hall. Are you okay?"

"She's taking the world's biggest dump," Serena said. "The Guinness Book people are on their way."

"I'm not taking a dump!" I said.

"Thanks for the news flash," some girl said, and my cheeks burned. I heard the stall on the far end open and close. She obviously wasn't taking any chances.

"I was just kidding, Erin," Serena said before she left.

Rosie laughed. "Well, if you're okay, I'm going to get to class."

"Wait!"

But she was already gone.

I unrolled more toilet paper, folding it carefully this time. After laying the "pad" in my underwear, I took another long piece of toilet paper and wrapped it around the pad and the bottom of my underwear a few times, like I was wrapping my ankle before a game. Then I tucked the loose end under the pad to hold everything in place.

Not bad. I pulled up my underwear and zipped and buttoned my jeans. It seemed to stay put. I turned and saw a few drops of blood in the toilet. I flushed, watching the brownish water disappear, feeling oddly sad that this was happening to me while I was alone, in a bathroom stall at school, with no one to tell.

Stepping out, I washed my hands, turning around to make sure you couldn't see any stains or bulges from the TP pad. Everything looked okay. It felt funny to have that bulk in my underwear but it was better than having leaks. I stared at myself in the mirror, trying to see if I looked any different. As I turned my face to one side, I wrinkled my nose.

News flash girl was taking a dump.

I decided to go to the office for supplies after language arts so I wouldn't have to explain a late arrival. But all during class I could feel things happening down there and I couldn't concentrate. Was it leaking out? Was it staining my jeans? Would people see?

"Erin? What do you think?"

I glanced up. Ms. Fehrmann had her eyebrows raised in a question.

I think I just had my first period and I'm freaking out a little bit.

"I'm sorry," I said. "I'm not sure."

"Did you read the story?"

What story? I knew I had read something last night but I couldn't remember what it was.

"You have absolutely no opinion on it?"

Clearly I *should* have an opinion on it.

"Lottery," Jilly coughed.

Lottery?

Oh. Right. We'd read "The Lottery" by Shirley Jackson. I remembered now. Who wouldn't? It was a weird, creepy story.

"I thought it was weird that everyone would go along with something so random," I said. "Maybe it was the law or tradition or whatever but when the winner of a lottery is stoned to death, it's time to take another look, don't you think?"

"Nice recovery, Erin," Ms. Fehrmann said. "With a little help from your friends." She glanced at Jilly, who was busy turning pages in her book.

After class, I stayed in my seat until everyone had left.

"Come on, Erin," Jilly said, heading for the door. "You're going to be late."

"Jilly, I —"

Jilly stopped and turned around. "What?" She tilted her head. "Are you okay?"

I shook my head and Jilly hurried over. "What is it?"

"I got it," I whispered, even though there was no one in the room.

"Got what?" Jilly asked.

"IT," I said. My period. I had my period. Me, Erin Penelope Swift. Finally.

Jilly's eyes grew wide. "Omigod! Are you serious? When? Where were you? Do you feel any different? Did it hurt? Are you using a tampon? Does anyone else know?"

"Shhh," I said, then explained what I'd done in the bathroom.

"That's pretty smart," she said. "I'll have to remember that."

"It would be better to always have supplies," I said. "But I need your help."

"Name it."

"Tell me if it's showing through." I stood up and walked down the aisle as Jilly examined my backside.

"I thought I saw something but it's underneath so I don't think anyone will notice."

"Good." But I pulled my black hoodie over my head and tied it around my waist so it hung down past my butt, just in case.

Jilly picked up her books and hugged them to her chest. "Wow," she said. "You got it."

The words "before me" hung in the air between us.

"Yours will come soon," I said. "Then we can borrow supplies from each other."

Jilly smiled. "You know that when women live together, their cycles will start to be in sync. That's what happened with my sisters and my mother."

"Weird," I said, wondering if my mom and I would ever sync up. "Well, I'd better get to the office." I grabbed my books. "Jilly?"

"Yeah?"

"Thanks."

She smiled. "Anytime."

Monday, September 29

THINGS THAT ROCK

* I got my period today & it wasn't completely humiliating. No white pants or people seeing & making fun of me, except the dump thing w/ Serena. She's trying 2 hard 2 be buddy-buddy . . . it's bugging me.

* Jilly was way cool abt it.

THINGS THAT MAKE ME WONDER

* I didn't tell my mom. I stood outside her office, staring @ the sign on her door—DO NOT DISTURB UNDER PENALTY OF DEATH BY EGGPLANT—wondering about the exact threat of the eggplant. Would she throw it at us? Force us 2 eat it? Make us wear it? I didn't find out cuz I didn't disturb her abt my period or anything else. I don't know why. I just didn't feel like telling her 2day.

* I met Blake @ the park & we made out next 2 a tree. It felt different. No big tingles. Maybe having yr period affects yr kissing feelings.

HOT—✪—METER

💔 **#1 Blake Thornton**—totally gorgeous 9th grade mountain surfer
#2 Dylan Beaumont—taken, but cute
#3 Mark Sacks—the hair, the butt in shorts—need I say more?
#4 Tyler Galleon—well, not exactly hot but definitely on the Cute-o-Meter, mostly cuz of that dimple I never saw before
#5 Mr. Perkins

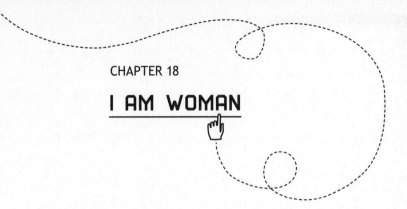

CHAPTER 18

I AM WOMAN

I FOUND MY PEK UNDER a pile of clothes in a corner of my room the next morning and stocked up with supplies from my parents' bathroom. I made it through the day like a pro, changing my pad every few hours and wondering if I would be brave enough to try a tampon next time.

No one had noticed anything different about me at breakfast, which was good because I would have been embarrassed to talk about it but bad because that meant it wasn't obvious that I had changed.

Jilly and I were talking about it on the bus when her phone chimed a text message.

"It's Blake," she said, "again." She handed me her phone, shaking her head. "Jon didn't even text me this much when we first started going out."

Miss u. Get 2gether this wkend?

I smiled as I read the text. He wanted to get together! So I had a no-tingle kiss. It was probably because I was so freaked out about my period. I still liked him, didn't I?

I sent him a quick reply. *Sure! Talk 2 u 2nite.*

When we got to school, Blake sent another text, asking if I wanted to double-date with Jilly and Bus Boy. I was texting him back when Kara and Mark walked by.

"You finally get a cell, Swift?" Mark asked.

"It's Jilly's," I said, sending a reply to Blake before turning the phone off and handing it to her.

"Blake has been texting her all morning," Jilly said. "I'm really sorry I gave him my number." She nudged me.

"Wow, that's great," Kara said, clearly thrilled that I now had a man in my life.

"The Bland Man," Mark said, raising his eyebrows at me.

"I've got to run," Jilly said, giving my arm a squeeze. "See you later."

"Glad things are going good with Bleak," Mark said after she left. He chuckled at his little joke.

"His name is Blake," I said. The "joke" felt different today. I didn't know if it was because Kara was there or because he'd used it so many times it was stale. Either way, I didn't like it.

"Oooh, sorry Miss Sensitive." Mark grabbed Kara's hand and strode off down the hall.

"What's his problem?" I asked no one in particular. I would seriously have to consider taking him off the Hot-o-Meter with an attitude like that.

"The same problem he's always had." Reede's voice made me turn. She opened our locker and put her bag inside. "He's into you."

"But he's going out with Kara," I protested. "We've been through this."

"He's confused," Reede said. "He doesn't quite understand what he's feeling, but when he does, look out. He'll be all over you."

"I think *you're* confused." Mark would never be "all over" me with Blake in the picture.

"Nah," Reede said. "He'll wait till your thing with Blake has run its course and then make his move."

I laughed. "You're crazy."

"Better than being boring," she said.

*   *   *

"So, how's Reede?" Mr. F squirted the windows outside the science lab on Wednesday and wiped them clean. It was the first of October and people were already talking about what they wanted to do for Halloween.

I frowned. I wasn't sure why Mr. F was asking me. Reede had been talking to him a lot; he had to know more about her than I did.

"She's a complicated girl," Mr. F said when I didn't answer. "But she's got a spark, doesn't she? Someone definitely worth knowing."

"I don't know if I'd call it a spark," I said, turning to the streaks on the window in front of me. "But she's definitely . . . something."

Mr. F smiled. "She's lucky to have you for a friend." He moved over to the other window and gave it a squirt.

I furrowed my brow. *Were* Reede and I friends? "Are you just saying that because you want me to be a positive influence on her?" I asked, thinking back to Ms. Moreno and my parents with Serena.

"I'm saying it because it's true," Mr. F said. "You're loyal and trustworthy and everyone needs that in their friends."

"You make me sound like a dog," I said and Mr. F laughed. But his words made me pause. I wasn't sure we were friends. I didn't think so. I still wasn't completely comfortable around her. I always felt a little off balance, a step behind, a lot younger.

"Well," he said, rubbing his nose with the back of his hand, "Reede Harper doesn't strike me as someone who is easily influenced."

I laughed. "You got that right." We knocked fists before I hurried off to lunch.

After the last bell, I headed to my locker. The area swarmed with the usual collection of Reede admirers. I shoved my way through the rather smelly throng.

"This is Reede's locker," one of them said.

"We're locker partners."

The boy eyed me with renewed respect. "Locker partner, huh?" he said. "You got her number? She's not giving it out."

"I'm not either," I said.

The bell rang again — reminding us that we only had five minutes to catch the buses — and the boys drifted away. I opened the locker as Reede hurried around the corner.

"Are they gone?"

I leaned way out, doing an exaggerated check of the halls. "Yep."

"Good." She waited for me to get my books, then reached in for her own. I watched her, wondering what it was about her that Mr. F thought was worth knowing. Probably not her ability to do mental makeovers, listen to her iPod in class without being caught, or claim that a guy liked another girl when he had a girlfriend.

I wondered if he knew she smoked and what he'd say if he knew she'd offered me a cigarette. I frowned. What was it about her that I should be noticing? I mean, she was nice but I didn't think she'd ever be a friend like Jilly or Mark or Rosie or even Tyler because even when she was in the middle of things, she was on the outside. On purpose.

"You finished counting my eyelashes?" Reede asked, poking me in the side.

"Sorry," I said, my cheeks warming. "I was just thinking, um, how great your eyes look and maybe I shouldn't have stopped you from doing your makeover on me."

"Really." Reede raised her eyebrows. "Very interesting. Let me see what you've got." She nodded her head down the hall.

"What?"

"Show me your stuff." She put a hand on one hip and cocked it.

I raised my chin at the challenge. Stepping away from the locker, I strutted down the hall, then turned back, using an exaggerated runway model hip swing-shoulder jut.

"Shake it, girl," Reede said, copying my movements. We shimmied and shook our way toward each other. When we came face-to-face, we collapsed against each other, giggling.

"What's the joke?" Jilly stood in front of us, scowling slightly.

"Oh, hey Jilly," I gasped. "Nothing. We were just being goofy."

"Well, we're going to miss the bus if we don't hurry." Jilly turned on her heel and strode down the hall.

"Forget the bus," Reede said, knocking her hip against mine. "Let's go to the mall."

That stopped me. "Now?" I'd never gone anywhere right after school without clearing it with my parents beforehand.

What would it feel like to break a rule?

"Now is always the best time," Reede said. "We could do that makeover."

"Well. . ." I hesitated, my mind ticking off all the reasons it wasn't a good idea.

"Oh, right," Reede said. "I forgot some people have to check in with Mommy."

"I don't have to check in," I said, annoyed. "*Some* people have to make sure they don't have other responsibilities." There. I'd stood up to her. Would she dis me and leave? Part of me wanted her to, because I was a little afraid to go without talking to my mom. But another part wanted to prove to her I was as cool as she was.

Reede laughed. "Fair enough."

Jilly had slowed down so I knew she was listening. She turned around. "Come on, Erin. Let's go." She placed her hands on her hips, a why-are-you-even-thinking-about-this look on her face. She reminded me of my mom, the way she narrowed her eyes and shook her head slightly.

I took a deep breath. For the next couple of hours, I was going to be Erin On Her Own, Erin Who Made Her Own Decisions. "I'm going to the mall," I said. "Want to come?"

Jilly snorted. "I don't think so." She spun around, practically running the rest of the way down the hall. She shoved through the doors and as they swung shut behind her, I had a flicker of doubt. Was I really going to go to the mall with Reede when I should be on the bus with Jilly, riding with the same people over the same route toward home? And how were we going to get to the mall? What was I going to tell my mom?

"Guess it's just us," Reede said, interrupting my thoughts. "Let's roll."

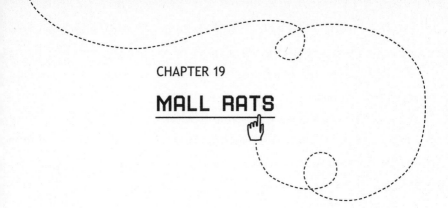

CHAPTER 19

MALL RATS

I'D ONLY RIDDEN THE PUBLIC bus once or twice and it was a long time ago, with my parents. I was surprised how well Reede knew the bus system since she'd only been in Colorado a few months. But I got the impression she went to the mall a lot. And what a great way to get around without having to rely on a ride all the time from your mom (too busy) or your brother (too expensive with the bribes). I'd have to try it out sometime. Of course, that assumed I wouldn't be grounded for life for going somewhere after school without telling anyone. I was itching to get to a phone without Reede around. I could at least leave a message so my parents wouldn't file a missing persons report.

As we headed for the mall restroom, Reede ran into someone she knew. While they talked, I bolted for the pay phones and left a message at home, saying I'd gone to the mall to help a new girl with a project. This was true. Reede was the new girl and I was the project.

I could relax a bit more when we entered the restroom, which always amazed me with its lounging area, seats in front of a mirrored wall, completely separate stalls with full-length wooden doors, and mouthwash and body splash you could use to freshen up.

"Love the outfit," Reede said, nodding to the layered shirts and jeans I was wearing. I'd bought them the last time Jilly and I had gone to the mall together. She had helped me pick them out. I had a little prick of guilt that I was here and she wasn't.

Reede cocked her head. "But we need to do more with your hair and face."

I smiled. I wasn't going to say no twice to a Reede Makeover.

She led me to a chair and took out the familiar makeup case I'd seen at school. She spun me so I faced her, my back to the mirror, while she worked.

"Ready for the unveiling?" she asked when she was finished. When I nodded, she spun me around and —

— I stared at someone I hardly recognized.

I was like one of those cover girls on a magazine, with eye liner, heavier eyeshadow that made my brown eyes look even darker, and lots of mascara. Regular Rule Follower Erin would have felt uncomfortable and wanted to wipe it off. But Make Her Own Decisions Erin felt transformed, wild, maybe even a little dangerous.

"Whoa," I said.

"You like?" Reede asked, smiling as she pulled up my hair on either side. Without waiting for an answer, she fluffed my hair with her fingers. "You got a comb?"

I produced one from my purse and she parted my hair on the side — something I never did — then pulled it back with a shiny clip. "Put these on," she said, holding out large hoop earrings. I never wore anything except studs or small hoops because the long stuff got in the way when I played sports.

"All done," Reede said as I stood up. I shook my head, enjoying the feeling of the metal earrings against my neck. I couldn't get over me. With my height, I could easily pass for fifteen or sixteen.

Reede tugged my shirts down around me, revealing more skin above my breastbone. "I think you're ready to meet your public."

I've never had so much fun at the mall. We spent most of our time following cute guys into stores without them knowing. Reede would act like she was buying something for her brother (she doesn't have one) and then would hold it up to one of the cute guys because he was "just the same size" as her brother.

Then she'd tilt her head. "You're actually bigger than he is," she'd say. "Do you work out?"

It sounded like a corny line to me but the guys would always flex under their shirts and say, yeah, they worked out and they were on the wrestling team or football team or whatever. It didn't take me long to be holding up shirts and flirting and talking about sports, especially basketball and soccer, which I knew something about. I felt like a different person and yet I knew I was me.

As we headed to Structure, I realized I hadn't thought about Blake at all. Should I feel guilty?

"You're not married to the guy," Reede said when I broke down and said something. "Nothing wrong with a little harmless flirting."

Which we did plenty of, especially with two guys we met outside Orange Julius. One of them, who was totally cute, even asked for my number. Not Reede's. *Mine.*

"She's got a boyfriend," Reede said. "But maybe if she breaks up with him—why don't you give us your number?"

I hid my amazement when he did, his admiring eyes following me out the door.

"I can't believe it," I said as we walked away. "Why didn't he ask for *your* number?"

Reede smiled. "Because you, my friend, are *sizzling.*" She licked her finger and touched my arm, hissing between her teeth. "You are such the It Girl." She glanced at her watch. "Wow. It's almost five o'clock."

"What?!" Panic jolted me. I still had to call my mom to pick me up. I was probably totally busted. "Omigod. You've got fifteen minutes to turn this It Girl back into It."

After I was back to Boring Erin, we headed for the bay of pay phones.

"You want to hang on to this or should I?" Reede waved the paper with the guy's number on it in my face.

I snatched it from her. "Do you think it's fake?"

"Only one way to find out," she said, snatching it back. She picked up the receiver, dropped some coins in, and dialed. "It went straight to his cell phone voice mail. But it was him." She held up her hand and I slapped it. "You're golden, girl."

I wondered how golden I'd be once I talked to my mom. I tried Chris on his cell first. If he came, it might go easier with Mom. But he didn't answer. My fingers shook a bit as I dialed our home number.

"I can't believe you went off without talking to me first," my mom said before I could even explain. "I think it's great that you went with someone to help her with her project, Erin, but you have to check in first. If you can't get ahold of me or your dad, you don't go. Those are our rules. It's as simple as that."

"Fine," I said, speaking low so Reede couldn't hear me. "I'll know for next time."

My mom sighed heavily on the other end of the line. "And how did you get there?"

I hesitated. I had a feeling she wouldn't like me taking the city bus, even though it was perfectly safe and people rode it all the time.

"Her mom brought us." The lie fell out of my mouth like an old piece of gum.

"Is her mother with you now? I'd like to talk to her."

"She's doing her own shopping," I said, shifting under the weight of the second lie. "We're supposed to meet her in a minute."

My mom sighed an irritated sigh through the phone. "Is she bringing you home or do you need a ride?"

"I need a ride."

After we'd made a plan, I leaned heavily against the wall.

"You okay?" Reede's voice was quiet next to my ear.

I shook my head and rolled my eyes. "You're lucky you don't have a mom freaking out about everything you do."

Reede glanced at me, then turned away. "Yeah, I'm lucky," she said. "My mom doesn't care what I do."

Something in her voice made me look at her. Her shoulders were hunched up and she didn't look at all like the confident, I'm-better-than-all-of-you girl who'd been strutting around school and the mall today.

But when she turned to me, she flashed her usual smile and I thought maybe I'd imagined what I'd heard in her voice or seen in the way she was standing.

Wednesday, October 1

I sent Jilly an e-mail 2 see if she was mad & she wrote back almost right away. I cut & pasted her answer here 2 remind myself that she can be a real brat sometimes:

As your friend I think I can be honest & tell u I think u r making a mistake. Maybe u feel cool hanging out w/ Reede but I hope u don't think she's your friend. I don't think she could be anybody's friend.

She doesn't even KNOW Reede. I'm wondering if she even knows ME.

I can't reply. I'm 2 mad.

THINGS JILLIAN GAIL HENNESSEY IS MISSING THAT SHE WOULD BE TOTALLY BUMMED ABOUT MISSING IF SHE KNEW SHE WAS MISSING THEM 💀

* A sophomore actually asked 4 my # & I got his & it wasn't a fake #.

* I didn't have instacrush on Mr. H.S . . . was this cuz of BT? Or just a sign of maturity . . . or insanity? Not sure.

GOOD STUFF TO BALANCE JILLY BEING ANNOYING ◎

* Reede e-mailed & said she had the best time w/ me.

* My mom seems 2 be over being mad @ me abt going w/o permission.

Check out that Hot-o-Meter! Can't quite bring myself 2 take Mark off, even tho he called me Miss Sensitive 2day.

My life feels a little less boring. I like it.

HOT—✪—METER

💗 **#1 Blake Thornton** — totally gorgeous 9th grade mountain surfer

#2 Greg @ mall — h.s. soccer player — yum

#3 Dylan Beaumont — taken, but cute

#4 Mark Sacks — the hair, the butt in shorts — need I say more?

#5 Tyler Galleon — well, not exactly hot but definitely on the Cute-o-Meter, mostly cuz of that dimple I never saw before

#6 Mr. Perkins

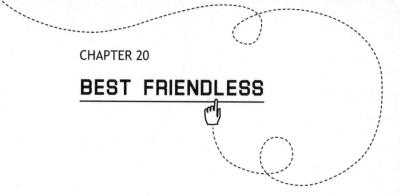

CHAPTER 20

BEST FRIENDLESS

I STOOD BY MYSELF AT the bus stop on Thursday morning, my arms crossed over my chest as I stared down the road. When I heard Jilly come up beside me, I waited for her to say something but she didn't. Was she waiting for *me* to say something after she'd totally reamed me in that e-mail?

Before I could decide what to do, Jilly's cell phone chimed a text. She glanced down and groaned loudly.

"Will you please tell your boyfriend to stop texting you on my phone?" She held the phone out to me, then pulled it back before I could take it. "Never mind. I'll do it." Her fingers flew over the buttons, eyes narrow, face pinched. I could only imagine what she was telling Blake. "There," she said, stuffing the phone in her pocket.

"Please don't be like this, Jilly," I said. "Come on. You're still my best friend."

She wrinkled her nose. "What? You think I'm jealous?"

"Well, why else would you be mad?"

Jilly snorted. "Give me a break. I'm not jealous of Reede Harper. I just don't know why you'd want to be friends with her." She shook her head. "You know she smokes." Her expression said she didn't think I knew and was hoping to shock me.

"I know," I said, and her face showed surprise. I shrugged like it didn't bother me, even though I'd freaked out about her wanting to smoke at my house. "So what?"

"So what?" Jilly said. "What's wrong with you?" She shook her head in disbelief. "And I can't believe you'd go to the mall with *her* and I have to practically drag you to go with *me*."

I bit my lip. "It was just —" I couldn't tell Jilly that it was partly because she didn't think I would go, that she assumed I'd come with her and not go off without talking to my parents first.

"Well," Jilly said, "I hope you had *fun*."

"I did," I said. "A lot more than I ever had with you."

Jilly's eyes flashed hurt but before either one of us could say more, the bus lurched to a stop and the door squeaked open. Jilly climbed on and slid into an empty seat, pressing up against the window. She stuck her earbuds in her ears, then cranked the volume on her Nano.

I flopped down in a seat in the last row. I felt bad about saying what I'd said but if she hadn't been so snotty, I wouldn't have said it.

"What's up with you and Hennessey?" Rosie asked when she got on, sitting down in the spot that would have been Jilly's if she wasn't being a turd.

"She's mad because I went to the mall with Reede."

"Oh."

I couldn't tell if that was an "Oh, that explains it" kind of oh, or an "Oh, so you went to the mall with Reede?" oh.

"We invited her but she didn't want to go."

"She'll come around," Rosie said. She held out her vocab book. "Quiz me?"

I nodded as I took the book. Why couldn't Jilly be as cool as Rosie about things?

*   *   *

After school, on my way to I-Club, I told Mr. F about Jilly being mad at me. I didn't mention what I'd said to her about having more fun with Reede at the mall.

"You and Jilly…" He couldn't finish. He gripped the broom handle, knuckles white. He sucked in a raspy breath as he clutched his chest.

I reached out to him. "Are you okay?"

He waved me away, taking in a few more breaths before the color returned to his face. "I'm fine, fine," he said. "Old age can really slow you down." He smiled weakly and I felt my return smile falter. "Don't you worry about me, Erin Swift," he said, jabbing a finger at me. "You've got enough to deal with." He nodded his head and pushed the broom again. "You and Jilly will work it out," he said. "Remember the wisdom of the Pop."

I nodded uncertainly. Last year he'd said good friends were like Tootsie Pops because they lasted a long time—unless you bit them.

I looked at him carefully. His cheeks seemed slightly pinker. "Things will be fine," he said, patting my arm.

"I hope you're right." I wasn't just talking about Jilly.

"Of course I'm right." He pushed the trash can into the gym as the first bell rang. "You'd better get going, young lady."

"Right." We knocked fists and I took a few steps before looking back. Mr. F's movements were slow and measured as he lifted the large dust mop. Like he was afraid the mop might break.

Or *he* would.

When I got home after I-Club, I couldn't get Mr. F out of my head. I called his house and talked to Mrs. F.

"Sometimes he overdoes it, Erin," she said, sighing. "I tell him he needs to slow down but you know how he is."

"So it's nothing serious?"

"Stubbornness can be pretty serious," she said, chuckling. "But I don't think you have to worry. You're sweet to call, Erin."

I felt better after we hung up and started thinking about what Mr. F had said about Jilly. It was stupid to be mad. This was Jilly, my best friend since kindergarten. I had to talk to her.

"I'm sorry, Erin," Mrs. Hennessey said when I called. "She's in the middle of something right now."

Yeah. In the middle of still being mad at me.

"Will you tell her I called?"

"Of course."

The doorbell rang a few minutes after I hung up.

"Erin!" my mom called up the stairs. "Blake's here."

Blake? What was he doing here?

"I hope it's okay that I came over," he was saying to my mom as I jogged down the stairs.

"Of course, Blake," my mom answered. "You're always welcome."

She walked back to the kitchen and I stood awkwardly in front of him.

"Jilly sent me a crazy text this morning and then I didn't hear from you," he said.

"She's mad at me," I said, "so you'd better not send any more texts."

"I wish you had your own cell phone," he said.

"I know," I said, but just as I said it, I had this random thought that maybe I was glad for once because I wasn't sure I wanted to be sending texts back and forth with Blake.

Where did that come from?

I looked at him. He was still cute but not as. I'd never noticed that one eye seemed a little higher than the other, and his eyebrows were kind of bushy. He stepped toward me.

"Hey," he said.

He had bad breath. Ugh.

"Hey," I replied, trying not to breathe through my nose.

Blake glanced over my shoulder toward the kitchen, then took my hand and led me into the living room. He kissed me and I kissed him back, trying to ignore the fact that bad breath meant a bad taste in my mouth. No way was I feeling the tingle. He put his arms around me and tried for some tongue action but all I could think about was that if I had to keep smelling his bad breath I might gag or worse.

I pulled away and smiled apologetically. "There are spies everywhere in this house."

Blake gave me a slight smile. "I should get back anyway—I've got a ton of homework." He turned back toward the door. "But let's plan something for this weekend. Tell your parents you're going over to Jilly's and we'll meet on our own."

He wiggled his eyebrows. Geez, this guy *liked* me. Me, Erin Penelope Swift. I *had* to like him back. I just had to.

"Sure," I said. "We could go back to DQ or maybe the Y."

"Too many people," he said, reaching out to squeeze my arm. "How about the park? Our tree spot?"

I gave him my biggest smile. "Sounds like a plan."

After he left, I went back upstairs and unloaded my backpack onto my desk—was there a teacher who hadn't given out homework? I was picturing myself alone with Blake at "our tree spot," trying to sort out my feelings, when the phone rang.

"Erin?" Mark's voice sounded weird.

"Are you okay?"

He sucked in a breath. "Can I come over?"

I guess he was talking to Miss Sensitivity again. I glanced at the stack of books on my desk, then at my assignment notebook.

"Sure," I said. "Come on over."

Thursday, October 2

Mark broke up w/ Kara. Said he didn't LIKE-like her anymore & things felt weird.

My hands r shaking as I type this—what's up w/ that?

Kara's totally bummed, even tho he said she said "I knew it" about 50,000 times. He wanted 2 know why she was upset if she already knew he was going 2 break up w/ her. Hello? Sometimes Mark is completely dense . . . don't think u r ever prepared . . . not that I know 1sthand—yet—but I definitely know what it's like 2 like someone & not have them like u back . . . doesn't matter if u r starting 2 feel like they don't like u anymore or u r starting 2 not like them . . . would still hurt 2 have them break up w/ u . . . just seems logical.

I could tell Mark felt bad cuz his voice was funny. But when we switched 2 talking abt I-Club & other stuff, he sounded happy. Guys r definitely different than girls. Jilly talked abt her breakups 4 days, b4 & after they happened. Mark was done in 5 minutes.

I hope Kara is okay.

HOT—✪—METER

🐾 **#1 Blake Thornton**—totally gorgeous 9th grade mountain surfer

#2 Greg @ mall—h.s. soccer player—yum

#3 Dylan Beaumont—taken, but cute

#4 Mark Sacks—the hair, the butt in shorts—need I say more?

#5 Tyler Galleon—well, not exactly hot but definitely on the Cute-o-Meter, mostly cuz of that dimple I never saw before

#6 Mr. Perkins

CHAPTER 21

RELATION SHIPWRECKED

KARA WAS NOT OKAY. IN fact, she was standing at my locker when I got to school Friday morning. She hadn't been on the bus so I figured maybe she was sick or pretending to be, after the breakup. But there she was at my locker, lips tight, eyes boring into me.

My heart sped up, and I almost turned around and ran the other way. But I needed to get stuff out of my locker, and I didn't want to be a wimp, so I kept walking. She usually didn't wear a lot of makeup but she had on a lot today. It wasn't really hiding her puffy eyes.

"Hey, Kara," I said, but I couldn't look at her. I focused on my combination, fumbling twice so I had to start over.

"You know, don't you?"

"Know what?" I said, but I sounded fake, even to me.

"He called you last night afterward, didn't he? God, I can't believe he called you." Her voice cracked on "you" and I bit my lip. How would she feel if she knew he'd not only called, but come over to my house? Sucking in my breath, I turned to face her. Her eyes were bright but she wasn't crying—yet. Good for her.

"I'm really sorry, Kara."

"I bet you are," she said, crossing her arms. "Now you can have him all to yourself."

"What?"

"Oh, quit acting so innocent, Erin," Kara said. "You've liked him for forever. Mark 'Cute Boy' Sacks." She wiggled her hips, her voice mimicking. "Oh he's a Hot tamale, oh, I wish I could kiss him instead of my pillow."

My cheeks burned. The things I wrote in my blog last year would haunt me forever.

Her eyes narrowed. "And I bet you made up this high school boyfriend just to make me think you didn't like him."

"I did *not* make up Blake Thornton and I don't like Mark, okay?"

She straightened up as if she hadn't even heard. "Well, *I've* kissed Mark and *you* haven't." Then her face seemed to sink into itself. "Have you?"

"WHAT?" Now I was mad. "I have *not* kissed him, Kara." That stupid kiss we had last year totally didn't count. Besides, that was before they started going out. "We're just friends." I turned back to my locker, pulling out the books I needed for first period.

"Yeah, right," Kara said. "Every time I'm looking for him, he's with you. When I called him, he was always talking to you. Erin, Erin, Erin. It's all about Erin."

I slammed the locker. "Mark and I are just friends," I said. "I'm really sorry he doesn't like you anymore, but it's not my fault."

Kara looked down. "Yes, it is," she said, her voice quiet. "You stole him away from me."

"I didn't," I said. "I don't like him like that."

"But," Kara said, the tears coming now, spilling softly down her cheeks. "He likes *you* like that."

When I got to history later, Reede stopped me at the door. "Told you."

I narrowed my eyes, still reeling from Kara's words. "Did you say something to them?"

"What?" Reede snorted. "Why would I?"

"You were so sure and now they're broken up."

"You thought I'd do something to make them break up?" Reede laughed. "They didn't need any help."

"So you didn't say anything to either one of them?"

Reede shook her head. "Promise." She held up two fingers, her face solemn. "I would never lie to a girl who is lusted after by high school guys."

I rolled my eyes but couldn't help a small smile. I believed her. She hadn't done anything to split them up.

"So you know that if you want him," she said, "Hot Hair is all yours. *He likes* you *like that*."

"Enough, Reede," I said. "I have Blake, remember?"

She eyed me carefully. "Not for long, though, right?"

"What?" I turned so she couldn't see my face. I would not let her predict this relationship like she was predicting everyone else's. "Blake is awesome. We're going out on Saturday."

"So you still like him?"

I groaned. "Of course I like him," I said. "I wouldn't be going out with him if I didn't, would I?"

"You would if you weren't sure how *not* to go out with him."

"You're crazy," I said, trying to ignore the way her words settled under my skin, pricking at me. "I feel bad about Kara," I said, switching the subject back. "She's really upset."

"I know," Reede said. "But she'll get over it."

I shook my head. Sometimes I just didn't get Reede. Didn't she care about anyone else's feelings? As I headed down the aisle, Mark smiled at me. I gave him a weak smile back and slid into my seat. He tapped me on the back with his pen, but I didn't turn around. I was all mixed up inside. Mark wasn't acting any different toward me. He was always tapping me on the back or throwing things in my hair. But now that he had broken up with Kara, and I was confused about Blake, it *felt* different and I didn't know how to act.

I kept my eyes on Mr. Perkins, but I didn't hear a word he said.

Mr. F was sweeping outside the office when I showed up during lunch.

"Well, if it isn't Erin P. Swift." He held out his fist and I knocked it with mine. "Mrs. Foslowski said you were checking up on me the other day."

I shrugged. "Just wanted to make sure you were okay."

"You don't have to worry about me, young lady." He smiled, handing me a dust rag. He wasn't moving as slowly today, which made me feel better. I dusted the wood around the receptionist's window, paying special attention to the corners. I could feel Mr. F watching me. After a minute or so, his broom brushed the wall near my feet.

"I don't suppose you came here to dust," he said.

"Not really," I said. "But I don't mind." I used a broken pen to dig some gunk out of a corner. "It's just that there's this girl."

"Jilly?"

I sighed. "No, she's still mad at me. A different girl."

"Ah," Mr. F said, brushing dirt into the dustpan.

I turned back to my work. "She was going out with this guy —"

"Mark?"

I ignored him. "So he broke up with her and she thinks he likes this other girl —"

"You?"

"Mr. F!" I smacked the rag on the wall. "Can I please finish my story?"

"Sorry. Go right ahead."

I could see a smile playing at the corner of his mouth. Sometimes

Mr. F could be really annoying. But he was so great to talk to I had to ignore his annoyingness. I started dusting the back of the bench that stood against the wall, sucked in a breath, and let it out. "So now this girl is mad at this other girl when the other girl didn't even do anything, you know? And if he does like the other girl—which I don't think he does—what is she supposed to do? It isn't her fault he might like her, right?"

He looked at me.

"Right?"

"Oh, I'm allowed to speak now?"

I smacked his arm. "Yeah."

"It isn't her fault."

I stopped wiping and looked at him. "Really?"

"Of course not," Mr. F said. "You can't help it if someone likes you, Erin."

"That's what I tried to tell her but —" My eyes narrowed. "Hey, you tricked me."

Mr. F laughed. "I did no such thing. I just said what I knew to be true, that's all."

"Maybe," I grumbled. "But it still felt sneaky." I finished wiping the back of the bench and started on the legs.

Mr. F dumped the contents of the dustpan into the trash.

"I told you I should have been prepared," I said.

"Would it really have changed anything, Erin?" Mr. F asked. "Would you have done anything differently?"

I shrugged. "I'll never know because I wasn't prepared."

Mr. F smiled and glanced up at the clock. "Bell's going to ring. Anything else?"

"No," I said, handing the dust rag back before knocking my fist against his. "But I may need some Tootsie Pops later."

*   *   *

Rosie and I found seats way at the back of the bus on the ride home. Jilly didn't even look at me as she sat down in the row ahead of us across the aisle, next to a girl who was on her track last year.

"Uh oh," Jilly said, nudging the girl, "relationship casualty at twelve o'clock."

Kara climbed on, keeping her gaze down as she sat in the first available seat near the front. She ignored all of the eighth graders in the back rows.

"I feel bad for her," Jilly said. "She's in my algebra class first period and she was a mess."

"Did she say anything to you?" the girl asked, wide-eyed.

I couldn't help it; I leaned slightly to my right so I could hear better. Had Kara mentioned our conversation this morning?

"Yeah," Jilly said. "She wanted to talk after class. I guess since Mark and I were together last year, she thought we might have some kind of dumped sisterhood or something."

I glanced up front. Kara sat rigid in her seat, her back straight, her backpack on her knees for easy grabbing when she reached her stop.

"What did she say?" the girl asked.

"She wanted to know how I handled the breakup," Jilly said. "Did I try to get him back and stuff." She sighed. "When I told her the breakup was mutual and I didn't want to get back together with him, she just shut up." She shook her head. "Then I told her that I knew it must be really hard for her, even though I had never been dumped before so I wasn't speaking from personal experience —" Rosie smiled and nudged me before flipping through her playlist — "Well, I didn't say that part because that would have been mean but, you know. I can imagine how it would feel. I imagine it all the time with my boyfriend, Jon."

Several minutes later, the bus screeched to a stop and we all jerked forward. I watched Kara stand up, heave her backpack over her shoulder, and step off without a backward glance. I felt bad for her, even though a teeny tiny part of me was happy. Weird.

"Do you think she'll be okay?" the girl asked Jilly.

"It will take awhile," Jilly said. "She is really in love with Mark. I just hope he doesn't start going out with someone else right away. That would be really bad." She glanced briefly in my direction, then turned to face front. What was that about?

I turned to Rosie, who shook her head. "It'll work out."

"What will work out?" I asked.

"It," she said as she leaned back and closed her eyes, her head nodding slightly to the music.

Friday, October 3

THINGS TO PONDER 🥪

✳ Does Jilly think Mark might ask me out? So does Reede!

✳ If he did ask me out, what would I say?

✳ Why am I even asking that question? I have Blake (bushy eyebrows). Blake is awesome (crooked eyes). I adore Blake (bad breath). I'm meeting him in secret tomorrow. (Why am I kinda dreading it?)

✳ Ack. I don't like MS that way anymore . . . u don't go out w/ some1 u don't even like, especially if u r supposedly going out w/ some1 else, even tho yr feelings about him might be changing.

✳ & even if I did like MS—which I DON'T—I couldn't go out w/ him. I couldn't make Kara feel the way I'd felt when Jilly & Mark were going out last year & it would be worse cuz at least Jilly didn't know I liked Mark . . . I know how Kara feels abt him.

✳ What IT was Rosie talking about? Kara not hating Mark or me? Mark asking me out? Jilly not being mad anymore? WHAT???

HOT—✪—METER
💟 **#1 Blake Thornton**—totally gorgeous 9th grade mountain surfer
#2 Greg @ mall—h.s. soccer player—yum
#3 Dylan Beaumont—taken, but cute
#4 Mark Sacks—the hair, the butt in shorts—need I say more?
#5 Tyler Galleon—well, not exactly hot but definitely on the Cute-o-Meter, mostly cuz of that dimple I never saw before
#6 Mr. Perkins

· 𝒬uiz ·

1. A boy u used 2 like broke up w/ a girl u know but aren't really friends w/. It's okay 2 go out w/ him:

   a. If she gives u permission.
   b. If 2 mos, 3 wks, & 5 days have passed.

c. Right away. They aren't going out & he's available.

d. Never, cuz even if u r not friends w/ her u know her pain.

2. If u go out w/ a boy when u know some1 else is crazy abt him, u r:

    a. Exercising yr free will.

    b. Proving that u aren't completely unlikeable.

    c. A total loser & every1 will hate u.

    d. Going 2 get hurt so it doesn't matter whether some1 else likes him or not.

3. People who make up quizzes abt going out w/ boys they don't like r:

    a. Creative.

    b. Stupid.

    c. Bored.

    d. Asking 4 trouble.

Answers to quiz: 1. d, 2. c. 3. b, c, d

Why am I even asking these questions??? What about Blake?

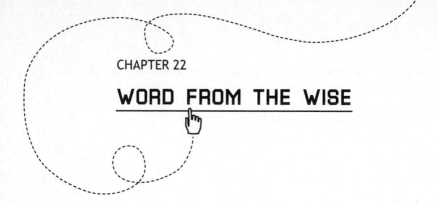

CHAPTER 22

WORD FROM THE WISE

BLAKE WAS ALREADY AT THE trees when I got there. He was leaning against one of them, his arms crossed over his chest, giving me a lazy smile. I set my bike against the nearest tree trunk and stood awkwardly next to it, giving a little wave.

"You're so far away," he said, but he didn't make a move toward me. That kind of bugged me, like he expected me to come to him.

"Not so far," I said, crossing my own arms over my chest and giving him what I hoped was a smile to match his.

"You're right," he said, pushing himself off the tree trunk and striding toward me. An instant later his arms were around me, his lips pressing against mine.

"Whoa," I said, pushing him away. His breath was okay. Minty, like he'd just brushed his teeth. But I still didn't feel like kissing him.

"What?"

"Maybe we could talk a little," I said. "You know, have a conversation."

Irritation flashed in his eyes, then disappeared. "Sure," he said, "what do you want to talk about?"

I sighed. What happened to the easy conversations we'd had at Jilly's unparty, at the bowling alley, and DQ?

"It doesn't have to be a specific topic," I said. "I just thought we could hang out."

"Fine." He shrugged and sat down on the ground. "Let's hang."

I sat down next to him as he picked at the grass blades, his shoulders hunched.

"What are you playing on the Wii these days?" I asked.

Blake sat up straight, his face suddenly animated. "*Battalion Wars,* man. It's awesome." He launched into a long description of the characters and storyline, tactics, and how he played. I asked questions every so often and then he asked me what I was playing on Playstation and pretty soon almost an hour had gone by. We were laughing and talking and we didn't kiss until we were getting ready to go. I gave him one kiss on the lips and before he could try for more, I had climbed on my bike.

"I'll e-mail you," he said as we rode our separate ways.

When I got back, Mr. F was in the garage, fixing our leaf blower.

"How's Jilly?" he asked as I sat down on the cement steps that led into our kitchen from the garage.

"Who knows?" I said.

"But weren't you just over at her house?"

Oops. I'd forgotten about my cover.

"Yeah, well, I tried to talk to her but she wouldn't talk to me so I just rode around for awhile."

Mr. F glanced at me, then back down at his work. "I see. Well, I'm sure it will work out."

"I hope so."

"And how's your young man?"

An image of Mark flashed through my mind, but I blinked it away, bringing Blake's face into focus. "Okay."

"Just okay?" He picked up a screwdriver.

"Yeah."

"Feelings fading?"

I looked at him, startled. "How did you know?"

"It happens to the best of us," Mr. F said, chuckling. "Even back in the old days we had that kind of thing."

"You did?"

"Sure," Mr. F said. "I remember in high school liking lots of different girls."

I furrowed my brow, trying to picture Mr. F young, liking girls who weren't Mrs. F. "Did you break a lot of hearts?"

"And had mine broken several times," Mr. F said. "But it's part of life."

"I don't want to hurt his feelings."

"If he likes you, there's no getting around that, Erin."

Sighing, I stood up to hold part of the blower so he could put it back together.

" 'Sometimes a friend is better than a boyfriend,' " I said. "Remember how you said that last year?" I had a feeling Blake wouldn't go for the "friends are better than a boyfriend/girlfriend" thing.

"No, but it sounds like something a wise man like me would say." He winked at me.

"More like a wise guy," I said, and we both smiled.

I gave him a big hug before he left, holding on a few seconds longer than necessary, hoping some of that wise man, wise guy stuff might rub off on me.

Sunday, October 5

THINGS THAT DRIVE ME CRAZY ⚡

✳ I don't know what 2 do abt BT.

✳ I can't talk 2 JGH abt what 2 do abt BT.

✳ I can't talk 2 JGH abt the whole Kara convo.

✳ I can't talk 2 JGH abt ANYTHING cuz she won't talk to me!

THINGS THAT MAKE ME WONDER ☿

✳ Mark flashed thru my mind when Mr. F asked abt my "young man."

✳ I want 2 take BT off the Hot-o-Meter.

ARGH. I NEED 2 TALK 2 JILLY!

HOT—✪—METER

♥ **#1 Blake Thornton** — totally gorgeous 9th grade mountain surfer

#2 Greg @ mall — h.s. soccer player — yum

#3 Dylan Beaumont — taken, but cute

#4 Mark Sacks — the hair, the butt in shorts — need I say more?

#5 Tyler Galleon — well, not exactly hot but definitely on the Cute-o-Meter, mostly cuz of that dimple I never saw before

#6 Mr. Perkins

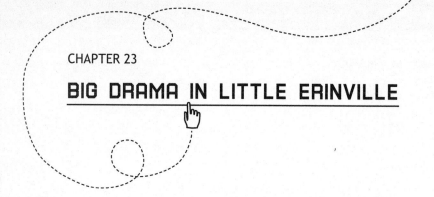

CHAPTER 23

BIG DRAMA IN LITTLE ERINVILLE

AFTER LUNCH ON MONDAY, TWO of Kara's friends kept looking at me while I was washing my hands in the bathroom. Then they started talking. Was I insane, or was this the stupidest conversation in the world?

THE KARA SIMPSON FIRING SQUAD
Place: South Hall Girl's Restroom
Time: Right after lunch and before Spanish
Players: Kara's curly-haired friend, her uncurly-haired friend, and me

ACTION BEGINS
Curly-haired friend: Just so you know, there's no way Mark could like you.
Me: I know. We're just friends.
(Both roll their eyes.)
Me: Why are you rolling your eyes? I'm agreeing with you. (Another set of eye rolls.)
Me: You can't have it both ways. Either you think he likes me or you don't.

Non-curly haired friend: I think he *thinks* he likes you but he really doesn't because how could he? (Waves hand up and down over me like evidence of my unlikeableness is scribbled on my T-shirt and jeans.)

Curly: And when he realizes he doesn't really like you, he'll come crawling back to Kara and she won't take him back.

Me: So she doesn't like him anymore?

Non-curly: She can't stand him.

Me: If she can't stand him, why does she care if he's friends with me?

Curly: Omigod. Don't you know anything?

Me: I guess not.

Non-curly: Well, we're not going to tell you.

Me: It makes no sense.

Curly: Not to you.

What??!!

I had to leave before my brain exploded.

And here's what I don't get. Boy breaks up with Girl. Girl still likes Boy. Girl doesn't want Other Girls around Boy, no matter what. OGs who know how Girl feels have some guilt about hanging out with Boy, even if OGs and Boy are just friends.

First of all, WHY do OGs feel like they can't be friends with Boy after a breakup? Especially if they were friends before Boy and Girl even started going out? Boys' relationships are so much simpler than girls'. Why can't we just shove each other, fart, go back to playing basketball, and be done with it?

I tried to apologize to Jilly on Wednesday when we got on the bus, but she immediately sat down with the same girl she was with last week when they talked about Kara. Fine. Be that way. I chatted with Rosie, who was nice enough not to bring up the Friend Freeze she had to be feeling across the aisle, while I tried hard to ignore how cold it felt.

During I-Club on Thursday, Reede and I were working on some animation for the home page. Well, I was working. She was watching and occasionally saying things like, "Is it supposed to be going backward?" I was just about finished when she asked me how things with Blake were going.

"Great," I said, trying to sound like they were. "You going out with anyone?"

"I'd never go out with anyone here," she said, laughing.

"That's not what I asked you," I said.

Reede looked surprised but before she could respond, Serena spoke up.

"If you two are finished planning your social life," she said, "could the Queen Bee please check out how us lowly worker bees did on the Contact Us page?"

"Well, Worker Bee," I said. "Have you tested it yet?"

Joe nodded. "Three times. It seems to be working but I wanted you to look it over."

"He doesn't trust me," Serena said.

Joe blushed. "That's not it. It's just that Erin's the leader of our group and —"

"No bickering, kids," Reede said. She leaned around me. "So, how's it look, Leader?"

I glanced at Serena, who was staring defiantly at her monitor. "I don't need to look at it," I said. "Serena could make an interactive form with two mice tied behind her back."

Serena looked up at me, startled.

"You're good at those forms, Serena," I said. "But if you want me to look at it before Ms. Moreno does, I will."

Serena clicked around the page, not really doing anything. "We did test the page three times," she said finally. "I guess we'll take our chances."

When the meeting was over, I stayed back to clean up. As I stepped out of the room, Serena was waiting for me.

"So," she said, "you really think I'm good at interactive forms?"

"Duh," I said. "You did most of them last year. Don't you think you're good?"

"Yeah, I guess I do." She smiled as she turned down the hall toward her locker, her head held a little higher.

Score one for the Positive Influence.

Mark was waiting in the hall when I turned the corner. "So how's your group working out?" he asked as we started walking toward the doors leading to the buses.

"I'm handling it," I said, shifting my backpack so it hung over my right shoulder, separating us. It was a little weird being with him knowing people thought he liked me, not to mention the crazy conversation I'd had with Kara's friends in the bathroom on Monday. But I still wanted our friendship. "Serena has been fine and Reede pretty much lets me run the show. It's weird, but I don't think she —"

I stopped talking and Mark stopped walking.

Kara stood at the intersection of the two hallways with her friends. She was staring at us.

"Uh oh," I said under my breath.

"I didn't know she had an after-school activity on Thursdays," Mark said.

"Yeah, well, I think I'm walking with her after-school activity." I picked up my pace so I was a few steps ahead of him. "See you later."

Mark caught up and grabbed my arm. "You don't have to leave just because she's here."

I glanced at Kara. I could almost feel the heat of her glare burning into my skin. "I don't want to cause any trouble."

Mark groaned. "Girls always make such a big deal out of everything."

I turned and looked at him. "Mark, this *is* a big deal. She really likes you. You broke up with her. She sees you with me and even though we're just friends, it hurts."

Mark sighed. His eyes shifted and his face relaxed. "She's gone." We started down the hall again. "This really sucks," he said. "I mean, am I not supposed to be with any friends who are girls because she'll get upset? What are the rules here?" He ran his hand through his hair and I had a brief peek at the eye underneath his bangs before the curtain closed over it again. "Is there some kind of a time limit on this? Like, after two months can I actually live my life without worrying about how it will make Kara feel?"

He had a point. "I don't know," I said. "I guess it shouldn't be so complicated, but it is."

"You're right," he said. "It shouldn't be." He shifted his backpack on his shoulder. "Why don't you girls go figure out a way to make it less complicated and then let us guys in on it."

I laughed. "I'll get right on that, Sacks."

He rolled his eyes. "Did you know she thinks I broke up with her because she thinks I like you?"

"Well that's dumb," I said, though a teeny tiny part of me hoped he'd say it wasn't.

Why?

I sighed and told him about the Harry and Sally thing.

"That makes no sense," he said. "We're proof you can be friends."

"I know." I didn't point out that we'd never really been just friends without one of us liking someone else. Darn Jilly and her stupid theories.

Jilly was sitting on my front porch when I got home. "Okay, so this is stupid," she said, standing up.

"Yeah, it is," I said, relieved. "I didn't mean what I said. I *do* have fun going to the mall with you."

Jilly laughed. "No, you don't. You hate it. And I'm sorry I've been acting so stupid and ignoring you."

"I knew why," I said. "It's okay." I smiled. "And I don't hate going to the mall. I just don't like all the shopping."

Jilly furrowed her brow. "So you didn't shop with Reede?"

"No, we —" How do you describe wandering around, following guys that you were pretending you weren't following, and flirting like crazy?

"You what?"

So I told her. She squealed at all the right places and asked all the right questions.

"Wow," she said, when I was finished. "I wish I could have been there."

"Me, too."

"Oh, I almost forgot," she said, pulling a cherry Tootsie Pop out of her pocket. "This is for you."

I took it and grinned, thinking about Mr. F and the wisdom of the Pop. I was glad that good friends lasted a long time, even when you gave them a little nip.

"I don't know what happened, Erin," Jilly said as we headed up to my room. "When I saw you totally laughing and having fun with Reede, I just flipped out. I mean, I was a little jealous last year with Rosie but there's something about Reede —" She shook her head. "I don't know. I don't really like her but you should be able to be friends with her if you want."

"Thanks. I think." We both laughed as we sat down on my bed. I took a breath and told her about Blake.

"So what are you going to do?" she asked.

"I don't know." Part of me wanted to keep seeing him because I liked the idea of having a boyfriend, of knowing someone was there, thinking about me, sending me e-mails and IMing me. I'd probably never have what Jilly had with Bus Boy so I should take what I could, right?

But I knew that wasn't fair to Blake.

I sighed heavily. "That's a lie. I do know what I'm going to do."

Jilly reached over and held my hand as I considered the fact that Erin Penelope Swift, the girl who never got the guy, was about to dump a really cute, really nice one who actually liked her.

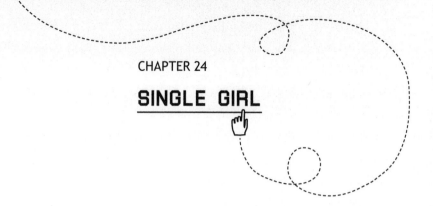

CHAPTER 24

SINGLE GIRL

ON SATURDAY I PLANNED TO meet Blake at the park, far from "our tree spot." I told my parents I was going to Jilly's again. It didn't really feel like a lie because I knew I'd go to her house afterward, when it was over.

I took my time getting there, putting off what I was about to do. My hands were sweating, my heart was pounding, and I was completely out of breath even though I was riding as slowly as possible without actually stopping completely. When I got to the bench where we'd agreed to meet, Blake was already there. His face lit up when he saw me and I felt like the biggest loser in the world.

I got off my bike and rolled it over to where he stood, putting it between us. He tried to kiss me right away but I pulled back.

"Hi," I said, looking everywhere but at his face.

"Hey," he said. "You want to sit down?"

"I'm okay." I rocked my bike forward and backward in front of me. *Say it, Erin.* "I wanted to talk to you, Blake."

I could feel his eyes on me. I knew I should look at him but I couldn't.

"Is your mom freaking about us?"

I bit my lip. It would be easy to use her as an excuse; that she was worried about us getting too serious. But that wasn't right.

I smiled. "My mom freaks about everything lately," I said, looking out across the park toward the playground. "But that's not what I wanted to talk to you about."

"Okaaay." I could feel his eyes burning a hole in my forehead but I still couldn't look at him.

"Blake, um —" I wrung my hands and look at the ground. "This is really hard."

"What's hard?" he said.

"I — well." Finally, I looked up at him. I took a breath. "I think I'd just like to be friends."

"Friends?" He rammed his bike tire against a bench. "What are you talking about?"

"I'm really sorry," I said. "My feelings — well, I don't know. I have a lot of fun with you and I still want to have that foosball rematch but —"

"Are you saying you don't like me anymore?" Blake interrupted. "*You*, Erin Swift, don't like *me*, Blake Thornton, anymore?"

"I like you," I said quietly. "Just not *that* way."

"How exactly does that happen?" His voice was steel and I knew if I looked up, his blue eyes would be icy. "It's only been a few weeks."

"I don't know," I said, my foot tracing a pattern in the grass. "It just did."

He snorted. "You like someone else, right?"

"No," I said. "It's not that."

He shook his head. "People told me not to go out with an eighth grader, but I thought you were different. More mature, like Jilly," he said. "Guess I was wrong."

That got my attention.

"So I'm not mature because I don't like you anymore? Is that what you're saying?"

He glared at me. "Whatever. I was going to call it quits anyway. You just beat me to it."

What? A minute ago he was about to kiss me.

"Then you must feel the same way," I said. "So it's not a big deal."

"*You're* not a big deal," he said, smacking his bike tire one last time against the bench before yanking it toward the path. "Have a nice life."

I watched him ride away, my heart sinking a bit. Had I made a mistake? Maybe if we'd spent more time together, the feelings would have come back. I was new at this relationship stuff. What did I know? Maybe I hadn't given it a chance and Jilly the Relationship Expert hadn't bothered to tell me. I almost raised my hand to call him back, tell him I was kidding, I was wrong, I didn't know what I was saying.

But I didn't. I just got on my own bike and pedaled straight to Jilly's house.

"What a jerk," Jilly said, when I got to her house. "Of course he's hurt but he should appreciate your honesty. At least you didn't do it in a text or e-mail like a lot of people do."

"Don't say anything to Bus Boy," I said. "It will just make it worse." I wanted to forget about it and move on but the scene kept replaying itself in my mind like a bad music video.

If only the music would stop.

Saturday, October 11

Got a bunch of e-mails from Blake. 1 said I led him on & he couldn't believe he'd wasted so much time on me. Hello? We were together like 5 times or something. It wasn't like we spent every minute 2gether. True we also spent time IMing, texting, & calling, but that's all part of it. I feel bad that he's upset but what does he want me 2 do, pretend I still like him? When I asked him that, he said no way, he didn't want me in his life @ all.

SO WHY DOES HE KEEP SENDING ME E-MAILS?

Talked 2 J again 2nite. Blake had already talked 2 Bus Boy. Told BB he "made a mistake going out w/ someone in middle school." SMACK. But BB was cool . . . guess he said I was really cool & he was sorry it didn't work out.

Man, is Jilly lucky or what?

So Blake is off the Hot-o-Meter 4 obvious reasons. I also took off Dylan cuz he makes me think of Blake, which is 2 bad cuz D's hot all by himself & deserved 2 be on the list.

This relationship stuff stinks. I'm not liking any1 else 4 a long, long time.

HOT—✪—METER

🖤 **#1 Greg @ mall** —h.s. soccer player—yum
#2 Mark Sacks— the hair, the butt in shorts—need I say more?
#3 Tyler Galleon— well, not exactly hot but definitely on the Cute-o-Meter, mostly cuz of that dimple I never saw before
#4 Mr. Perkins

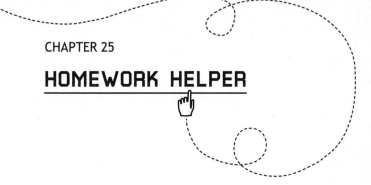

CHAPTER 25

HOMEWORK HELPER

"HEY, SWIFT." MARK WALKED DOWN the hall toward me before the first bell on Monday. This was it. The first day we both didn't like someone else and I was praying there would be no energy surges or sparks flying. The breakup with Blake stunk and I just wanted to be crush-free for awhile.

But I did want Mark to notice my new look. Lame, I know, but I couldn't help it. One thing I learned from Jilly was that when you are feeling kind of down or bummed out, looking good can help. To get me out of my "eighth grade girls aren't as mature as ninth grade SORE LOSERS funk," I spent some serious time getting ready this morning. My hair was doing what I wanted it to, I was zit-free, and I was wearing a jean skirt that flattered my slightly-existent hips. Shaving had gone well—no nicks or cuts—and I'd even put on a little more makeup—not as much as I'd had on at the mall, but I did try the same shimmery eye shadow Reede wore sometimes.

When I'd come downstairs, my mom had stared at me. "Isn't that skirt a little short?"

"No, it's fine," I said. Couldn't she just tell me I looked good? Or ask why I was making a special effort? Not that I wanted to tell her I'd lied to her and had gone to the park to break up with Blake. But still.

"You look —"

"Beautiful?" I said, twirling around. "Wonderful?"

"Older." My mom had sighed.

"I am older, Mom." I had squeezed her arm. "Get used to it."

But now I was standing in front of Mark and he didn't seem to notice anything. Which was kind of annoying because Jilly and I both saw the looks I was getting — on the bus and as we walked into school. They were the kind of looks Jilly always got but I'd never gotten until today.

Except from Mark.

"Any chance I can get some algebra help?" he said. "I'm really confused."

I sighed. Why did I want Mark to notice how I looked anyway? We were just friends and no way did I want any kind of relationship right after the Blake Break.

"When did you want to get together?" I asked.

"You got something after school?" he asked. "Maybe I can just come home with you."

My first thought was, Mark Sacks and me on the bus together? I mean, he came over sometimes but not on the bus. My second thought was —

"Kara's on my bus."

Mark sighed an irritated sigh. "So, when's the deadline? How long do I have to change my life so I don't hurt her feelings?"

I pulled my books out of my locker. "Why don't you try talking to her about it?"

Mark looked at me like I'd just said he had to stop watching ESPN. "I don't think so."

"I think you should try," I said. "She'll probably appreciate your honesty."

"She'll probably get mad at me."

"Probably," said a third person.

We both turned to see Reede standing behind us. She was wearing a tight black shirt and jeans that dragged on the floor, almost completely hiding her scuffed black boots.

"They always get mad," Reede said, reaching in front of me for her own books. "But they get over it." She looked from Mark to me. "Wow, Erin. You look great."

I blushed. "Thanks."

"Doesn't she look great, Mark?"

Mark barely glanced at me. Obviously my hot factor was not registering on his meter. "Yeah," he said. "Okay, so I just don't think I have to ask Kara's permission to go do homework with someone."

"Well, aren't you the lucky study partner." Reede raised her eyebrows at me before turning to Mark. "You don't have to ask permission," she said. "But like Erin said, just give her a heads up so she doesn't freak out when you get on the bus."

"Maybe I should just go home first and ride my bike over," Mark said. "But it'd be easier for me to just go home with you." He groaned. "Why do girls have to be like this?"

"We like to drive you crazy." Reede laughed as she walked down the hall. "Good luck."

"Fine, I'll say something," Mark said. "But I know she's going to get mad."

"Then just come over later," I said.

"No," Mark said. "This is stupid. I should be able to go home on the bus with you."

The first bell rang.

"Let me know how it goes," I said.

*   *   *

When Mark told Kara, I guess she said, "What a surprise." Then: "Gee, thanks for the news flash but I'm not even going to be on the bus today. I have a dentist appointment."

So at least he didn't have to see her on the bus. Mark and I took the seat in front of Rosie and Jilly and I ignored Jilly making her lovey-dovey face at me.

"See?" I said as the bus pulled away from the school. "That wasn't so bad."

Mark leaned back and crossed his arms. "Whatever. I just need help with algebra."

When we got to my house, we tossed our backpacks next to the kitchen table and I started pawing through the cupboard for snacks. I tossed a box of Goldfish to Mark and he caught it neatly, setting it on the table. Then he helped himself to a glass of water.

"Here," I said, holding out a stone-hard, half-eaten muffin Chris had left on the counter from breakfast that morning. "Chris wanted you to have this."

Mark laughed, taking the muffin from me. "He's a thoughtful guy." He turned it around in his hand before holding back as if it were a football. "Go long."

I grabbed the trash can from under the sink and hustled to the other side of the kitchen. I stopped in the doorway leading to the hall.

"Or short," Mark said as he measured the distance with his eyes. He sent the muffin in a perfect end-over-end toss.

Thunk. Right into the trash can.

"Two points," I said.

"Oh, that was easily a three-pointer."

"No way," I said. "You're, like, eight feet from it."

"But we're in a smaller area overall." Mark opened his arms to survey the kitchen. "Everything is on a smaller scale."

"But the basket is huge compared to the muffin," I said. "Cheater."

"Meanie."

I laughed.

"So, where *is* the Muffin Man?" Mark asked, grabbing a handful of Goldfish and tossing them back.

"Who knows?" I said, putting the trash can back under the sink. "He's always got something after school."

"Well, hello, Mark." My mom came into the kitchen to refill her water bottle.

"Hi, Mrs. Swift."

"Thanks for helping us carry boxes the other day," she said. That was when he'd come over to tell me about Kara. "It was nice to get the basement cleared out."

"No problem," Mark said.

Mom smiled at both of us. "Study hard."

Mark and I sat side-by-side at the kitchen table and worked through his algebra.

"I don't see where you're having a problem," I said when we'd finished. "You got every single one right. I hardly helped at all."

"Well, it was enough for the lightbulb to go on," Mark said. "I don't know why but it just made more sense when you explained it." He smiled at me, then nudged his elbow against mine. "You're in my elbow space."

I nudged him back. "No, you're in mine."

We nudged back and forth until we both were rubbing our sore elbows. Then we looked at each other and our eyes caught. My heart fluttered a little, like old times. I had a flash that maybe we were about to kiss and I couldn't believe I had just thought that because didn't I just have a horrible experience with Blake Thornton and I was not going to like anyone for a long, long time?

But then the doorbell rang and Mark's mom was standing there, ready to take him home, and I wasn't sure what the flutter meant or if there would have been a kiss or if maybe I'd imagined the look in his eye as I stood on my porch, waving good-bye.

And in the next minute, none of that mattered because Chris pulled up with someone in his car who wasn't his girlfriend, Bethany. And when this someone stepped out of the passenger seat, my heart triple-flipped and then stopped beating.

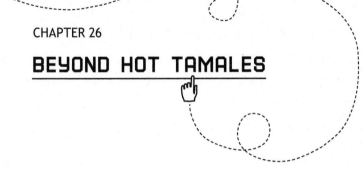

CHAPTER 26

BEYOND HOT TAMALES

OMIGOD. OH YOUR GOD. HE *was* a god.

The guy standing a dozen feet away in the driveway had deep tanned skin, brown eyes, and dark hair tied back in a ponytail.

I couldn't breathe.

"Erin, right?" The god boy smiled. It was a smooth, easy smile. My heart flipped again at my name coming from those lips, softened by a southern accent. How had he known? Were we meant to be together? Why wasn't I getting a vibe on his name to prove we had some psychic connection?

"Yeah," I said, choking it out.

"Your brother told me to be on the lookout for his little sister. I'm Jeff." His eyes dropped briefly to my chest before returning to my face. I fought the urge to cross my arms over my perky little middle school breasts. But I didn't want him to know I'd seen him look.

"Hi," I said. No psychic connection after all. Just an annoying brother who probably said stupid things about me. Even though I came up past the god boy's shoulder, I suddenly felt very small. *Little sister* implied *young, baby, don't bother.* And why should he? If he was a junior like Chris, he was three years older than me. I might as well be in preschool as far as he was concerned.

"Just show him your alien markings and go back to your spaceship," Chris said, nudging me out of the way to go inside.

"Shut up," I said automatically as I followed them inside. Chris went immediately into the family room and flipped on the TV. Jeff lingered in the kitchen, where I caught the faint scent of his cologne mixed with boy smell.

"I'd be interested in those alien markings." Jeff turned and raised his eyebrows at me in a way that sent a tingle down my spine.

My cheeks warmed and I dropped my gaze. Some of the new welcome-to-teenhood sproutings on various parts of my body were definitely alien markings. But no way was I showing them to anyone.

"Massey, it's on," Chris called from the other room.

"Be right there." Jeff looked at me. "Got anything to drink?"

"There's soda in the fridge." I motioned to it.

He pulled out three cans of Coke, popped the top on one, and handed it to me.

"Thanks," I said. For a second, I thought he was going to invite me to go sit somewhere with him. Then he took a long gulp from his can. "See you soon, Swift the Younger." I watched him walk into the family room, his shoulders wide, his muscles large and taut. Man, oh man.

"Little sister's cute," I heard Jeff say.

Chris snorted. "Little sister's little," he said. "She's in eighth grade."

I strained to hear what Jeff said next but Chris had turned the sound back on, drowning them out.

That night I leaned against my window, looking out at the night sky. I kept hearing Jeff's words, *Little sister's cute.* I couldn't believe this high school god thought I was cute. I mean that Greg from the mall was all right but Jeff was . . . I don't know. Beyond wow. And Swift the Younger. How cool was that?

"Erin." My mom's voice was soft behind me. "I didn't want to scare you."

"Hey, Mom." I glanced over my shoulder but didn't move from the window.

"How was your study date with Mark?"

I blinked once, twice. *Mark who? Blake who?*

"Fine," I said, turning back to the night sky. "Just fine."

Monday, October 13

Jeff Massey. Jeff Massey.

Omg. Omg. Omg.

I can't stop thinking abt him. I keep seeing that body, that smile, those eyes. I keep hearing his voice saying I'm cute.

Little sister's cute. Little sister's cute. Little sister's cute. Little sister's cuuuuuute.

Did I say I wasn't liking any1 else 4 a long time?

Did I say I don't care what I said?

Jeff Massey is so hot, I can feel my skin burning. ♥ ♥ ♥ ♥ ♥

HOT—✪—METER

♥ #1 Jeff Massey
♥ #2 Jeff Massey
♥ #3 Jeff Massey
♥ #4 Jeff Massey
♥ #5 Jeff Massey
♥ #6 Jeff Massey
♥ #7 Jeff Massey
♥ #8 Jeff Massey
♥ #9 Jeff Massey
♥ #10 Jeff Massey

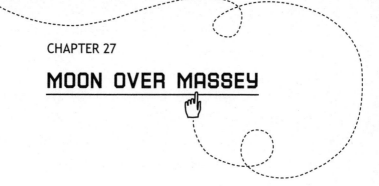

CHAPTER 27

MOON OVER MASSEY

I WAS STILL IN SOME kind of Jeff Massey haze when I got to school the next day. I didn't even tell Jilly about him because I wanted it all to myself, at least for a little while. Besides, it was just a crush and he was way too old for me and I didn't want another relationship anyway.

Right?

"Something going on with you, Erin P. Swift?" Mr. F squirted Windex on the glass outside the library and wiped it down.

"Nope," I said, turning so he wouldn't see my face. Did he know? Did it show?

"Um hm." He said it in a way that told me he didn't believe me.

Later I passed Reede near the gym. All she said was, "You're over one and into another. Is it the Hottie with the Hair?"

When I shook my head automatically, she grinned. "New blood. I like it." How does she *do* that?

But besides Mr. F and Reede, no one else seemed to notice. I got through the day with only a few teachers tapping their desks to get my attention and Mark teasing me once — "Earth to Erin" — right before history class. I could smell his BO and when he flipped his hair back, it kind of annoyed me and I didn't know why. I looked at him. Three zits had erupted on the sides of his nose and he had a black thing between his teeth. They were nice teeth, and he'd never had braces, but still. The black thing. The zits. The wrinkled shirt. How could I have ever thought he was a hot tamale? He looked like a little kid. It was a good thing we were just friends.

"You've got a thing," I said, pointing to his mouth.

"Thanks." He rubbed his teeth with his finger, then bared them at me. "Is it gone?"

"Yeah," I said, looking away quickly as I walked down the hall.

He fell into step beside me. "So, I heard you and that dude broke up."

I shrugged. "It just didn't work out." An image of Jeff Massey sprung before my eyes. Those muscles, those eyes, that amazing ponytail. The way he said my name, and smiled a little crooked smile when he joked about my alien markings. It might have been flirting. If only I'd had a good comeback. If only —

"Hello? Erin?" Mark snapped his fingers in front of my eyes. "Anybody in there?"

"Sorry. I guess I'm a little distracted."

"Yeah, I noticed." He glanced at me. "So tell me how long I need to wait before I ask someone else out."

Jeff and his ponytail disappeared in a poof of imaginary smoke.

"You already like someone else?" I shook my head. "And I thought girls switched crushes fast."

"I liked her before but only kind of realized it," Mark said, stopping to look up at a READ poster outside the library.

I stopped too, my eyes following his gaze. "Uh huh."

"Then I thought I didn't," he said, "but now I think I do." We started down the hall again.

"It's like this undercurrent of liking that kind of came up to the surface," he said. "Like those hot springs in the mountains."

"Undercurrent of liking?" I said as we turned down the hall. "Where did you get that?"

Mark's face turned red and he shrugged. "I kind of made it up."

I laughed. "It figures." I felt almost giddy with relief. I had absolutely no feelings for Mark Cute Boy Sacks. No sparks, no undercurrents, nothing. I felt free.

"So, how long do you think?"

"I don't know," I said, trying to ignore the flashes of Jeff's face that kept popping up. "I thought you were taking a break from the whole girlfriend thing."

"Yeah, that was my plan but now I don't know."

"Huh." I wondered if Jeff might come over again and how I could find out without asking Chris, who would totally make fun of me or tell me I was stupid. "Well, do you know if she likes you? Do you think she's waiting for you to ask her out?"

He paused, looking away so I couldn't see his face. "I thought she did," he said finally. "But maybe I'm wrong."

"Oh," I said, keeping my eyes glued to the head of the person in front of me. Was he talking about *me*? No, he couldn't be. We had just had that whole "we're proof we can be friends" talk. I must have misread his look. "Do you want me to see if I can find out?" I asked. "Jilly's a master at that kind of thing."

"That's okay," Mark said. "Taking a break is a good idea." He stepped ahead of me into the classroom.

I slipped into my seat and opened my folder, peeling back the papers to expose the blank back of the folder itself. Using my blue sparkly pen I wrote *JM is hot* in large, looping letters.

Tuesday, October 14

HOT—✱—METER
♥ #1 Jeff Massey
♥ #2 Jeff Massey
♥ #3 Jeff Massey
♥ #4 Jeff Massey
♥ #5 Jeff Massey
♥ #6 Jeff Massey
♥ #7 Jeff Massey
♥ #8 Jeff Massey
♥ #9 Jeff Massey
♥ #10 Jeff Massey

THINGS THAT ARE REALLY ANNOYING

✱ Like an idiot I broke my promise & asked
   Chris abt Jeff . . . "not gonna happen"
   was his parting phrase b4 he went out
   w/ Bethany.

I hate my brother.

THINGS THAT MAKE ME SMILE

✱ Jeff always talks 2 me when he calls 4 Chris
   on the home phone & I answer.

✱ Calculations: Jeff will turn 17 in May & I'll turn 14 in April so he's 35
   mos older than me—no big.

THINGS I DON'T WANT TO THINK ABOUT

✱ JM is basically THREE YEARS older than me—big. & even bigger after
   Blake the Butt said what he said.

✱ There r 35 Masseys in the online white pages 4 Denver. But he could
   be unlisted. And it's not like I'm going 2 call or go by or anything, but
   it would be nice 2 know where he lived.

Erin P. Massey
Erin P. Swift-Massey
Ms. Erin P. Swift and Mr. Jeffrey Massey
request your presence at their . . .

Yes . . .

Jeff
+
Erin

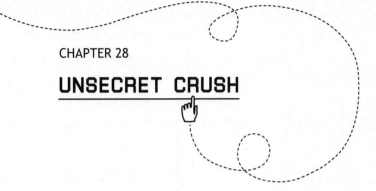

CHAPTER 28

UNSECRET CRUSH

JILLY AND I WERE COMING out of PacSun at the mall on Saturday. She was teasing me about whether we should shop or boy watch when I saw a familiar ponytail across the mall.

"Omigod." I pulled Jilly back into the store and hid behind a rack of jeans near the window. "Don't move."

Jilly looked at me. "Why are you whispering? Does he have super hearing?"

I looked at her. "How do you know it's a 'he'?"

"Duh." She peered out between the size fours. "So, who do we really want to see even though we're hiding?" She sucked in her breath. "Omigod. Look at that guy."

I moved a pair of jeans away from my face. Jeff Massey stood near a planter with two other guys. "Which one?" I said, hoping my voice sounded casual.

"The hottie with the ponytail," she said. "Who else?"

My heart pounded. No way was Jilly going to like someone I liked again. It just wasn't going to happen. "What about Bus Boy?"

"I can still look," Jilly said. "And man, I don't want to take my eyes off that one."

"Excuse me, ladies."

We looked up. One of the sales people stood next to the jeans rack, looking down at us. "Did you need help with something?"

"Yeah," Jilly said. "Can you get that guy's phone number for us?"

"Jilly!" I smacked her on the arm as we stood up.

The sales clerk leaned to one side, glancing through the window toward Jeff. "Wow. I might get it, but I don't think I'd be handing it off to anyone else."

Jilly nudged me and giggled as we moved toward the center of the store.

"Aren't you two a little young for him?"

"He's only thirty-five months older than me," I blurted out. Then clapped a hand over my mouth.

"Say what?" Jilly's eyes bored into mine.

"I think this is my cue to leave," the sales clerk said. "Let me know if you need any help—with *clothes*." She walked away before either of us could say anything.

Jilly was still staring at me.

"I, uh, see —"

"Well, if it isn't Swift the Younger."

Jilly and I turned toward the voice at the same time. Jeff Massey stood a few feet away, his arms across his chest. His muscles bulged and I felt that tingle again.

"Uh, hi, Jeff."

Jilly elbowed me.

"Oh. This is my friend, um —"

"Jillian Hennessey," Jilly interrupted. "I'm Swift the Younger's best friend."

"Nice," Jeff said. He thumbed over his shoulder. "Roy and Brandon."

We exchanged hi's. I wanted to say something, but I couldn't think of anything that wouldn't sound stupid or immature. But if I didn't say something, Jilly would and then he'd fall in love with her and she'd be taking away someone else I liked, even though she had Bus Boy and wouldn't go out with Jeff.

"Hey, I got the Green Street Majority CD," Jeff said to me. "Your bro said they were one of your finds."

I smiled. "Yeah. I came across them online. Chris says they're awesome in concert." I cringed. Why did I say that? Now he'd know I was a baby, too young to go to a rock concert.

Jilly stepped forward. "Erin is totally into the music scene," she said. "She knows bands no one has even heard of." I looked at her in surprise. Jillian Gail Hennessey was bragging about me to the hottest guy in the entire world.

I laughed. "She's exaggerating."

Jeff smiled. "I have a feeling you've got good taste."

I looked him right in the eye. "Oh, I do." I was about to say more when Jilly grabbed my arm.

"Well, we've got to bust," she said. I almost said, *We do?* but she shot me a warning look.

"See ya next time, Erin," Jeff said.

"See ya," I said as Jilly dragged me out the door.

When we were out of earshot, I turned to Jilly. "Why'd we leave?"

"Because they were about to," she said. "It always best to take off first. Leaves them wanting more." She steered me down the mall. "But don't think that gets you off the hook," she said as we ducked into Seal. "You are in so much trouble. I can't believe you didn't tell me about him. And what was that good taste thing?"

I groaned. "Was it too much? Was it too middle school?"

"It was perfect," she said. "He ate it up. Now tell me what's going on."

"Nothing, unfortunately." I told her how we met. "That's why I didn't say anything."

"A hottie in your house that you have a major crush on?" Jilly said. "Who listened to your music advice through your brother? Erin, this is News with a capital N."

"Okay, okay," I said. "I'm sorry."

She shook her head. "Man, if I wasn't so in love with Jon . . ." She smiled at me. "But I am and this guy is yours. You saw him first." She furrowed her brow. "I wonder if he's seeing anyone."

"Probably," I said. Who was I kidding? I didn't have a chance. Even if I was in high school, I could never go out with a guy like Jeff.

"We'll find out his status," she said. "But first, I need to try on some jeans."

It took Jilly exactly three hours to find out where Jeff lived, that he'd had at least one serious girlfriend back in North Carolina and had gone out with two girls since he'd been here — one a senior who was a cheerleader. He also liked grits, hated chocolate (who hates chocolate?), and was obsessed with the homemade burritos you could buy outside the Broncos games.

"You didn't find out boxers or briefs?" I teased as we sat on her bed. I had no idea who she'd talked to to get all this information, and I wasn't sure I wanted to know.

Jilly laughed. "No, but I probably could."

"I don't want to know," I said, putting my hand up.

Jilly rolled over on her stomach. "Well, it sure doesn't sound like he's going out with anyone right now."

"That doesn't mean he'll go out with me." Why were we even having this conversation? As if my parents would let me go out with anyone for real yet, let alone a junior in high school.

"You never know," Jilly said, propping herself up on her elbow so she could look me in the eye. "But even if he doesn't, it's still fun to be talking about it. You know, imagining what it would be like. Making things up until there's something real to talk about."

I liked how she said "until," like it was only a matter of time.

"Let's make some things up," I said, grinning.

Saturday, October 18

I wish I'd told Jilly abt Jeff earlier. We had fun planning stupid, impossible ways 4 me 2 c him again. Some of Jilly's ideas:

✱ Set up an appointment 2 shadow @ Wash High & ask him 2 be my guide. Can u say . . . obvious?

✱ Call him & ask if he wants 2 go 2 a movie. Can u say . . . no guts & rejection central?

✱ Hide in Chris's trunk the next time he goes 2 c a local band, because Jeff will probably be there. Can u say . . . suffocation?

✱ Send him a mystery invitation 2 a restaurant & be waiting. Can u say . . . stood me up?

Mark & I shot hoops today & well . . .

THINGS THAT ARE WEIRD ABOUT PLAYING HOOPS W/ A GUY YOU USED TO HAVE A MAJOR CRUSH ON WHO NOW MAY HAVE A MAJOR CRUSH ON YOU WHEN YOU HAVE A MAJOR CRUSH ON SOMEONE ELSE

✱ He looks different, even tho he hasn't done anything 2 look different.

✱ He seems . . . young.

✱ He checks u out when he thinks u don't know.

✱ He acts nervous around u.

✱ U find yourself giving him shots cuz u don't want 2 risk getting tangled going up 4 a block.

✱ U can feel that he wants 2 say SOMETHING & u say stupid stuff so that he won't say SOMETHING.

✱ U feel bad & aren't sure why.

············ **Flirting True or False** ············

During a basketball game, r the following situations considered flirting?

❏ He punches u almost every time u check the ball.
❏ He holds yr gaze longer than feels normal 4 just friends.
❏ He teases u abt yr strong-arm jump shot w/ a look he's never used b4.
❏ When u give him a high 5, he holds yr hand a few secs b4 letting go.

I have no idea what 2 do w/ this info — darn that Harry & Sally.

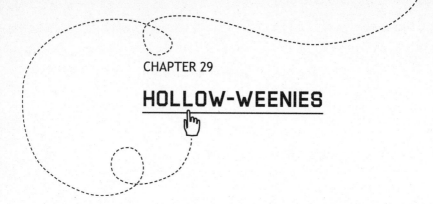

CHAPTER 29

HOLLOW-WEENIES

"THERE'S SOMETHING WRONG WITH MY life when even my parents are going to a fun costume party and I'm not," I said to Rosie as I put the first *Twilight Zone* DVD into the player. Jilly was going to some big Halloween party with her family and Bus Boy would be there too. Mark was going to a party with a girl from C Track and Tyler and Carla were going to the same one.

"I don't want anyone else over besides Rosie," my mom had said before they left. "No boys. No other girls. No one else. I mean it."

"I *know*," I had said. "You've said it a zillion times." What did she think I was going to do, throw a big party like Chris had? Hardly. He'd ruined it for me by getting reported on by the nosy neighbors. I knew they were all on high alert, probably with binoculars trained on the house whenever my parents were gone.

Rosie set the popcorn and Coke on the coffee table. "You could have gone to lots of parties, Erin," she said. "You didn't want to."

"I didn't want to hear my mom say no one more time," I said. "Besides, even if I could have gone, I didn't want to risk seeing Blake or Kara or someone else who might hate me."

"They don't hate you," Rosie said. "They're just feeling dissed. They'll get over it."

"You keep saying that," I said, pressing Play before flopping down on the couch next to her, "but so far they aren't."

"Well, there isn't a lot you can do about it so why keep stressing?"

I groaned. "You sound like Mr. F."

Rosie smiled. "I'll take that as a compliment."

The phone rang. Mark.

"Aren't you at the party?" I asked.

"It kind of blows so far," Mark said. "What are you and Rosie doing?"

"Watching *Twilight Zone* and eating popcorn."

"Sounds like more fun than I'm having." He sounded wistful.

"I wish I could invite you over but you know the rule about having evil boys over when my parents aren't home."

Mark laughed. "Yeah, I know. I could sneak in the back, though. They'd never know."

He was probably right. So why wasn't I telling him to come on over?

"What about the girl you went with?"

"She's off with her friends. Hasn't talked to me all night."

"Ouch."

"Not really," Mark said. "I mean, she's nice and all but it's not like we're going out or anything."

There was silence on the phone between us.

"So, I'll come in through the back."

I groaned silently. "How will you get here?"

"I'll find a way."

I glanced at Rosie. She was giving me the eye: *Just tell him.*

I shoved the phone at her and scooted over on the couch.

She shoved it back. "Don't even think about handing off your dirty work," she whispered, covering the mouthpiece of the phone with her hand.

"But I don't know what to say," I protested.

"If you don't want him here, you need to tell him."

"I can't tell him I don't want him here," I whispered, hoping Mark couldn't hear me. "That's mean."

"You know what I mean."

I bit my lip.

Rosie put her hands under her armpits and flapped. "Bawk, bawk."

I scowled at her.

"Fine," I said, snatching up the phone. "Are you there? Sorry. I dropped the phone." I took a deep breath. "I'd really like you to come over but I don't want to blow it with my parents. I'd like to be able to go to the next concert everyone goes to and stuff. You know?"

Silence.

"Yeah," Mark said finally. "You're right."

After I'd hung up, Rosie shook her head. "You make things too complicated, Erin."

"Let's just watch the show."

But we had barely gotten past Rod Serling's doom and gloom introduction when the doorbell rang. I pressed Pause and jumped up.

"We'll get it," I shouted up to Chris, who was probably trying to wrangle his wild hair. I picked up the bowl of candy from the table in the foyer while Rosie opened the door.

"Do a trick or be my treat."

Jeff Massey was leaning against the brick wall, arms crossed.

"What exactly would that involve?" Rosie asked.

Jeff smiled his easy smile. "I can't reveal that unless you agree."

We laughed.

"Want some candy, little boy?" I asked, holding out the bowl of treats.

"Hmm," Jeff said, wiggling his fingers above the bowl before plucking a Snickers from beneath several Pops. "Thanks."

"Massey." Chris appeared next to us in the doorway.

"Christopher. Ready to roll?"

"Where are you guys going?" Rosie asked as Chris stepped past us onto the porch.

"Some party Chris knows about." Jeff cocked his head. "What about you two?"

"We're hanging out," Rosie said.

"Yeah," I said. "No parties here. My mom has already called twice to make sure we're" — I made quotation marks in the air with my fingers —"'okay.' Besides," I said, "Chris was already caught twice, ruining any chance I might have. The neighbors are all spies now, thanks to him."

Jeff laughed. "I've got an older sister and she did the same thing to me." He looked over his shoulder across the street. "Should we give them something worth spying on?"

"Nah," Chris said. "Let's get out of here. Bethany will wonder where we are."

"You'll have your chance at a party," Jeff said to me, nudging my arm.

I could still feel the nudge after we closed the door and headed back to the family room.

"Wow," Rosie said as we plopped back down on the couch. "He is one hot tamale."

"I know," I sighed. "What am I going to do?"

"Whatever you can," Rosie said, grinning at me before turning up the volume on the TV.

Wednesday, November 19

I can't believe it's been so long since I wrote in my blog—since b4 Halloween! 2 much going on, I guess.

HALLOWEEN HIGHLIGHTS

* Rosie & I ended up having a lot of fun. We called the guy Rosie likes & he made us laugh.

* When we called Mark @ his party, he was suddenly "2 busy" 2 talk 2 us. We didn't ask "busy w/ what." Talked 2 Tyler, who seemed distracted 2. I think he likes some1!

* Jilly called from her party 2 tell me she was having the best time, that Blake was there, acting like he was w/ a girl but she could tell he wasn't & was just doing it so she would tell me & I would be jealous. Guess what? I'm not.

THANKSGIVING THRILLS

* Loved sitting in the audience @ this year's Thanksgiving play 2nite . . . no stupid corn cob costume, no singing in a chorus, no blog disaster like last year . . . cast was most of my friends: Jilly & Serena both had leads, Carla had graduated from the veggie chorus 2 be 1 of the daughters, & Steve played the dad. Kara was the narrator & spent most of her time staring @ Mark, who sat w/ us in the 2nd row.

THINGS THAT MAKE ME SMILE

* Steve and Mark were totally flirting w/ Carla & Serena after the play.

* This girl—ME—had not a twinge of jealousy. No doubt another sign of my growing maturity.

HOT—✪—METER

♥ #1 Jeff Massey
♥ #2 Jeff Massey
♥ #3 Jeff Massey
♥ #4 Jeff Massey
♥ #5 Jeff Massey
♥ #6 Jeff Massey
♥ #7 Jeff Massey
♥ #8 Jeff Massey
♥ #9 Jeff Massey
♥ #10 Jeff Massey

* Jeff has been over 3 times since Halloween. Even w/ Chris giving me the evil eye, I managed 2 talk 2 him every time . . . abt music & school & how he used 2 go canoeing in NC.

I'd love 2 be in a canoe w/ him.

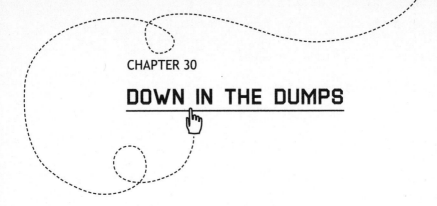

CHAPTER 30

DOWN IN THE DUMPS

THANKSGIVING PASSED WITHOUT TOO MUCH excitement. We went over to my grandparents' house with some relatives for dinner, then watched college football where all the dads fell asleep in their chairs and Chris and my cousins and I decorated them with pieces of popcorn while they snored on.

The next week was crammed with studying for exams and I-Club stuff—we still had a lot to do before our February or March launch. Mark stopped me in the hall a few times but we didn't talk long because I was always in a hurry and, if I was honest, because I didn't want to give him a chance to ask me out or do anything weird. We were *friends* and I was insane over Jeff Massey and I wanted to keep it that way, nice and simple.

"You are one hard person to pin down," Mark said the Wednesday before we officially got out for winter break. "What's up?"

"Just crazy," I said, not slowing my pace as I headed to my locker. "Studying, working on the website, you know."

"Yeah, well let's do something over the break," he said, matching my pace.

"Sure," I said. "Call me."

"Why don't you call me?"

I looked at him. "Okay," I said. "*I'll* call *you*."

"You'd better," he said, shoving me playfully before turning down another hall toward his class.

"Right," I muttered, just as the bell rang.

"I think Jon is going to break up with me," Jilly said the second we sat down on the bus that afternoon.

"Not again," I said. "Jilly, you've got to stop doing this to yourself. Besides, even the stupidest boy wouldn't break up right before Christmas and Bus Boy is not stupid."

"So you think he's going to break up with me *after* Christmas?"

"Jilly!"

"Okay, I'm sorry. I'm just getting this weird vibe."

"You're just being paranoid," I said. How many times were we going to have this conversation? "Just think how excited he's going to be when you give him his present." She had gotten him this cool speaker setup for his iPod. It must have cost her all of her savings.

"You're right," she said, sighing. "I know you're right. Still —"

"Stop it, Jilly," I said. "You're going to marry him."

Over the break, I saw Jilly almost every day and Mark, Rosie, and Tyler a couple of times at the Y. The day before Christmas Mark gave me a present — a necklace with a basketball on it.

"I didn't know we were giving each other presents," I said. "I didn't get you anything." I wasn't sure how I felt. I mean, it was jewelry, which usually meant romance, but it had a basketball on it, which wasn't very romantic. But the basketball was silver, which was.

So what did that mean?

"That's okay," he said. "This isn't much. I just saw it and thought you might like it." He looked at me closely. "It doesn't mean anything, Erin. It's just something I saw."

I wasn't sure if I was disappointed or relieved. "Okay. Thanks." I put it on and he smiled.

"Looks good," he said.

I felt guilty so I gave him a gift card to Sports Authority the day after Christmas. He thanked me but didn't seem too excited about it.

"I thought you could pick out something you want," I said.

"Sure," he said. But I had a sinking feeling he was bummed because I hadn't picked out something for him, like he'd picked out something for me, even though he said it was something he'd just seen and decided to get for me.

Can we just have an uncomplicated friendship, please?

Our first week back after the holiday, I was walking toward the lunch room when I spotted Mr. F cleaning the floor outside the boy's bathroom. He straightened up slowly. His breath came faster, like he'd climbed a long flight of stairs.

"You okay, Mr. F?"

"Fine, fine," Mr. F said, brushing away my question with a rag.

"But you seem —"

"Mr. Foslowski, there you are!" Puppet Porter rushed toward us. "There seems to have been a slight . . . incident in the science lab. I was just about to page you."

"I'm on my way," Mr. F said, reaching for his cart. His movements were slow and deliberate, like he was unsure if his body would do what he wanted it to do.

"See you later, Mr. F," I called after him.

He waved his hand but didn't look back and didn't say anything.

It was the first time I could remember that we didn't knock fists.

"So, my parents said I could bring a bunch of friends up on the ski train in February for my birthday," Carla said, handing out invitations near her locker that afternoon. "Who's in?"

How fun would that be, riding up on the train to Winter Park, going to the snack car, hanging out with everyone before and after a great day of skiing?

"Me," I said, along with everyone else.

"Think your parents will let you?" Mark asked.

I scowled. Did he have to bring that up? "They'd better," I said, "or I'm sneaking out."

"Now you're talking," Tyler said, grinning. "We'll help."

When I got home after I-Club, Jilly was sitting in the living room, her face blotchy with tears.

"Jon broke up with me."

"WHAT?" I dropped my duffel and ran to her.

She blew her nose into an already-damp tissue and took a breath. "I told you he'd been acting weird."

"I'm sorry," I said. "I really thought —"

"I know," Jilly said, interrupting me. "And you were always right about me being paranoid before. But not this time." She explained how he'd called and asked to come over.

"He told me he really liked me but felt it wasn't fair to either of us to be with just one person. I asked him if he liked someone else and he said no but I don't know if I believe him."

"Well, he's always been honest with you," I said. "If there was someone else, I think he would tell you."

Jilly looked at her hands. "I don't know which would be worse. Having him break up with me for someone else or because I'm not enough."

"I don't think that's it, Jilly," I said. "He said he still likes you."

"But not *that* way." She shook her head. "How does that happen? One day he likes me and the next day he doesn't? It doesn't make any sense."

How exactly does that happen? Blake's voice echoed in my head.

"Sometimes feelings just–change. I'm so sorry, Jilly."

She started crying and I ran to get her some more tissues, trying not to think about Blake and how he must have felt when I broke up with him, even though we didn't go out very long.

Jilly blew her nose again and I squeezed her hand. We sat for a while in silence. Then she straightened up.

"We'd just made it to our one year anniversary. How could he?"

"The dog," I agreed.

Jilly tried to smile but it was more like a grimace. "And he gave the present back. He said he didn't feel right keeping it." She shook her head. "I gave it to him. He should have kept it." Blowing her nose again, she looked at me. "Why does he have to be so nice? I can't hate him when he's so nice."

I didn't know what to say to that so I just put my arm around her and squeezed. We sat for a few minutes, with Jilly's head on my shoulder, listening to the clock tick above the mantle. When I looked up, my mom was standing quietly in the doorway, watching. I raised my eyebrows in question.

"I was just wondering," she said quietly. "If anyone would be interested in a DQ Blizzard in spite of the cold weather."

I looked at Jilly. She looked at me. "I'm in pain," she said, "but I'm not dead."

Tuesday, January 6

THINGS THAT STINK 🌪

✱ Jilly got dumped. She's never gotten dumped b4. It's so weird that I dumped someone & she got dumped. It seems backward.

THINGS I KNOW 💟

✱ I don't ever want 2 feel the way Jilly is feeling right now.

✱ I don't ever want 2 make any1 else feel that way & I think I did.

THINGS THAT MAKE ME WONDER ⊚

✱ How DO feelings just stop? Like mine 4 Blake or Bus Boy's 4 Jilly? And how do they start? Like Mark's 4 me and mine 4 JM. I know it would be better if I didn't like JM cuz I have 0 chance but I can't help it. I can't stop thinking abt him or imagining us 2gether. I can't stop hoping maybe we WILL get 2gether.

✱ Why can't we turn feelings off & on like a faucet? It sure would make life easier.

CHAPTER 31

ON THE NOSE

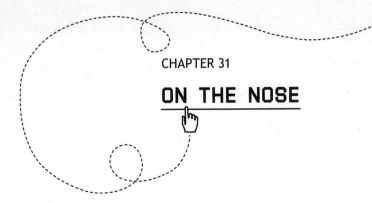

I HAD JUST FINISHED MY homework on Wednesday and was getting a snack when the front door banged open. I heard voices; Chris and —

Jeff Massey. Man of my dreams. Coming into my house the day after I'd written about him in my blog (okay, any day he came would probably be a day after I'd written about him in my blog but this felt especially meaningful).

I was having gymnastics heart again. I placed my hands on the fridge to steady myself. *Easy, Erin. You can do this.* I ran my fingers through my hair and rubbed my lips together. I hadn't put on much makeup today and I'd changed into a really old pair of jeans because I'd started my period. But I couldn't run up and change or he'd see me.

I pulled my Nano out of my pocket and popped the earbuds in my ears. That way I could look like I was here without knowing they were. I'm so brilliant.

"Hey, Erin," Jeff said, smiling as he entered the kitchen.

"Hey!" I hoped I sounded surprised to see him. "Where's Chris?"

"Bathroom," he said. He walked closer to me. He was so close I could see the dark stubble on his chin, could smell sweat and the sweet scent of detergent wafting up from his body.

"What are you listening to?" He tugged at my headphone wire.

I blinked, pulling out my right earbud. Cleaning it off, I handed it to him and he stuck it in his ear, nodding his head to the beat. I nodded along with him. We were sharing the same musical experience, our ears connected by a thin wire running between us. Electricity shot through me.

"Very cool," Jeff said. "Mind if I check out your playlist?"

"Sure." I pulled the Nano out of my pocket, then cleaned off the left earbud and handed them over. He listened for several minutes, walking around the kitchen, flipping to different songs. Then he gave it back.

"Very nice, Erin Swift. Thanks."

"Anytime," I said, surprised at how comfortable I felt. I wasn't stuttering or flipping out or worried about what to say.

"So, what do you know about Winter Park?" Jeff asked.

"It rocks," I said. "It has lots of different runs for different levels. So does the other mountain—Mary Jane—but Mary Jane also has a lot of extreme black runs. For the crazy people."

He laughed. "I don't think I'll be doing any of those. I'm going up with a bunch of people on the Winter Park ski train," he said. "I'll need to find someone to ski the baby hills with me."

My heart skipped a beat. "I'm going on the ski train, too," I said. "February fourteenth."

"No kidding?" Jeff said. "That's when we're going."

Oh. My. God. The ski train with Jeff Massey on Valentine's Day.

"Cool," I said weakly. "Maybe I'll see you."

"Maybe you can tell me which runs won't make me look like a fool," Jeff said as Chris came in. "We don't exactly have real mountains where I come from."

I'd rather show you. "I'm sure you'll do fine."

"You probably tear up the mountain," Jeff said as Chris handed him a Coke.

"Chris is a much better skier than I am," I said. "But I like it."

"She's a good skier." Chris rubbed my head.

"Stop," I said, ducking away. What was I, three years old? Sheesh. "Gotta go," I said, remembering Jilly's advice about leaving first.

"Hey, Erin."

I turned at his voice. He stepped toward me so we were just inches from each other, then tapped me on the nose. "See you around."

Wednesday, January 7

I'm never washing my nose again.

HOT—✪—METER

💘 #1 Jeff Massey
💘 #2 Jeff Massey
💘 #3 Jeff Massey
💘 #4 Jeff Massey
💘 #5 Jeff Massey
💘 #6 Jeff Massey
💘 #7 Jeff Massey
💘 #8 Jeff Massey
💘 #9 Jeff Massey
💘 #10 Jeff Massey

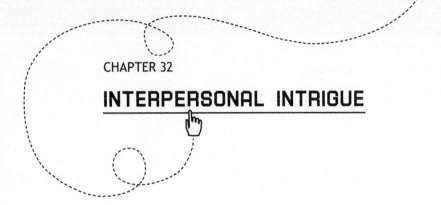

CHAPTER 32

INTERPERSONAL INTRIGUE

JILLY DIDN'T WANT TO GO to a Wash High basketball game when I asked—okay *begged*—her to go with me. It had been over a week since I'd seen Jeff and the nose touch had just about worn off. Rosie was going to the game but I also needed a best friend boy expert to back me up. I knew Jilly was worried about seeing Bus Boy, who would probably be there. She was now trying to get over him, rather than get him back.

"Aren't you worried that Blake might be there?" she asked.

"Who cares?" I said. I had Jeff Massey. "You know, this is your chance to show Bus Boy you aren't sitting around crying about him."

"True." Jilly furrowed her brow, considering. "Okay, I'll go. But if this turns into a disaster, you'll pay big time."

We ended up sitting way up high, away from my mom and dad, who were chatting it up with some of the other parents. Jilly spent most of her time updating me on the fact that she didn't see Blake anywhere and pretending she wasn't scanning the crowd for Bus Boy.

"I guess I should be glad he isn't here," she said. "But I feel like torturing myself so I wish he was."

Rosie patted her knee, then looked at the court. "That's Eddie Abeyta," she said, pointing to one of the shorter guys on the opposing team. "He's wicked fast and an incredible ball handler. They're going to need to watch him."

I smiled. I could always count on Rosie to talk about other things besides boys. I turned my attention to the court and soon was caught up in the pregame action, especially when Jeff appeared.

The team was running layup drills and Jeff was making his easily. I loved the fluid way he sprinted to the basket, all one movement, as if the basketball was a part of his body until he released it, letting it bounce off the backboard and drop through the basket. He was even more exciting to watch when the game started, and I found myself moving back and forth between admiring how he played and just admiring *him*.

At halftime, we headed for the snack bar. Juggling our food in our hands, we wove through the crowd. As we got near the door of the gym, Jilly froze and grabbed my arm. Blake was walking toward us with his arm around some girl. His face registered surprise when he saw me. Then he looked pleased with himself.

"Hey, Blake," I said, playing it cool. Inside my stomach did a little dance.

"You know her?" the girl asked him.

"Not really," Blake said as he steered her to the snack bar line. He looked over her shoulder to sneer at me. I just shook my head.

"Oh, puh-leez," Jilly said as we stepped back inside the gym. "He's so not over you."

"Not even close," Rosie said.

"*You're* saying that?" I asked Rosie, surprised. I didn't think she noticed things like that.

"I'm not blind," she said, shrugging.

When we got back to the bleachers, I scanned the bench. Jeff was looking right at me, grinning and toasting me with his water bottle.

He waved and I waved back. Then he elbowed Chris, who turned around and shook his head at me.

"He waved at you!" Jilly squealed. "In front of everyone."

I just sat there, grinning like a fool.

Washington won in overtime so the crowd was pretty pumped after the game. Rosie had seen a friend and went to talk to her. Jilly and I hung out near the bench looking for people we knew. I had tried to get Reede's attention after the game but she was taking the long way around from the top bleachers and didn't see me.

"Have you seen Jon?" Jilly asked for the tenth time. "I haven't seen him and I'm glad."

"You're miserable," I said. "And you'll be even more miserable if you see him."

Just then the team trickled out of the locker room. Jeff sauntered out, freshly showered, hair slightly damp against his skin. He was surrounded by people — mostly girls but some boys.

I turned away so he wouldn't see me staring.

"This is crazy," I said. "What am I doing?"

"Just have fun with it."

"Says the girl who is suffering from the effects of having fun," I said to Jilly.

"I plan to have fun again," she said. "It'll just take time." She squinted across the gym in Jeff's direction. "He's walking toward us," she said, smiling as if she was saying something completely different. "Okay, now he stopped to talk to some girl. Uh oh. I think she might — she might — no, it's friend only."

"He's coming around the bend," I said, "along the fence, leading by a length —" I spoke in a fake announcer voice, and we both started laughing.

"He's — he's —" Jilly gasped but she was still laughing too much to get the words out.

"Must be a great joke." Jeff Massey stood behind us, smiling that lopsided smile.

You mean nothing to me, my brain said, while my heart did the thumpity-thump.

He put one arm around me and one around Jilly. "Thanks for coming to the game, girls."

I feel nothing — except the solid weight of his arm on my shoulders, the closeness of his face to my own, the warmth of his body against my side.

I swallowed hard. "It was really exciting," I said with a squeak. "You did great."

Jeff laughed, squeezing my shoulder before letting go. "I can get around the defense when I need to." His friends chuckled. "I understand you're a pretty decent player, Swift the Younger. Maybe you can teach me some of your moves." He faked a pass to me and I pretended to catch it before the crowd sucked him into their midst and he was gone.

"He was so flirting with you," Jilly said. "That whole 'moves' thing. He *likes* you."

"He does not," I said. "He's just a big flirt." But I loved that he was flirting with *me*. I sighed. "We'd better go find my parents."

As we turned toward the bleachers, I nearly collided with someone.

"Sorry," I mumbled, then nearly had a heart attack as I looked into a familiar face. "Sacks! Hey!"

Mark glanced at me before looking past me at the crowd leaving the gym. "Who was that guy you were talking to?"

"Just a friend of Chris's," I said.

Jilly looked over my shoulder and her eyes got wide. "He's here."

I glanced back. Bus Boy stood near the opposite set of bleachers, talking to some guys.

"Don't go, Jilly," I said. "Stay here." I hoped it sounded like I was trying to help her get over Bus Boy, to be strong. But I was really saying: *Please don't leave me alone with Mark.*

"I just want to say hi," she said. "That's all. Show him I'm mature and handling things, just like you said."

"Jilly."

She squeezed my arm. "I'll be right back."

Traitor.

I shifted uncomfortably next to Mark. "So, what a nail biter, huh?"

"Yeah," Mark said. "Man, I couldn't believe it when Standiford made that three-pointer to tie. That was awesome."

I relaxed as we talked about the game, the best plays, who was on or off their game. By the time Jilly came back, we were laughing about last year at MBMS when I tripped in a game, fell flat on my face, and Steve got a picture of it and put it on the MBMS Intranet.

Jilly didn't look so happy, though.

"So?" I asked.

"So he was happy to see me but he was in total friend mode. No BF vibe at all." She crossed her arms over her chest. "Is he walking out with anyone?"

I glanced over her shoulder. "He's with a bunch of people."

"Boys and girls?"

"Yeah."

"But not any one girl," said another voice.

I whipped my head around. Reede stood behind us, sipping a Coke.

I furrowed my brow. "How can you tell?"

"Just the way he's walking and talking. See the distance between him and that blonde girl? And how she's holding her purse in the hand that's closest to him? She doesn't want him to touch her."

"Interesting," Mark said.

Something about his tone made me look at him. Reede seemed about to say something when her eyes widened. "Uh oh. Here comes the 'rent who doesn't approve of me. Later."

I looked up to see my mom walking towards us.

"Mark! It's good to see you."

"You too, Mrs. Swift."

"What a game," my dad said to Mark. "That three-pointer was amazing." He and Mark talked for a few minutes while Jilly and I exchanged looks.

"Um, Dad?" I asked. "Jilly has to get home to help her mom."

"Oh, right," my dad said. "Good talking to you, Mark."

"You, too, Mr. Swift." But Mark was looking at me. I dropped my eyes and he turned and walked away, shoulders scrunched, his pants dragging the floor.

"Okay," Jilly said, grabbing my arm. "That was a little too much excitement for one night."

My dad looked at us but didn't say anything. I had a feeling he and my mom both knew Jilly wasn't just talking about the game.

Friday, January 16

THINGS THAT STINK 🌪

* Reede thinks my mom doesn't like her.

* I don't think my mom likes her.

* I'm still madly in love w/ JM.

* I think Mark knows I like JM.

THINGS THAT ROCK 🎸

* I'm still madly in love w/ JM! Why should I try 2 stop? I should enjoy it, like J said.

* Only 1 more month till ski train — Jeff will be on the same ski train — it's fate.

* Jeff put his arm around me @ the game. Sure he put the other 1 around Jilly but he kept mine on longer & looked @ me more.

* All of us r going 2 a movie this weekend — except Jilly & Reede . . . Jilly had something w/ her sis & I think Reede didn't want 2 be seen w/ a bunch of 8th graders. Sometimes she's really weird. I mean, SHE'S in 8th grade. Just cuz she acts older & hangs out w/ older people — why can't she hang w/ us 2?

Whatever. It'll be fun, but I wish I was going w/ JM — alone.

HOT—✪—METER
💔 #1 Jeff Massey
💔 #2 Jeff Massey
💔 #3 Jeff Massey
💔 #4 Jeff Massey
💔 #5 Jeff Massey
💔 #6 Jeff Massey
💔 #7 Jeff Massey
💔 #8 Jeff Massey
💔 #9 Jeff Massey
💔 #10 Jeff Massey

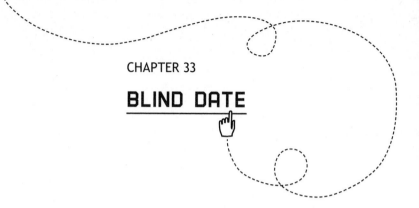

CHAPTER 33

BLIND DATE

THE THEATER WAS ABOUT HALF-FULL when we got there. We picked a row in the middle and settled in with our snacks — Rosie, me, Mark, Steve, Carla, and Tyler. Mark passed a huge tub of popcorn back and forth and then the previews came on. I settled back to watch. A few seconds into the third trailer, Rosie tapped my arm.

"Ex. Two rows back." She jerked her head over her shoulder.

I looked. Kara sat with two of her friends, laughing as she watched the previews. I raised my eyebrows at Rosie. Since when was she the relationship drama police?

She shrugged. "Just thought you should know."

I sighed. They were totally going to think I was on a date with Mark, even with our big group. Maybe I should try to switch seats with Rosie. But that might call attention to us. Better to play it cool, I thought, as I sank low in my seat.

"What are you doing?" Mark asked.

"Just trying to get comfortable." I scooted my butt back and forth to prove my point.

During the movie, my elbow sometimes touched Mark's as one of us reached for the Coke we were sharing, but I got away quickly and all was well.

I started imagining touching elbows with Jeff Massey, or feeling that hard bicep pressed against my arm. He'd smile over at me in the dark, lean in, and kiss me. He might drop his arm around my shoulders like he did at the game. Or maybe he'd reach out and take my hand in his, squeezing gently, neither of us sweating because we were so comfortable with each other.

My hand.

Someone was touching it.

No, someone was *holding* it.

I glanced down. Mark's hand covered mine. It couldn't be an accident because my hand was on my knee, nowhere near the Coke cup. He squeezed my hand and held on. I glanced at Rosie, but she was into the movie.

Mark Sacks was holding my hand. How many nights last year did I imagine a scene just like this one? And now it was here and all I could do was feel uncomfortable and wish it was Jeff's hand. I didn't want to hurt Mark's feelings but I didn't want to hold his hand either. I decided to tie my shoe, even though it didn't need tying. I pulled my hand out from under his and leaned down. When I sat up, Mark had settled back, his elbows on the armrests.

I scooched my elbow behind his. "No hogging the armrest," I whispered into his ear.

He turned so his face was millimeters from mine. "Okay." His soft buttery popcorn breath warmed my nose. Oh, no. He was going to kiss me. Mark Sacks was going to kiss me and half the school would see and why wasn't he Jeff Massey?

I leaned down for a sip of Coke and his lips brushed the side of my head. He let out an impatient sigh and sat back hard in his seat.

We watched the rest of the movie without any whispers and I could tell Mark was trying not to touch me. He even stopped drinking the Coke, just sat with his arms over his chest.

When the movie was over, we all went to the bathroom, then waited in the lobby for Tyler to get a popcorn refill "for the road."

Rosie shook her head. "Where does he put it all?"

"Bottomless pit," I said, smiling as I tried to catch Mark's eye. But he was busy talking to Carla, who seemed completely enthralled with him, even though Steve was at her elbow, staring at her. Then Carla said, "Uh oh," and we all turned to look.

Kara and her friends stood in the lobby, watching us. Kara flipped her hair over her shoulder and strode toward the main doors, her friends hurrying to keep up.

"You need a ride?" Mark asked Carla.

"My mom could take you," Steve chimed in.

"Um, no, I'm okay." Carla seemed flustered by all the attention. Her eyes flicked to me before she dropped them to the ground.

"Okay," Mark said. "See ya." And he left the theater.

Tyler stepped up then, tossing back a handful of popcorn. "So, did I miss anything?"

All three of us looked at him.

"Okaaayy," he said slowly. "I think I'll wait outside with Sacks."

When I got home I hopped on the Internet. My Buddy List showed Mark online.

Webqueen429: Sacks, you there?

The cursor blinked at me accusingly.

I watched his status. A second later, it changed from *Online* to *Away.*

Sighing, I closed the program and went up to my room.

Saturday, January 17

THINGS THAT BUM ME OUT

HOT—✪—METER

♥ #1 Jeff Massey
♥ #2 Jeff Massey
♥ #3 Jeff Massey
♥ #4 Jeff Massey
♥ #5 Jeff Massey
♥ #6 Jeff Massey
♥ #7 Jeff Massey
♥ #8 Jeff Massey
♥ #9 Jeff Massey
♥ #10 Jeff Massey

✳ I tried 2 call Mark but his mom said he was out . . . think he was there & didn't want 2 talk 2 me.

✳ Jilly said I handled it just fine & he needs 2 wake up & get a grip on reality but I still feel guilty.

THINGS THAT MAKE ME SMILE

✳ Rosie said Mark's being a baby & maybe we should give him a pacifier. Gotta love her.

✳ Jeff called 4 Chris & I got 2 talk 2 him . . . thanked me 4 coming 2 the game . . . said he hoped he'd c me again. Yes!

QUESTIONS TO FRUSTRATE ME

✳ Why did Mark have 2 hold my hand & try 2 kiss me?

✳ Why is he ruining things?

✳ He totally agreed w/ the Harry & Sally thing & now he's totally blowing it. Why can't he just be my friend?—Guess what? On Monday, I'm going 2 find out.

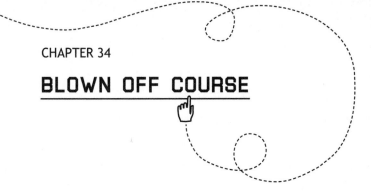

CHAPTER 34

BLOWN OFF COURSE

"GOOD LUCK." JILLY GAVE MY arm a squeeze as she left me near Mark's locker Monday morning. "I hope you know what you're doing."

"I don't," I said, "but I have to try something."

My heart raced when I saw Mark walking down the hall with two guys I didn't know too well. When he saw me he stopped, then set his mouth in a straight line and kept coming.

"Can I talk to you?" I asked, stepping back as he opened his locker.

Mark glanced at one of the boys. "You do the algebra homework?"

I bit my lip. He was acting like I wasn't even there.

"Do I ever do the algebra homework, bro?" the boy asked. He glanced at me, then back at Mark. "Want us to meet you later?"

"Nah," Mark said, pulling out his books and closing his locker. "I'm done here."

I stood there, staring at his locker, feeling like an idiot, feeling like a whole canyon had just opened up between us, not just a dozen feet of linoleum.

Tuesday wasn't much better than Monday. Mark ignored me in class and he and Tyler sat with some other people at lunch.

"I didn't know he could hold a grudge," I said to Rosie. "What else don't I know?"

"Just give him space and a chance to get a reality check," Rosie said.

After school we had an I-Club meeting. We were counting down to the big launch next month so everything was being checked and double-checked. It was a good thing everyone was so busy. No one noticed that Mark and I never said a word to each other.

Except Reede.

"I feel a chill in the air," she said as she leaned over my shoulder, watching as I made some color adjustments to the website background.

"Yeah, well it's not coming from me," I said.

"Told you he's into you," Reede said. "But don't worry, it'll work out."

"What will work out?" Serena sat down at the computer next to mine, pulling up the Contact Us page she was working on last week.

"Nothing," I said.

Serena clicked a few things on the screen. "This doesn't have anything to do with the fact that Mark Sacks hasn't been within twenty feet of you all day?"

Okay, so maybe other people had noticed.

"Can we just focus on our pages?" I said.

When it was time to go, Mark and Tyler were the first two out the door. I gathered my stuff and told Rosie to save me a seat on the activities bus.

Mr. F was pulling a trash can and bucket out of the custodian's closet when I walked up. He looked down the hall, where Mark stood with a group of guys. "It looks like there's trouble between two of my favorite people."

"I guess I blew it," I said. "Somehow I sent him the wrong signals and I don't know how I did that."

Mr. F tugged a tissue out of his pocket and wiped his brow. "Some-times people see what they want to see, not what's really there."

"I guess." I walked with him for a few steps. "What should I do?"

"Be his friend."

"He won't let me."

"Give him time and don't give up," Mr. F said.

I glanced at the clock on the wall. "Oh, geez, my bus is going to leave," I said. "Thanks, Mr. F. See you tomorrow." We knocked fists and I took off.

That night I got to talk to Jeff because Chris wasn't home yet. Ap-parently he wasn't picking up his cell so Jeff had called the house. I was so excited that at first I couldn't say much except "uh huh" when he asked me a question, even when I didn't hear the question. I just liked listening to him so I leaned back against the couch and closed my eyes, letting the sound of his voice wash over me.

"So, you really eat raw pig's eyes in the morning?"

"Uh huh — what?"

He chuckled through the phone. "Just making sure you were listen-ing. I didn't realize I was so boring."

"You're not boring," I said quickly, afraid he might hang up. "I was just distracted by the TV. I'm turning it off." *Whew. Okay. Get a grip, Erin. Think of something to say.* "So, are you ready for the Winter Park trip?"

"I went up skiing last weekend and will probably go up again this weekend," he said. "Hope I won't look too bad in front of the ladies."

Twinge. But of course there would be other girls. Girls his own age. What was I *thinking*?

Mature. Be mature. "You're a good athlete. You'll do fine."

"Thanks, Swift the Younger," Jeff said. "I appreciate that. So maybe I'll see you on the train. And on the slopes. You wouldn't laugh at a North Carolina boy, would you?"

"Never," I said.

"Cool. Tell your bro to give me a call when he gets in."

The next day I was determined to give Mark his space and be his friend. I didn't avoid him but I didn't approach him either. I felt him staring at the back of my head all through history but he never poked me with his pencil or flipped my hair. And when the bell rang at the end of class, he jumped out of his seat like he'd been shot out of it. Unfortunately, he didn't have a good grip on his books and stuff so everything went flying. I picked up some papers that had slipped under a desk and handed them to him. He took them without a word.

"I'm still your friend," I said, "even if you're not mine."

He tried to get around me but I stepped over, blocking his exit.

"This is stupid," I said. "Why can't we be friends?"

Mark shook his head. "I guess *I'm* stupid," he said. "I thought you felt . . . whatever."

"I'm sorry if I did something to make you think . . . something," I said. "I didn't mean to." I sucked in a breath and let it out. At least we were talking, even if it was about as comfortable as sitting on the pushpins that Serena put on my chair in second grade. "It's just, well, it took me by surprise," I said. "But I don't want to ruin our friendship."

Mark pushed me aside. "Too late."

I followed him out into the hall. "It doesn't have to be."

He stopped so suddenly, I nearly ran into him. Whirling around, he faced me. "Is it that guy from the game? Do you like him?"

The question threw me off guard. "I—I don't know."

"You don't know? How can you not know?" He shook his head, disgusted. "You like him, Erin. It's obvious. But get a grip. He's in *high school*."

"So?"

"So, he'll never go out with you."

My stomach clenched. "I don't even like him, okay?"

"Right," Mark said, turning away. "Just don't do something stupid."

"You're stupid!" I shouted, not caring how immature it sounded to say that. I stomped away, my eyes pricking. Blinking quickly, I tried not to sniffle until I was way down the hall, far away from stupid Mark Sacks and his stupid comment.

Wednesday, January 21

I can't believe Mark said those things 2 me.

Jerk.

What does he know, anyway? Nothing. He doesn't know abt my convos w/ Jeff, how we tease each other or anything.

I didn't think it was possible, but I think I hate Mark Sacks.

HOT—✪—METER

- 💔 #1 Jeff Massey
- 💔 #2 Jeff Massey
- 💔 #3 Jeff Massey
- 💔 #4 Jeff Massey
- 💔 #5 Jeff Massey
- 💔 #6 Jeff Massey
- 💔 #7 Jeff Massey
- 💔 #8 Jeff Massey
- 💔 #9 Jeff Massey
- 💔 #10 Jeff Massey

CHAPTER 35

ERIN'S EXCELLENT ADVENTURE

I WAS HOME ALONE SO I made myself some hot chocolate before spreading my books out on the kitchen table to start my homework.

"Oh, great." I looked at the papers in my hand. Somehow I'd gotten Mark's history study sheet along with mine when his papers flew everywhere after class today. As I tried to decide what to do, the doorbell rang. Holding Mark's worksheet in my hand, I hurried to the door and peered through the peephole.

"Reede?"

She stood on my front porch, grinning like she'd won the lottery. "You're going to love me," she said. "Guess who's sitting in that car, ready to take you for a ride?"

I looked around her. Jeff Massey was leaning across the front seat of a cool new sports car. Cloth top, too—a convertible. He waved at me through the passenger window.

"Oh, my God!" I said. "Are you kidding me?"

"I never kid about hot guys," Reede said.

"How did you know? I—him—you know."

"I have my ways." She glanced around me into the house. "Is your brother here?"

I shook my head. "He's out somewhere with Bethany. Is that why Jeff is here?"

"I saw him at a stoplight and told him we should give you guys a ride."

"But now he won't want to if it's just me."

"Sure he will," Reede said. "You're hot. Besides, guys can't resist showing off new wheels. It's in their genes."

I smiled.

"Once we're on our way, I'll have Jeff drop me off at Tower Records," Reede said.

"No!" I protested. "You have to come, too. Really. It's fine with me."

"Well, it shouldn't be," Reede said. "Buck up, Swift. Can't you handle being alone in the car with an older guy you have the hots for?"

My cheeks warmed. Did I have the "hots" for Jeff? That sounded so . . . unromantic.

"Of course I can handle it," I said, turning back into the house. "I was just trying to be a good friend." I folded up Mark's worksheet and slid it into my back pocket.

"Yeah, right," Reede said. I wasn't sure if she meant that as a *Yeah, right, no way are we friends* or *Yeah, right, no way is this about friends, it's about you being too chicken to be alone with Jeff Massey.* "And Jeff's *that* way." She jerked her thumb over her shoulder.

"I need to call my mom and tell her where I'm going."

Reede gave Jeff a just-a-minute finger and followed me inside.

I dialed my mom's cell quickly. When she didn't pick up, I left a message. I also left a note on the white board on the fridge.

"Very Brady Bunch," Reede said, tapping the white board with her polished nail.

"Let's go." I didn't want her to start in about how lame my life was compared to hers. I grabbed my jacket and followed her out the door.

When I got to the car, I leaned down to look at Jeff through the passenger window. "Chris isn't here."

"He's missing out," Jeff said. "Hop in." He raised his eyebrows above those amazing brown eyes.

"Reede can —"

"— sit in the back," Jeff and Reede both said.

Omigod. Jeff wanted me in the front with him.

"Good," I said, trying to sound confident, even though my body was shaking with nervous excitement. "I was about to call shotgun."

Sliding into the front seat, I breathed in new car smell. Music blasted through the speakers, the car thumping in time. As Jeff peeled away from the curb, I reached for my seatbelt, then stopped. He wasn't putting his on. It felt weird not to have the strap across my body but I didn't want to look like a baby. I pretended I was admiring the seat and turned back to the front.

"Check this out," Jeff said, pointing to the GPS system. Then the stereo system, where his Zune was connected.

"It's amazing," I said as he rounded a corner.

We dropped Reede off in front of Tower Records. I thought it was extremely cool of her to do this and mouthed *thank you* to her.

"Have fun," she called, giving me the thumbs up before waving good-bye.

Jeff laughed and so did I. I wasn't sure what we were laughing at — how crazy it was to think he and I might have a good time together? Or just because it was fun to be in an amazing car no matter who you were with?

Jeff turned to me. "So, where would you like to go?"

"Uh." Where *did* I want to go with Jeff Massey in this incredible car? I shifted in my seat, suddenly remembering the worksheet in my back pocket. "If you wouldn't mind, I have some homework I needed to take to someone."

"Lead on," Jeff said, turning up the volume on the stereo.

* * *

Several minutes later we were idling at the curb in front of Mark's. "I'll be right back," I said as I opened the door.

"And I'll be right here." Jeff drummed his hands on the steering wheel.

"Be home, be home," I murmured as I strode up the walk.

He was.

"Erin," Mark said when he opened the door. "What are you doing here?"

"I found your study sheet stuck to mine in my backpack. I thought you might need it." I held out the paper.

"Oh, thanks." He squinted, looking over my shoulder. "Who brought you?"

I turned around, just as the passenger side window rolled down and Jeff leaned over, waving. I waved back.

"Just that *high school* guy."

Mark stared at Jeff for a second, then turned back to me, his face dark with anger. "I can't believe you'd come here with him, knowing —" He stopped and pressed his lips together. His nostrils flared as he breathed hard through his nose. "Just don't come crying to me when you get hurt."

"I'm not going to cry and I'm definitely not going to get hurt," I said. "You're just jealous."

Mark bit his upper lip, then looked right into my eyes. "You're right," he said finally. "But that doesn't mean I'm wrong." He stepped into the house and closed the door, leaving me alone on the porch.

Jeff honked from the curb and I turned and ran down the walk.

When I climbed into the car, I looked up at Mark's house, checking to see if he might appear at one of the windows. But they were all like blank eyes, staring back at me. "Whatever," I mumbled. Then I took a deep breath and turned to Jeff. "Let's see what this thing can do, Mr. Massey."

"Push that button," Jeff said as we turned the corner at the end of

Mark's street. I leaned forward and pressed a black button on the dashboard. The roof started to rise.

"Whoooeeee," I shouted, throwing my arms in the air.

"Whoooeeee," he said back, and we both laughed.

Soon we were speeding down the highway, the cold wind whipping my hair around my face. I stopped trying to push it away, just let it go, ignoring the occasional sting as the tips pricked my cheeks. I felt wild and free, as if I could lift right out of the car and fly away.

I laughed out loud and let out another whoop.

Jeff grinned. "Cold?" he shouted, blasting the heater vents at me.

"Perfect," I said, holding out my cold palms to feel the hot air against them.

Once, Mark's angry faced popped into my mind and I felt a little twinge. Maybe I had been a little mean bringing Jeff to his house. But he was mean first. I pushed his face away and cleared my mind, enjoying the wind, the powerful feel of the car roaring beneath us, loving Jeff just a foot or so away from me.

"You having fun?" Jeff shoved me playfully.

"Yeah!" I tried not to grin like an idiot. I could totally be alone in a car with a guy I had the hots for. Totally.

We sped along, bouncing to the music, shouting the occasional comment over the noise—

—until it all came suddenly to a halt. Literally.

"Crap," Jeff muttered as red, white, and blue lights flashed behind us. He pulled over to the shoulder of the highway and I cowered by the door, my heart pounding so fast, you would think I was on the most wanted list, afraid of being recognized.

But I calmed down as Jeff talked to the officer, who had this fabulous red hair she tied back in a ponytail. He was so polite and respectful and I felt proud to be with him. He *yes, ma'am*ed and *no, ma'am*ed all over the place with his sexy southern accent and I was sure she would melt into the asphalt — even though it was only about forty-five degrees out — because that's what I felt like doing.

But she didn't melt. She didn't even drip. And even though she was very nice, she was rock solid. Not only did Jeff get a ticket for speeding, which meant he'd lose points off his license, but he also got a second ticket because neither of us was wearing a seatbelt. Colorado law on the highway. Jeff tried to tell the officer he was from North Carolina but she held tough.

"You've got a Colorado driver's license and your car is registered here," she said. "We expect you to know the laws of your new state."

"Yes, ma'am."

"I'll help pay," I said after we were on our way again. I was embarrassed that he'd gotten in trouble with me in the car, but oddly exhilarated too.

"Don't worry about it," he said. "I'll charm them out of it." He flashed me a smile, then asked me to pick out a playlist from his Zune. I was disappointed when we turned down my street and he pulled up in front of my house. I wanted to keep driving with him forever.

"Thanks for the adventure, Erin Swift," he said.

"It was a blast," I said. "Sorry again about the tickets."

"No worries," he said, squeezing my knee. He left his hand there, sending electricity up my thigh. He held my eyes for a moment and I saw — what? — something that made me shiver. I smiled.

"So, yeah," he said, patting my knee once before returning his hand to the steering wheel. "Maybe we'll do it again sometime. Tell your bro I'll catch him later."

"Right," I said, hardly able to contain myself. He totally wanted to kiss me. I could tell. I wasn't sure what stopped him — my age, the fact that he was friends with my brother, or something else — but, for that moment, he had *wanted* to.

That's all I needed to know.

Thursday, January 22

ONE THING I DON'T KNOW WHAT TO DO WITH 🛷

* In btween being a total butthead, Mark admitted he was jealous of Jeff.

THINGS THAT SEND ME OFF THE PLANET 💫

* JM totally wanted 2 kiss me yesterday!!!!! I KNOW he did. Next time we're together, he WILL . . . or maybe I'll kiss him. Wahoo! Maybe on the ski train, in front of Mark & every1.

* Chris heard abt my "spin" in Massey's new 'stang . . . couldn't believe I got 2 ride in it b4 he did . . . that we rode w/ the top down. Wicked, he said.

* Chris didn't say anything abt the tix, which means Jeff didn't tell him. How cool is that? Most guys would totally brag abt speeding & getting pulled over but Jeff didn't.

* I rode in a hot sports car w/ Jeff Massey w/out wearing a seatbelt, got stopped by cops, & got away w/ it. We share a secret. It will bind us together 4ever.

* Jilly squealed @ all the right places when I told her . . . she called me Wild Girl.

* Reede went crazy when I told her . . . told me I was smokin'.

THINGS THAT ARE KIND OF ANNOYING BUT NOT ENOUGH TO BRING ME BACK TO EARTH 🌍

* Mom was pretty cool when I got home but freaked abt the top being down on Jeff's car. Like I might get pneumonia or something from the cold air.

HOT—☼—METER

♥ #1 Jeff Massey
♥ #2 Jeff Massey
♥ #3 Jeff Massey
♥ #4 Jeff Massey
♥ #5 Jeff Massey
♥ #6 Jeff Massey
♥ #7 Jeff Massey
♥ #8 Jeff Massey
♥ #9 Jeff Massey
♥ #10 Jeff Massey

* Mom asked if I had a crush on JM. That makes it sound SO middle school. I'm in LOVE. But I didn't tell her that. I told her we were just friends . . . she said good cuz he's a lot older & she didn't want me 2 get hurt & btw, don't 4get u can't date till u r a lot older & not guys who r almost 3 years older than u. I KNOW. She gave me this lecture w/ Blake . . . blah, blah, blah.

* And what's w/ this getting hurt thing? R she & Mark in on this 2gether? They both need 2 stay out of my biz!

* Mom also pulled some twisted adult psychology: "That's my smart girl. I never have to worry about you."

Ugh. Why did that feel like a bad thing?

Probably cuz I'm wild. I'm smokin'. I SO rock.

CHAPTER 36

SLOPELESS IN DENVER

FEBRUARY WAS MBMS EIGHTH GRADE girls' basketball. We practiced once a week and had a game once a week so I had to fit it in around I-Club. It wasn't Jamball or Gold Crown but it was still fun. We had some decent players and won our first game easily. Our second game was on a Wednesday at home so a lot of people stayed after school to watch and hang out.

When the game was over—we won—and we'd showered and changed, I headed back into the gym. Mark was talking to Carla near the water fountain, which I had to pass to get to my parents. My shoulders tensed. Would he say something mean? Would I? How did it come to this?

As I got nearer, Mark glanced up. Our eyes met briefly before he stepped closer to Carla to let me pass, even though there was a good five to six feet between us. *Hello?*

Mark turned his back. "So, do you think you can?" he asked Carla.

"I don't know." She glanced at me. "Hi, Erin."

"Hey, Carla."

Mark reached out and squeezed Carla's arm. "Let me know, okay?"

Carla looked flustered. "Yeah, okay."

He walked away without even a backward glance at me. Carla and I stood awkwardly for a few moments.

"So, good game," Carla said.

"Thanks." I could tell something was on her mind so I stayed where I was.

Finally she cleared her throat. "Look," she said, "Mark just asked me to play basketball with him Friday after school. I know you two aren't going out or anything but I don't know. I feel like I need to ask you if it's okay."

I felt like someone had punched me in the stomach. Mark was shooting hoops with someone besides me? And someone who didn't even know how to play? He hated playing with newbies. Did he *like* Carla now? Or was he just trying to make me jealous? And why was I even asking these questions? Jeff Massey and I bonded over a speeding ticket and he almost kissed me. I didn't have time for this middle school drama.

"You don't need my permission," I said, the MES (Mature Erin Smile) coming easily. "Have fun."

The Saturday of the ski train, I woke up with my throat so swollen I could barely swallow. My head and nose felt like someone had stuffed them with cotton before shoving my head into a trash compactor.

"I'm sick," I whispered hoarsely into the phone when I called Jilly. "I can't go." I was crying, too, which only made the stuffiness worse. I couldn't believe I wasn't going to be on that train. I'd gotten online and researched Jeff's car and was all ready to talk to him about it. And I was seriously thinking about kissing him. I had planned to just ignore Mark and have fun.

"But you have to go," Jilly wailed. "Who's going to sit with me?"

"Sit with Mark," I said. "I'm sure he'll be glad I'm not going."

"Oh, Erin, I can't believe it," she said. "Do you think it had something to do with driving eighty miles an hour with the top down in that convertible?"

"No," I said. "But my mom sure thought so." When she came to check on me this morning, she shook her head. "I can't believe he was so irresponsible. What was he thinking? It was freezing out."

"Mom, three people in my homeroom were out sick last week with this same flu. I'm sure it wasn't the car."

"I'll report in as soon as I can," Jilly said before we hung up.

My mom got me some orange juice and vitamin C and put me back to bed. I was able to sleep most of the day, but fitfully. One minute I was hot, tossing my covers off, the next I was shivering as if I sat in a tub of ice cubes.

Chris avoided me all day. "I don't want to catch what you've got," he said. "I've got too much going on."

I slept, watched TV, read, and listened to Jilly's messages, which didn't say much except "having fun, but we miss you" because she knew my mom might listen to them first.

I imagined Jeff on the train and on the slopes, heartbroken without me, barely able to have a good time knowing I was practically on my deathbed because of course he knew about my illness with our amazing psychic connection. Maybe he had stayed in the lodge all day worrying about me, ignoring any girls who might be around, waiting until he could check in on me because he didn't get cell service on the mountain and —

"Erin?" Chris knocked on the door later that night. "You alive?"

I burrowed deeper under my covers. "Barely."

"Jeff's on my cell," Chris said, raising an eyebrow in. "He wants to talk to *you*."

Omigod. He was really calling. But how was I going to talk to him? I sounded like I had beans up my nose.

"Erin? Do you want to talk to him or not?"

I held out my hand for the phone.

"Hello?"

"Erin? Jeff." Oh, that voice. "Missed you on the train. Your cute little friend from the mall told me you were sick."

"Yeah," I said. "It stinks." It came out more like "it thinks" which made me feel stupid. And how cute did he think Jilly was? Cute enough to take for a ride in his Mustang? Now that she and Bus Boy had broken up, she was fair game.

"And," Jeff said, interrupting my panic attack, "I thought you'd like to know that I was able to lower my fines and drop the points for the tickets."

Our secret. "So you charmed them," I said. "I'm not surprised."

"Yeah, well."

He paused and I could sense he was going to hang up. *Quick, Erin. Come up with something.*

"Um, so I meant to ask you if your Mustang is a GT? I can't remember."

"Yeah, it is." His voice perked up. "That's cool that you asked." He started explaining some of the features under the hood. I remembered a few from my research but others were a complete mystery. I listened to his voice, smiling contentedly. ". . . so I went with the V-8."

"That's great, Jeff. Wow."

"Well, I hope you feel better," he said. "Who knows? Maybe we'll hit the slopes together sometime."

"That would be great." It would be beyond great. It would be stupendifabulous.

"Okay, can you put your bro on now?" Jeff asked. "I'll talk to you later."

Sunday, February 15

THINGS THAT ROCK BEYOND ALL ROCKING 👄

* I may have a ski date w/ Jeff Massey.
  Okay, we didn't talk abt an actual date
  but maybe we'll hit the slopes 2gether
  like he said. Man . . . riding the lift
  together . . . skiing thru trees . . . maybe
  getting "lost." Oh, yeah.

HOT—✪—METER

💘 #1 Jeff Massey
💘 #2 Jeff Massey
💘 #3 Jeff Massey
💘 #4 Jeff Massey
💘 #5 Jeff Massey
💘 #6 Jeff Massey
💘 #7 Jeff Massey
💘 #8 Jeff Massey
💘 #9 Jeff Massey
💘 #10 Jeff Massey

Jilly called & told me every1 missed me on
the ski train—except Mark I'm sure—he still
h8s me . . . J said MS started out skiing w/ Steve & Tyler but then went
off w/ Rosie & Carla cuz they were better skiers . . . Jilly was stuck w/
Steve . . . said he made her laugh a lot & she had fun but being w/
Steve made her miss Bus Boy.

J said she saw JM in another train car & he was w/ a ton of people, lots
of girls but not 2 worry . . . said none looked like a gf. He said hi 2 her
& asked where I was & then—as we know—he CALLED ME.

Erin P. Massey . . .

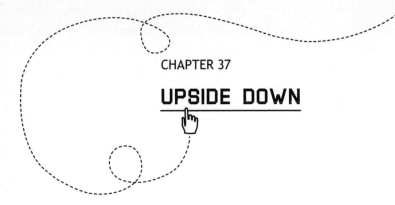

CHAPTER 37

UPSIDE DOWN

THE OFFICIAL MOLLY BROWN MIDDLE School website launched without a hitch on Tuesday, February 24. Well, no hitches except the pictures Steve posted of Carla in her Thanksgiving play costume, spitting out something all over the floor. You wouldn't have known it was her if you hadn't seen the play but pretty much everyone at school had so they all knew.

"That wasn't supposed to go live," Steve said when Carla came storming into the computer lab after school. "I was just showing it to a few people."

"Steven." Ms. Moreno sighed. "Didn't you learn anything from your mistakes last year?"

"I—I—"

"You gave me that unsweetened chocolate after the play on purpose," Carla said, poking her pen at his chest, backing him up against the wall.

"I didn't know it was unsweetened," Steve said, holding up his arms to ward off another poke. "It was an accident."

"Like it was an accident that you had your camera right there, ready to take a picture of me gagging and spitting?"

Steve looked guilty. "But you're so cute when you're spitting."

Carla's face registered surprise—and maybe a little pleasure—before she got back to business. "Nice try, Anderson, but you're dead meat. Erin's going to help me get back at you when you least expect it." She turned to me. "Right, Erin?"

"Absolutely," I said.

"I don't want any flame wars," Ms. Moreno said. "You people settle this thing in a mature fashion—offline."

"How about Sumo wrestling?" Tyler said and everyone laughed, easing the tension.

Steve glanced at Mark. "A little help?"

"You dug yourself into this one, dude," Mark said.

"But you're not going to let Swift get back at me, are you?"

"Swift does what she wants," Mark said, turning away to close down his computer.

"So, I heard about a raging party on the 12th." Reede and I were at our locker Friday morning. "We are totally going."

I wrinkled my nose. I had never been to a party that I could have called "raging." It sounded a little out of my league. Reede shoved me with her shoulder, smiling mischievously.

"Your joyriding buddy is going to be there."

"Jeff? Jeff's going to the party?" My heart skipped a beat. "How do you know?"

"I have my sources," Reede said, looking mysterious. She squinted, thinking. "I guess you'll need a cover since your parents are . . . you know."

I frowned. Of course *she* wouldn't need a cover. Her parents were totally cool.

"A sleepover or something," Reede continued. "Parties like this don't start until late."

"Parties like what?" Jilly had come up, with Rosie close behind.

"High school parties," Reede said.

Jilly stared at me. "No way are *you* going to a high school party."

"Why not?" I asked, suddenly determined to go.

"Well, you're — you know — not really —"

"It's not something you would do," Rosie finished. "You'd have to lie to your parents."

"I've lied to my parents before," I said, sounding braver than I felt. "Besides, I'm so sick of not getting to do things." I turned to Reede. "I'm totally going."

"That's my girl," Reede said, throwing her arm around me. "Who else is in?" she asked, looking at Jilly and Rosie.

"Not me," Rosie said. She looked me in the eye, shaking her head slightly. I felt a surge of irritation at her disapproval. She was the one who said I should do anything I could to get Jeff when she was over on Halloween.

I looked at Jilly, ready to fire back if she gave me grief, too.

"You really want to do this, Erin?" Jilly asked.

I sucked in a deep breath. "Yes."

"Okay," she said. "I'll be your cover."

By the time school got out, Jilly had the entire party plan worked out. I would pretend to spend the night at her house — perfect because we slept over at each other's houses so much, our parents never called to check in. And she was lending me her cell so I could call my parents on it and they could call me. They'd see her name on the Caller ID and assume I was with her.

Brilliant.

"And if they call the house number," she said, "I'll tell them you're in the bathroom and then call you so you can call them."

"But what if your parents answer?"

"They won't," Jilly said. "I always answer. They're always joking that it's my phone, even though I have a cell, that no one ever calls them."

I hugged her. "You're so awesome. I owe you big time."

Monday morning we sat in history, watching Mr. Perkins go nuts about the Civil War. He had images of soldiers from both the north and the south projected on the board and was discussing the south's position when the loudspeaker buzzed. Mr. Perkins flicked off the LCD projector and turned on the lights.

"Please excuse the interruption, but we have an important announcement." Mrs. Porter's voice sounded higher than usual. "Mr. Foslowski, our long time custodian, suffered a heart attack last night and is in the hospital."

The classroom seemed to collapse in on itself. I felt like I was looking down a long dark tunnel. I gripped my desk for support as people around me started talking. It was all I could do to keep from falling over.

"He is not allowed visitors but would welcome cards and notes from students," Mrs. Porter continued. I blinked rapidly, then took a breath, the room coming back into focus. If he wanted cards, that meant he was okay, right? I waited for Mrs. Porter to say more. I thought I heard her blow her nose. "Mr. Foslowski has been a valuable part of our school community for nearly twenty years. We ask each of you to keep him and his family in your thoughts and prayers. We will keep you apprised of his condition and of what we can do to support them." Another voice said something and we heard Mrs. Porter again, clearly talking to someone else while the intercom was still on. "Yes, I said 'prayers' over the loudspeaker and if the ACLU wants to come after me, so be it. This is Mr. Foslowsi."

The speaker crackled again, then went dead. We listened to the hum of the radiator and the clock ticking the seconds slowly by.

Mr. Perkins cleared his throat. "I think it would be best to take the rest of the class to write something to Mr. Foslowski if you are so inclined. I will collect them at the end of the period and make sure they get to him."

No one moved for several seconds. Then Rosie took a piece of paper out of her folder and started to write. A few others did the same.

I picked up my pen, then dropped it. The room seemed to grow warmer by the second. I felt like I couldn't breathe.

Mr. F had a heart attack.

Mr. F was in the hospital.

I bolted from the room, hardly hearing Mr. Perkins calling after me.

"They can't mean *me*," I said to my mom when she came to pick me up. Mrs. Porter knew about my family's friendship with Mr. F and had agreed to let me go home early. "I want to see him." I *needed* to see him. Needed to make sure he was really okay.

When we got home, Dad and Chris were waiting for us in the living room.

"He's in intensive care right now," my dad said as my mom and I sat down next to each other on the couch. "No one can visit except immediate family."

"I *am* immediate family," I said.

My mom brushed her hand over my head. "I know you feel you are, honey, but the hospital doesn't see it that way."

Dad sighed. "We'll keep checking. Every day."

"He'll be okay," Chris said. "It's Mr. F."

"Right," I said, but I covered my face with my hands.

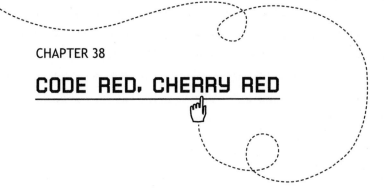

CHAPTER 38

CODE RED, CHERRY RED

THE WHOLE WEEK WAS A blur. I went to class, went to I-Club, did my homework, and worried about Mr. F. But then sometimes I'd forget he was in the hospital and I'd look for him and see strangers washing the windows and wiping the floors and then I'd remember he wasn't here to talk to.

But I did get to chat with him for a few minutes Thursday afternoon.

"Don't let them mess with my closets," he told me when I mentioned the new custodians.

"They had to hire two to take your place," I said.

"Of course," he said, and we both chuckled. His ended in a cough and I gripped the phone hard.

"Are you okay?"

"Yes, yes," he said impatiently. "Everyone is making a big deal out of nothing. This heart is as strong as ever."

I smiled. "You'd better be right. It's not the same without you."

"I appreciate that, Erin P. Swift." He sounded tired but cheerful and I felt better.

In addition to keeping an eye on the temporary custodians, I watched Mark and Carla. It seemed like every time I turned a corner, they were together, heads nearly touching, talking and laughing, and it hurt. Mark had been one of my best friends and now he wasn't anything. I hated it; hated him for not handling everything better.

I was glad I had Jeff and the party to focus on. Friday afternoon I sat in my room, staring out the window. I was picturing myself at the party, seeing Jeff across the room, having his eyes light up as I walked over to him. He'd put his arm around me and introduce me and we would look at each other, remembering our shared times in the Mustang, knowing we'd have lots more.

The following Tuesday we heard that Mr. F had moved to a different room where he could have visitors. Everyone cheered. I was impatient to get home to see if I could visit but Mrs. F beat me to it by calling my parents first.

"Jacob would like to see Erin tomorrow," she said. "But no one else from the school," she told my mom. "Just Erin."

Hospitals stink. Not just because Mr. F was in one, but they just smell. They're full of sick people, except for the maternity ward, and they have that hospital smell that makes you want to turn around and run right back out and suck in the cool, fresh, outside-the-hospital air.

But I didn't run back out because Mr. F was in there.

"He's pretty weak," the nurse outside his room said. "Please limit your time."

"Thank you," my dad said.

As I looked at the door, my legs seemed to turn to rubber. I hung back, clutching my mom's arm for support. "I can't go in," I whispered.

"Take a deep breath," my mom said. "Give yourself a minute."

I glanced up at her. "I'll need more than a minute." I'd need an hour. A day. Maybe a whole year to get up the courage to walk in and see Mr. F in a hospital bed. I thought I could do this, but now I realized

I couldn't. Maybe he didn't want to see me. Maybe Mrs. F had gotten it all wrong and he said everyone from school *except* Erin.

"It's okay to stay out here, Erin," my dad said. "We can go in and explain."

I frowned. The thought of my parents going in and saying I was right outside but didn't have the guts to come in was too much.

"No," I said. "I'll go in."

"He'll look different," my mom said. "But he's the same person." She wrapped her arms around me and hugged me tight. "And that's who you'll see," she whispered into my hair. "The person he is inside. The person you know in your heart."

Tears sprang to my eyes and I squeezed them shut, breathing deeply into her shoulder. Then I pulled away, wiping my eyes.

"Do I look like I've been crying?"

My mom brushed her finger under my eye. "You look like you've been caring."

"Come on, Mom," I said. "Do I have red eyes or not?"

"No," she said, smiling. "You look fine."

"Okay," I said, taking a deep breath. "Let's go."

"Well, look who's here," Mr. F said when we stepped into the room. He had tubes running every which way—out his nose, from his arm, one snaking out beneath the thin white sheet that covered him. My stomach clutched, but I put the MES (Mature Erin Smile) on my face and kept walking.

"I feel like a science experiment," he said, lifting his tube-infested arm.

"You look like one," I said and everyone laughed, which helped. I stood next to the bed and he raised his fist. I knocked it with mine, trying not to notice the way the tubes taped to the top of his hand wiggled.

"So glad you came." Mrs. F gave us all a hug.

Mr. F patted my hand. "I'm worried about my Tootsie Pops. Those can't fall into the wrong hands."

I smiled. "I can bring them here if you want."

"I'd appreciate that," he said. "So, how's Reede?"

"Fine," I said, glancing briefly at my mom. "We've been hanging out."

"Good," Mr. F said. "She needs the kind of friend you can be. Remember the wisdom of the Tootsie Pop." He rearranged himself in the bed. "And the website? How's that going?"

"So far, so good," I said. "Steve keeps doing crazy things, but it's working."

Mr. F started to say something but ended up wheezing.

"Are you okay?" I reached for his hand, squeezing it tight.

"It's all this stuff they're doing to me," he said when he'd caught his breath. "Can't breathe, can't talk, can't hardly eat or use the facilities."

My mom squeezed my shoulder from behind. "It's time for us to go anyway."

I gripped his hand and we held each others' eyes. Then he released his hand and dropped it to the bed.

"I'll be back with the Tootsies," I said, knocking his tubed-up fist.

"I'll look forward to it," he said. He was smiling when I left, his face slightly pink instead of the gray we'd seen when we first arrived.

On Monday I got the Tootsie Pops from Mr. F's closet and brought them home. Mom and I bought more Tootsie Pops and I put the new flavors on top.

We went by to see him on Tuesday but he was sleeping. Out in the hall, I held out the jar of Tootsie Pops to Mrs. F but she shook her head.

"Would you mind bringing them when you come back?" she asked. "I want him to see you and the Tootsie Pops at the same time."

I looked at my mom, who opened her PDA and clicked around.

"We can come on Friday," she said.

I nodded. Friday was the party but it would still work if we went right after school. I needed to be at the bus stop at six forty-five to make the transfers so I could meet Reede at eight o'clock at a restaurant near the party house to change.

"See you then." Mrs. F squeezed my arm and stepped back into Mr. F's room.

CHAPTER 39

PARTY GIRL

I WAS OVER AT JILLY'S house the night before the party because I had insisted she dress me. This was too important to leave in the hands of an amateur like me. As she walked to her closet, she said, "So Chris is definitely not going to be at this party?"

I shook my head. "I heard him making plans with Bethany. They thought about going but decided to go to a movie instead. Just the two of them."

"Well, that's good. Can you imagine if you ran into him? He'd kill you on the spot."

We laughed but inwardly I shuddered. Seeing my brother would be the worst.

Jilly laid out three outfits on her bed. I chose a black lacy V-neck and jean skirt. I gulped. The skirt was a lot shorter than any of mine.

Holding the outfit up in front of me, I turned from side to side. "Well?"

"If Jeff doesn't go crazy for you, he's crazy," Jilly said as she put the clothes in a bag. "Go get him."

On Friday, butterflies fluttered in my stomach as I thought about what I was going to do that night. I could hardly concentrate on our history test. I kept picturing myself in Jilly's outfit, talking easily with older guys before chatting with Jeff in a cozy corner of some house.

When I got home that afternoon, my mom was in the kitchen, talking on the phone.

"That's fine," she said. "I understand. We'll be there around six." She hung up the phone and looked at me. "You won't be able to go to Jilly's until later, honey. That was Mrs. Foslowski. Mr. Foslowski has a test scheduled for four so she'd prefer we didn't come until six."

Six? That ruined everything. There was no way I could get to the hospital, visit with Mr. F, come back here, and make it to the bus stop in time to meet Reede.

"Isn't that kind of late?" I said. "Won't he be eating dinner or something?"

"Margo felt like this was the best time so that's when we'll go."

I called Reede for help.

"The next set of buses for your transfers won't get us to the party until ten thirty or later," she said. "That's just not going to work. Isn't there any way you can get out of it?"

I sighed. How could I not go see Mr. F? I still hadn't given him the Tootsie Pop jar.

But how could I not go to this party?

"I'll be there," I told her. I'd just have to figure something out.

"What's wrong with you?" Chris said as I picked at my food. We were eating dinner early so we could get to the hospital in time. My party clothes were folded neatly in a backpack near the front door. Would I get to wear them?

"Nothing," I said. "It's just that I'm kind of feeling bad about visiting Mr. F right after a test. He'll probably be tired." I looked at my mom. "And you look tired."

My mom sighed. "I am pretty exhausted. I was up until one a.m. meeting a deadline. I don't do those late nights very well anymore."

My dad patted her arm.

"Maybe I could call Mrs. F and see if we can come in the morning," I said. "Mr. F will probably feel a lot better after a full night's sleep."

My mom smiled. "That's very thoughtful, Erin. I think we'd all be a little fresher tomorrow."

I smiled, ignoring the guilty twinge in my stomach when she'd called me thoughtful. It *was* a good idea, even if it wasn't just about Mr. F.

"You know we'd love to see you tonight," Mrs. F said when I called. "But tomorrow would probably be better for all of us."

"Can I talk to him?"

"Oh, I'm sorry, Erin, but they've still got him downstairs for that test," she said. "I'll tell him you called."

"I'll try to call him later," I said. I could at least do that. "Tell him the jar is completely full of Tootsie Pops. New flavors, too."

Mrs. F laughed. "I'll tell him."

An hour later, I stood at the front door with my backpack slung over one shoulder. "I'll pick you up at ten so we can get to the hospital right away," my mom said when I pretended to set out for Jilly's. "Are you sure you don't want me to give you a ride? It's kind of cold out."

I shook my head. "It feels good. And it's only a few blocks."

"Okay," she said. "Call us when you get there."

I couldn't look back at her as I headed down the street. Even though we weren't always seeing eye to eye, I had never lied quite this ginormously before. But sometimes you have to make your own decisions. Try new things. Take risks. At least that's what I kept telling myself as

I walked quickly down the street toward Jilly's, where I would double back and head for the bus stop. Besides, it wasn't hurting anyone. I'd go to the party and have fun, come back, sneak into Jilly's house, and we'd see Mr. F in the morning.

Everything would be fine.

I made the bus transfers no problem and called Jilly from a pay phone after I got off at the last stop. That was her idea—she didn't want her number showing up on Caller ID. She could always say the pay phone number was a wrong number. I had told her she'd make a good spy.

"I just got off the last bus," I reported. "I'm not far from the restaurant where I'm supposed to meet Reede."

"Nervous?"

"Very."

"You've got more guts than I do, Erin."

I smiled, but inside my stomach was twisting in on itself.

"So, tell me again what you're going to do if Jeff is with another girl," Jilly said. She had made me rehearse this with her over and over. "That way," she had explained, "if it happens, you won't freak out. It'll be a bummer but at least it'll feel a little bit like you've already been through it." I had no idea Jilly's drama background would come in handy with relationships and guys.

"I'm going to smile, say hi, then turn and talk to the first cute guy I see, as if I don't care."

"Right," Jilly said. I heard voices in the background. "Time for dinner. Call me later."

I hung up the phone and hurried down the block, picking up my pace as I spotted Reede.

"Hurry up," she said when I got to her. "It's freezing."

The restaurant was so crowded, no one even noticed us as we wove our way through to the bathrooms in the back.

Reede was already dressed in a skimpy tank, black skirt, tights, and boots. She added more makeup and some different earrings while I changed in a stall. Then she did my makeup.

"You have eyelashes to die for," Reede said as she rubbed some shimmering shadow below my brow. Then she added some body jewels to my neckline and some to my left bicep.

She tugged at my shirt and my eyes dropped to my chest in the mirror. Jilly's shirt was tighter than any of my shirts and I was very aware of my perky petes standing out there for everyone to see. I hoped they—and I—were ready for prime time.

Twenty minutes later we stood on the sidewalk in front of a house that seemed to pulse with a life of its own. Muted music wafted through the open front door and people were streaming in and out, each one with a cup or bottle or can in hand. The laughter and shouting got louder as we got closer. I hesitated at the walkway leading to the front steps.

My first high school party. Was I really doing this? Me, Erin Penelope Swift, rule follower, good girl, positive influence?

"This is your night," Reede said, as if reading my mind. "Strut it."

Taking a deep breath, I nodded. Then I swung my hips towards her and we both laughed as we walked up the front steps.

The music seemed to shake the house. People were everywhere, pushed up against the walls in the entry, spilling out of the kitchen, filling up the living room where a big screen TV glowed. I grabbed Reede's hand, afraid I'd lose her in the crowd. She shook it off so I had to keep my eyes on her blond head as we nudged our way to the stairs, where more people sat or stood.

"'Scuse us," Reede muttered, stepping over a pair of legs and narrowly missing a foaming cup of beer on the next step. We reached the second floor, where the music was only slightly less booming; we still had to shout to be heard. After wandering around for awhile, she shook her head. "Let's go back downstairs."

I followed, eager to find Jeff and see what he thought of my stuff.

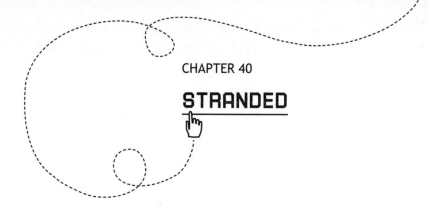

CHAPTER 40

STRANDED

IN THE FEW MINUTES WE were upstairs, the population seemed to have doubled downstairs. The staircase was now completely filled and we had to squeeze our way through. I got stuck against the wall as two girls shoved their way up. One of them did a double take, staring at me.

"You've got to be kidding," she said, eyes roaming my body. "What are *you* doing here?"

"Who is it?" her friend asked.

Amanda Worthington ignored her. "Is your brother here?"

"Excuse us," I said, "we're looking for someone." I pushed past her and moved as quickly as I could down the stairs. "Great," I shouted to Reede as we got closer to the music. "Now everyone is going to know we were here."

"Who was that?" Reede shouted back.

"Serena's sister."

Reede shrugged. "Who cares? You'll be the cool one for coming to this party." I didn't want to think about who else would know once Amanda started talking. We stashed our backpacks behind a sofa in the living room and Reede put her hands on her hips, surveying the crowd. Suddenly she stiffened, swearing under her breath.

"What is it?" I asked.

"Nothing," she said, her eyes glued to something or someone across the room. "I just need to take care of something. We'll hook up later, okay?"

"WHAT?"

"I just need to talk to some people," she said.

"Why can't I come with you?" I hated the slight whine in my voice. But I didn't want to be left with all these strangers. Older strangers. With beer and cigarettes and who knew what else.

Reede's eyes flashed with annoyance. "Grow up, Erin. This is a chance to prove you're not just another middle school infant." She stared at me. "I didn't make a mistake inviting you, did I? You can handle being here without a babysitter, can't you?"

I stared back, my heart pounding—with anger at her for abandoning me and defiance at her challenge. "I don't need a babysitter," I said. "Just go."

Her furrowed brow smoothed out and she smiled. "That's my girl," she said. "We'll find each other later."

No, we won't, I thought as she walked away, waving without looking back before being swallowed up in a sea of swaying bodies. My mind spewed out a few choice names for her. I thought about going after her and saying them to her face when I felt a hand on my butt. I turned to see who had touched me, but there were too many people and no one was looking at me. I ducked around two guys, knocking one on the elbow. Beer sloshed across my shoulder.

"My bad," I mumbled, brushing my shirt off. Great. Now I smelled like beer. I took a breath, the anger I'd had at Reede slipping away, leaving me feeling weak and alone. Did I look as clueless as I felt? Were people staring at me, knowing I was in middle school, that I'd never been to a party like this?

I skimmed faces, hoping to find Jeff, but they were all people I didn't recognize.

Until I looked to my right.

Blake Thornton stood across the room, his arm around a girl. It was a different girl from the one he had been with at the basketball game. I tried to duck behind someone but he had already seen me. His face registered surprise as he checked me out, then he smiled slightly, turned, and kissed the girl. And kept kissing her.

I slipped away, shrinking against the end of the wall separating the living room and dining room. Let him come up for air and see me not watching his stupid make-out session. Who was the immature one in this picture? I adjusted my skirt and crossed my arms over my chest, continuing my scan for Jeff.

"You go to Washington?" An unfamiliar voice shouted in my ear over the music, the stink of beer wrinkling my nose. I could feel his chest against the back of my shoulder and I stepped forward, putting some space between us before I turned around.

The guy was about four inches taller than me, his muscles bulging under a tight T-shirt. His brown hair was gelled, his face rugged with a few days' worth of stubble.

"Uh, no," I said, sidestepping to a folding chair. If I had to, I could jump over it and throw it back at him. "I go to a private school."

He wiggled his eyebrows. "One of those all-girls schools?" he asked, moving toward me. "You must be ready for a little action." He took another step and I gripped the top of the chair, ready to heave it and make a break for it. He walked toward me, his beer sloshing in his hand.

"So, what's your name?" He was just a few feet away. I could see a scar on his nose and a tiny diamond stud in his left ear.

I lifted the chair a few inches off the ground —

"No way. Erin?"

I whipped around and found myself looking into Bus Boy's friendly blue eyes. I was so relieved to see a familiar face I nearly threw my arms around him.

"Hey!" I moved so he was between me and Mr. Action. Mr. Action looked at me, then at Bus Boy. Shaking his head, he turned and got sucked into the crowd. I heaved a sigh of relief. "Wow. Thanks, Bus Boy."

"Um, do you think you could call me Jon?"

I smiled, still giddy with relief at having someone I knew, someone I trusted, standing right next to me, even if he had dumped my best friend. I resisted the urge to tie our arms together with a shoelace or something. "Sorry. Old habit." I squeezed his arm, needing contact. "You really saved me from that guy. Thanks."

"No worries." He looked past me. "Is Jilly here?"

I shook my head. "She's —" I was about to tell him she was just hanging out at home. What kind of friend was I? "She had other plans," I said, shrugging.

Bus Boy's face sagged. "Right. Okay. Well, can I get you something to drink?" He held up a Coke can. "Or are you not allowed to talk to me because Jilly and I broke up?"

I couldn't just let that slip by. "You mean because *you* broke up with *Jilly.*"

Bus Boy smiled. "If you want to get technical. But she's obviously moved on so it doesn't matter, does it?"

Oh, geez. I was really bad at this stuff. Had I blown it by letting him think she was out with another guy? But she didn't want to get back together with Bus Boy. She'd told me that.

"Is that just Coke?" I asked, changing the subject.

Bus Boy laughed. "Yeah. I don't drink."

"I'd love a Coke," I said. "I'll come with you." Being seen with a guy was probably okay. In fact, maybe it would improve my cool factor. Bus Boy was definitely cute. I would probably have him on my Hot-o-Meter if he wasn't Jilly's ex.

Just as I popped the top on my Coke, Reede stumbled by, wearing some guy around her shoulders. I thought I recognized him as one of the guys she was with at the Washington High basketball game. Her smile froze when she saw me, her eyes glassy and a bit unfocused. She'd been drinking.

"Reede," I said.

"Who's your friend?" the boy-collar asked her, pointing at me.

"Just someone from school," Reede said, avoiding my gaze.

"We sure miss Harper," Boy Collar said to me, squeezing her in a bear hug. "You'd still be with us, baby, if you hadn't —"

Reede turned and kissed him full on the mouth, shutting him up before pulling him backward through the crowd. I scowled. Just someone from school? Is that how she saw me? Wasn't I good enough for her other friends? And where did he miss her from? That didn't make any sense.

"I can't believe her," I murmured, turning back to Bus Boy. But before I could say anything else, my heart triple-flipped.

CHAPTER 41

OPERATION ERIN P. MASSEY

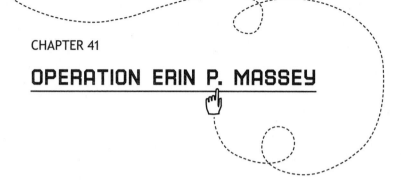

JEFF MASSEY SAT ON THE arm of a couch, talking to a girl next to him. Another girl was leaning over the back, her chin on his shoulder, like a parrot perched on a thick branch. A couple of guys sat around a coffee table in front of Jeff, trying to bounce a quarter into a glass.

What should I do? I couldn't just walk over there. He had girls all over him. But this was what I'd come for, right?

I glanced past Jeff. The back wall was a row of windows, with a sliding glass door leading out to a patio. I could see people standing underneath gas heaters outside. Perfect. I could act like I was heading out there and had to pass the couch on my way and Jeff Massey, hunk of the universe, just happened to be sitting right there.

"I think I'm going to see what's out back," I said.

"Besides the keg?" Bus Boy asked.

I smiled. "You never know."

He glanced at Jeff. "Want some company?"

Did I? I didn't want Jeff to think I was with Bus Boy. But if things didn't go well, it would be nice to have Bus Boy right there. Before I could make up my mind, Jeff looked up.

His eyes roamed up and down my body before his face broke into a grin. "Erin! Wow." He motioned me over. When I got closer, he grabbed my wrist and pulled me onto his lap. I could smell his beer breath but it didn't bother me; he was still the most incredibly gorgeous guy I'd ever seen.

Parrot-Head Girl stood up and sat on the back of the couch, glaring at me.

Jeff wrapped his arm around my waist. "She's thirteen going on thirty," he said to Parrot-Head.

Did he have to mention my age? But at least he thought I acted older. Besides, I was sitting on his lap and she wasn't. I tugged my skirt down as one of the guys on the floor peered up at me.

"I'll be fourteen next month," I said, immediately regretting how lame it sounded.

"She's adorable." Parrot-Head Girl spoke in a way that said I was anything but. She tried to pat my head but I ducked and she missed.

"Want some?" Jeff held his beer out to me.

I looked at the amber bottle. I hated the taste of beer, but I didn't want to look like a middle school infant in front of all these people. Besides, Jeff's lips had been on the top of that bottle. If I put my lips there, it would almost be like we had kissed.

"Is it cold?" I asked.

Jeff grinned. "Ice."

I took the bottle from him, smiling.

"Erin." Bus Boy shook his head at me.

I ignored him, putting the bottle to my lips. I tilted it back, took a big swig—

—then gagged and sprayed a mouthful of beer all over Jeff.

"Crap!" He shoved me off his lap, sending me sprawling against the guy on the floor who'd been playing with the quarters. The guy grabbed the coffee table, tipping it over on top of both of us. The beer bottle flew out of my hand and smashed against the wall, showering everyone nearby.

"Aaaa!" People screamed and wiped themselves off.

I struggled to get free but I was stuck under Mr. Quarters and the table. I pushed hair out of my eyes and looked up at Jeff. "I'm—I'm sorry."

Jeff just scowled and kept wiping his shirt.

Someone pinched my thigh and I slapped the hand away.

Then people started giggling and pointing at me. I struggled to get free just as a pair of sleek black boots stepped in front of my nose.

"My, my, what have we here?"

I looked up into the face of Amanda Worthington, her perfectly plucked eyebrows arched over her blue eyes.

"Erin Swift making a fool of herself? How unusual." She shook her head, then stared at me. "No froggie undies for *you*, eh?"

I looked down and froze in horror. Jilly's jean skirt was bunched up around my waist, the pink hearts on my black underwear like little neon lights flashing: *Look here! Look here!*

I struggled to pull the skirt down, squirming to break free of the guy and the table. Where was Bus Boy?

"Swift?" Parrot-Head asked. "As in Chris Swift?"

"Oh my God!" another girl cried. "Is that the girl who did that blog thing last year?" She turned to Parrot-Head, cracking up. "How many pairs of froggie underwear ended up in Chris's locker after that stuff went around?" The BN strikes again. Chris was going to kill me.

"Oh my God!" a third girl shouted. Was there an echo in here? "She's *that* girl?" She smacked her hands against the couch, throwing her head back in laughter. She started talking to Jeff and I knew he was getting an earful about the YOHE and my personal, private, no-one-will-see-but-me blog.

He wrinkled his nose, then laughed. Hard. He looked back at me, shaking his head. He started to say something but then stopped as Parrot-Head said something else to him. He cracked up again and I wanted to melt through the floor. Jeff Massey—Man of My Dreams,

Sharer of Musical Taste, Fellow Criminal, Flirt Extraordinaire—was laughing . . .

. . . at me.

Jilly hadn't prepared me for *this*. I squeezed my eyes shut, holding back prickly tears. I had to get out of there. Mustering the last of my strength, I pushed into the back of the guy on top of me. He grunted and rolled, setting me free. I stood up a bit wobbly, adjusting my skirt once more. A few guys whistled but I ignored them.

I felt a hand on my arm and was about to dig into it with my fingernails when I recognized the voice.

"Sorry," Bus Boy said in my ear. "Some girl pulled me away to help her with —" He stopped talking and looked at me, concern in his eyes. "Are you okay?"

I shook my head.

Bus Boy grabbed my hand and I clutched his arm with the other, stumbling after him as my vision blurred with tears. He pulled me through the throngs until we were safe in the living room, far from the scene of my latest humiliation. I flopped down in the first empty chair and wrapped my arms around my knees, hiding my face.

"They're jerks," Bus Boy said, sitting on the arm of the chair. "Don't waste your time worrying about it."

I took a breath, sniffled, and looked up at him. "Thanks for not abandoning me."

"You're welcome." Putting his hand on my shoulder, he spoke gently. "I need to go find the guys I came with, but I'll be right back." I must have looked as panicked as I felt because he squeezed my shoulder. "I won't be gone long. I promise. Do you want me to call anyone?" He held up his cell.

"I've got a phone," I said, holding up Jilly's cell. I leaned back against the cushions. It felt good to sit here, away from just about everyone. I looked around at all the people in the next room—talking, dancing, drinking, making out and probably other things I didn't want to think about. I shouldn't have come. I didn't belong here. I didn't want to be here.

I glanced down at the floor, spotting a purple Tootsie Pop wrapper all wadded up.

Mr. F. I'd forgotten to call Mr. F.

I checked Jilly's phone. Ten-thirty. It was too late to call.

I blinked back tears. I should have gone to visit him. I should never have come to this stupid party. I wanted to go home. Who could I call at ten-thirty? Or text?

Text. That was it. I couldn't text Jilly because I had her phone. So who?

Taking a deep breath, I flipped open the phone.

I know u h8 me, I typed. *But I need help. Pls call-E.*

I flipped through the phone book until I found Mark's cell number, then pressed Send.

After I got my backpack from behind the sofa, I returned to the chair, bouncing my legs up and down as I stared at Jilly's cell, willing it to ring. What if Mark's phone was off? Or maybe he was ignoring me. Why would he care? He totally hated me. He probably knew he was right and was having a good laugh about it. *Look,* he was saying to anyone who would listen. *I told her not to come crying to me when she got hurt and here she is doing it.*

I looked at the display and let out my breath. I was just about to call Bus Boy and beg a ride when the phone rang.

"Thank you," I whispered into the phone. It was so good to hear Mark's voice, I nearly burst into tears. He listened while I explained where I was. I didn't tell him about the NOHE (Night of Humiliating

Events)—I was sure he'd hear about it soon enough through the wireless, textable grapevine. "I just want to go home," I said, my voice ragged with near-tears. "I don't know what to do."

"I'll figure something out," he said. "Just stay where you are. I'll call you back."

Closing my eyes, I took a deep breath and lay on the arm of the chair, covering my face with one arm. I promised myself I would never do anything like this again if I could just go home. I kept peeking at the phone under my elbow, making sure the ringer was on. Mark wasn't calling back. Twenty minutes went by. Then thirty. Mark had no plan. He had abandoned me too.

I tried to call Bus Boy but he didn't pick up. I could beg a ride off a stranger but what if they were too drunk to drive and I couldn't tell? And how would I tell them how to get to my house? I hadn't paid attention on the bus. I wasn't sure I could give directions.

Tears welled up again and I dropped my head in my hands, sobbing.

"Erin?"

My eyes flew open. My brother stood looking down at me, eyes dark. I wiped my own eyes, streaks of black mascara and eyeshadow smearing my fingers. Bethany sat down next to me and put her arm around me. "You okay?"

"What are you doing here?" I asked.

"Mark called me," Chris said.

"Don't be mad at him," Bethany said. "He didn't know what to do so he called Chris. He figured that was better than telling your parents or his. He didn't want you to get in trouble."

I nodded, wiping my face again before picking up my backpack.

"Did you come with anyone?" Bethany asked.

"Let me guess," Chris said, "That chick who smokes got you here."

"I just want to go home," I said.

Chris's cell rang as we headed outside. He looked down at the display. "It's Mom and Dad."

"Did you tell them where I was?" My eyes burned into him.

He shook his head.

"Don't answer it," I said. "Just take me to Jilly's."

Chris sighed. "It might be about something else." He flipped open his phone. "Hello?"

I could hear my mom's voice, high and loud, her words tumbling over each other so I couldn't make them out.

"Yeah," Chris said, looking at me. "I've got her."

I dropped my head.

My life was over.

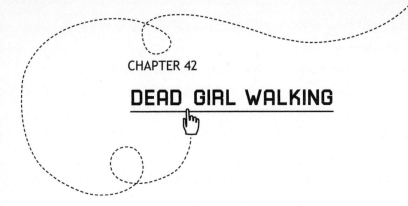

CHAPTER 42

DEAD GIRL WALKING

"ARE YOU OUT OF YOUR mind?" My mom's whole body shook as she stood in front of me in our living room.

"I'm sorry," I said for the zillionth time. It didn't seem to make any difference.

"Sorry isn't enough," my dad said, pacing nearby. "What you did was beyond irresponsible, it was dangerous." He leaned over and grabbed me by the shoulders. "Do you have any idea what could have happened to you? On a bus across town at night? Not to mention that party. My God." He held my shoulders before a look of disgust came over him.

"You've been drinking!"

"No!" I tugged at my shirt. "I wasn't drinking. Honest. Someone spilled beer on me."

My mom grimaced.

"Reede abandoned me once we got to the party," I said. "I didn't know how we got there so I didn't know how to get back. I wanted to come home."

"Don't put this off on Reede," my dad said. "You made the decision to go with her. You could've called us if you wanted to come home."

"And you *lied* to us," my mom said, her eyes blazing. "Right to my face you told me you were spending the night at Jilly's. And you changed our visit with Mr. Foslowski so you wouldn't miss this party!" She shook her head.

Something inside me snapped. "I wouldn't have to lie if you didn't treat me like a baby!" I said. "I've never done anything before to show you you couldn't trust me but you still kept saying no to everything I wanted to do. You never let me do anything!"

"Don't you *dare* blame this on us," my mom said, eyes blazing. "What you did was wrong. Totally and completely wrong." She stopped pacing and looked right at me, dropping her voice so I could barely hear it. "I don't even know you anymore."

She turned on her heel and strode out of the room and up the stairs.

The room was quiet except for the refrigerator humming in the kitchen and the rush of hot air from the heater vents beneath the table against the wall. The silence was worse than the yelling. Way worse.

My dad stood looking at me for a moment, then turned his back. "Go to bed. We'll talk about consequences in the morning."

I stood by myself in the living room for a few minutes, my body numb, my mind blank. And then my anger took over.

I snuck into the family room and blasted off a nasty e-mail to Reede. Then I picked up the phone. I didn't care how late it was, I was going to say a few things to her. I carried the phone down to the basement closet, which used to be my Defcon 4 place to go when things got a little bad and I needed to get away. My fingers shook as I punched in her number and I rehearsed what I would say if one of her parents answered; but all I got was some scratchy answering machine. When I heard the beep, I just let it all out.

"Reede, this is Erin. I don't care who hears this. I can't believe you left me alone at that party and went off with some guy and got drunk." I took a breath. "I got in so much trouble because of you! You are such a —"

"— oh, tragedy," Reede's voice startled me and I almost dropped the phone. "I was grounded for a few weeks for going to a party," she mimicked, "my life is over." I could almost see her rolling her eyes. "It's not my fault you couldn't handle it. Besides, I should be mad at you for leaving without me."

"You blew me off!"

"Don't be such a baby, Erin. You should be thanking me for giving you the experience of your life."

"What?" My anger rose. "I didn't know anyone. I was pinched and grabbed and humiliated —" I stopped, not wanting to relive it. "I thought you were my friend," I said, fighting against the stupid tears filling my eyes.

There was a pause. "You thought wrong," Reede said. "Now go back to your perfect family and take your punishment like a good little girl."

Click.

"I hate you!" I said, tossing the phone. It cracked against the back wall of the closet before dropping to the carpet. I slid down the wall, sobbing into my arms. When I'd cried myself out, I got up slowly and crawled my way up to bed.

It was still dark when my parents woke me up. I sat straight up, my heart pounding. The clock said four a.m. I'd only been asleep for a couple of hours.

"What's wrong?" I said. "What is it?"

I couldn't see their faces in the dimness but I heard my mother's voice, quiet and sad.

"Margo Foslowski just called."

My sleepiness made me stupid. Was she calling to change our visit? Why couldn't she wait until later? And why were my parents waking me up to tell me?

"Mr. Foslowski —" My mom's voice broke and she covered her face with her hands.

Dad reached over and took my hand. "He passed away, honey."

I stared at him, felt his warm hand around my fingers. It suddenly felt hot. The whole room felt hot.

"No," I whispered. Then louder: "NO." I pulled my hand away and scrambled around my dad to stand next to the bed. "You're lying," I said, clenching my fists at my sides. "You're saying that because of what I did last night. I can't believe you'd do that. I hate you!"

"Erin." My mother stepped toward me but I backed away. "Honey, we'd never lie about something like this. Mr. Foslowski —"

"Don't say it again! Don't you dare say it!" I held up my hand, stopping the words, wanting to stop what I already knew was true. "Don't say it! Don't say it! Don't say it!" I repeated it over and over, willing myself to concentrate only on those three words — don't say it. Don't. Say. It. Dontsayit — until they didn't make any sense, until they weren't words anymore but just a jumble of sounds that had to come out of my mouth so the pain and hurt couldn't come in.

I don't know how long I kept it up but at some point I realized I was kneeling on the floor, my arms across my stomach, rocking back and forth, sobbing and mumbling, my dad's strong arms around me.

MR. F WAS DEAD.

There. I could say the word now, at least in my mind.

He was DEAD.

I covered the jar of Tootsie Pops on my desk with a towel.

Then I lay on my bed, rain pounding against the window, like a monster trying to get in.

I didn't think it would ever stop.

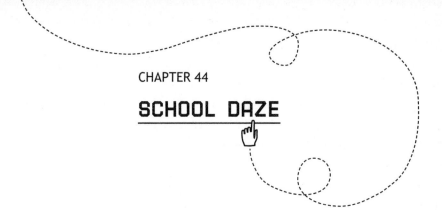

CHAPTER 44

SCHOOL DAZE

THE RAIN FINALLY STOPPED BUT the monster had gotten in.

It was huge, thick, suffocating. It squeezed me in muscled arms until I could barely breathe. It made my heart heavy, filling it with sand while my mind spun with images and thoughts that weighed me down even more—the lies, all the lies, and going off to a party while Mr. F lay dying in a hospital bed. I was angry one minute, drenched in sorrow the next.

I stayed home from school for two days. My parents didn't know what to do with me. I knew they felt bad about Mr. F but they were still upset about the party, especially my mom. She could hardly look at me and when she did, her face was full of anger and sadness mixed together in a way that made her look like someone I didn't know.

"I know you feel terrible about Mr. Foslowski," she said to me at lunch the second day I stayed home. "We all do. He was a good man, a dear friend. But that doesn't change what happened Friday night." They had grounded me—from the phone, from the computer, from everything—and my mom only talked to me when she had to, like when I was helping Mrs. F, or she had to give me a phone message, or tell me to set the table.

It was a relief when Jilly came over with pictures from the Foslowskis' so we could put photo posters together for the memorial service.

It felt good to do something for someone else, and for a few brief hours, I was free of guilt.

I trudged up the stairs onto the bus behind Jilly on Wednesday morning. My parents wanted me to go to school before Mr. F's funeral on Friday. Something about helping me get back to normal. Like there was such a thing.

I stood in the bus aisle, staring down at Jilly's backpack so I wouldn't have to look at anyone. The fluffy kitty face she had attached to the zipper swayed slightly back and forth and focusing on it calmed me. People were whispering behind their hands as we passed but I kept my eye on Fluffy Kitty. She was my guide.

"Are you okay?" Jilly whispered as we sat down in the back of the bus.

I shook my head. She reached over and squeezed my hand. Tears filled my eyes. I was so tired of crying. I wiped them away fiercely, flinching at the sting on my chapped cheeks.

"I'm really sorry you got in trouble about the party," I said to change the subject.

"Quit apologizing," Jilly said. "I'm sorry I blew your cover." It turned out that after Mark had called Chris and while Chris was on his way, my parents had called Jilly's to tell me we were going to see Mr. F at nine instead of ten and it was the one time Jilly didn't answer. Busted.

"But they took away your cell phone," I said to Jilly.

Jilly shrugged. "Not forever. I'll survive."

I told her about Bus Boy, how great he'd been in both of my moments of need, how I thought he wanted to get back together with her.

"He's a good guy," she said, sighing.

"Do you want to get back together with him?"

She shook her head. "It's been fun joking around and flirting with different guys, hanging out with my friends. I hope we can be friends someday, though. I miss talking to him."

The bus screeched to a stop and Rosie got on, sitting in the seat in front of us. She turned around. "I feel so bad about Mr. Foslowski," she said. "I just can't believe it." Jilly gave her a look but it was too late. Tears sprung to my eyes.

"I was supposed to visit him on Friday," I said. "But Reede made me go to that stupid party." I turned away, my vision blurry.

"It's okay, Erin." I felt Rosie's hand on my arm.

"It's not okay!" I shouted. "I hate her!"

I knew Rosie and Jilly were exchanging looks over my head and I hated that too. "Just leave me alone," I said, covering my face with my arms.

When we got to school, Jilly and Rosie walked on either side of me and slightly ahead, like bodyguards. As we approached the doors, a guy I hardly knew stepped in front of us, blocking our way.

"Did you really go to Autumn Browne's party and flash your underwear?"

Jilly shoved him at the same time Rosie ordered: "Move." If I hadn't been so numb, I might have been impressed. I'd never seen Jilly act tough before.

"What's your problem?" he said, but he stepped out of the way.

As I passed, he said, "I heard the cops came. Were you there for that?" He didn't wait for an answer. "They arrested a bunch of people. I heard Reede Harper was caught stealing a portable DVD player. Had it under her shirt." He shook his head. "How stupid can you be?"

"Unbelievable," Jilly said when we finally got into the building. "I can't believe she stole a DVD player. Did you know about that?"

"No," I said. And I didn't really care. I hoped she rotted in juvenile detention. Mr. F was dead and it was Reede's fault I didn't get to see him one last time.

When we got to the top of our hall, Jilly stopped. "Do you want me to come with you to your locker?"

I stared down the long hall. It seemed to go on forever and ever without any end. I didn't want to be here. Didn't want to walk around the halls and not see Mr. F.

How could my parents think this was a good idea?

Jilly squeezed my arm. I knew what she was talking about. I shook my head. If I had to face Reede, I wanted to do it alone. I didn't want her to think I couldn't handle it by myself. "I'll see you in language arts."

Jilly hugged me. "Good luck."

I approached my locker slowly, relief flooding me when I saw Reede wasn't there. But Mark was. He looked at me expectantly, like he was waiting for permission or something.

"You okay?" he asked.

I shrugged.

"I'm sorry," he said. "About Mr. Foslowski. About the party."

"Why?" I said. "You didn't do anything."

"You're not mad at me for calling Chris?"

I shook my head, dropping my backpack at my feet. "I was already busted." It suddenly seemed so long ago. It didn't really matter anymore.

"I'm glad you texted me," he said.

Something in his voice made me look at him. Mark Sacks. Former crush, possible former friend. A guy who was always there for me, even when I wasn't there for him.

"Me, too," I said finally. "You were the only person I wanted to talk to." I took a breath. "So you're not mad at me anymore for—you know?"

He shook his head. "It was stupid to be mad. You can't start liking someone just because they want you to." His hair had fallen back over one eye and his smile filled his face. He was so cute. How could I have forgotten how cute he was? Even the new zit next to his nose was cute.

Just as the bell rang Carla came up, standing beside him. He smiled at her. Like they shared a secret or were about to.

Mark glanced briefly at me. "See you later?"

"Yeah," I said, trying to smile at Carla. I didn't think it was possible to feel any worse than I already did. Part of me wanted to yell: *How can you go on with your lives? How can you start going out as if nothing has happened?*

And why hadn't anybody told me about them? Carla should have talked to me like she did about playing basketball. But why should she? Why should anybody tell me anything?

And why did I care?

I turned and dialed my combination, hoping they'd wait to hold hands or whatever until they were out of sight. Flinging open my locker, I grabbed the door to keep it from banging against the locker next to it.

"Omigod."

The locker had been stripped bare of all but my two photographs and my books. I hadn't realized how much of the locker held Reede's stuff until now. Her mirror and white board were gone. So were the magnets that held photos and notes and scraps of song lyrics. Her books were cleared off the shelf. There was absolutely no sign she had ever been there. It was as if she'd never existed.

I pulled my books out quickly, slammed the door, and headed down the hall.

"You look freaked," Rosie said, falling into step beside me. "What's up?"

"Reede's gone," I said, explaining about the empty locker. *And Mark is going out with Carla and nobody told me. And Mr. F's dead and I still can't believe it.*

"People are talking," Rosie said. "Everything from her getting arrested to running away to moving back to San Jose."

I pressed my lips together. Any of those was fine with me.

Fourth period we had a history test. As I bit the end of my pen, Mr. Perkins stopped at my desk and squatted down so we were eye to eye.

"I know you've been dealing with a lot, Erin. If you don't get a passing grade, we'll talk about a makeup."

I gave him a grateful look. "Thanks."

After I turned in my test, I stood for a moment next to Reede's desk. Part of me wished she was sitting there so I could hit her or wrap her earbud cords around her neck.

As I trudged through the day, I ignored all the party and underwear comments. After the YOHE, I had a lot of practice with this kind of ignoring. I headed for the bathroom before my last class. I needed a quiet place for a few minutes and hoped the bathroom would be empty.

It wasn't.

"I wouldn't have believed it if Serena's sister hadn't seen you with her own eyes." Two of Serena's friends stood at the sink at the far end, looking at me.

The other one raised her eyebrows. "She said you were so magazine cover, she hardly recognized you." The girl laughed. "Of course, that was before you flashed everyone your cute little heart undies and then —"

"Shut up, Jo." Serena banged out of one of the stalls, striding straight towards both girls. "Just shut up, okay? My sister's a jerk."

I looked at Serena, surprise making me forget how I felt for a moment. But she didn't look at me; her eyes were trained on her friends.

Jo smiled uncertainly, giving Serena a little shove. "You've got to admit it was funny. Don't you wish you could have been there? Don't you wish —"

"Mr. Foslowski died," Serena said evenly. "Does anyone care about that?"

The girls' expressions changed. "Well, yeah. Of course. We were just —"

"Leaving?" Serena asked. "Good."

The girls hurried out the door, tossing dirty looks at Serena.

Serena turned to me, her voice soft. "You okay?"

I shrugged.

"You want to be alone?"

I nodded.

"You got it."

She pulled the door open and stepped out, planting herself in front of the doorway with her arms across her chest, daring anyone to cross her path. As the door closed behind her, my eyes filled with tears of gratitude.

"Thank you," I whispered, even though I knew she couldn't hear me.

Wednesday, March 24

Dad gave me this notebook. "Sometimes it helps to write things down," he said. "With your hand and not a keyboard." I guess that was nice of him, even though he was the one who banned me from the keyboard he was talking about.

It's funny, but when I type in my blog I use shortcuts and stuff, but in this notebook I write everything out. You'd think it would be the opposite since I type faster than I write. Weird.

Even though I'm grounded, Jilly is allowed to come over because of Mr. F but no one else and I can't go to anyone's house. Today she came over and told me she tried to e-mail Reede and the message bounced back. When she tried to call, the phone was disconnected. I don't know why Jilly is trying so hard when she never even liked Reede in the first place. When I asked her she just said she couldn't explain it. "I know you're mad at her but something isn't adding up," she said. "Besides, you told me Mr. F kept saying she was worth knowing." I guess she's a detective in addition to being a spy.

I told her Mr. F was wrong. That Reede was probably his biggest mistake ever.

I thought yelling at Reede and telling her how I felt would make me feel better.

But I feel worse. Even though she replied to my nasty e-mail with one of her own and said those mean things to me on the phone, I only want to strangle her sometimes. Other times I just feel crazy sad.

I don't understand that. And I don't really feel like writing about it either.

CHAPTER 45

MESSAGES

I COULDN'T BELIEVE ALL OF the people at the funeral. Old people. Young people. People in between. The whole church was filled with people who cared about Mr. F and right away I noticed a whole row of kids directly behind the row for the family—the kids in the photos in his closet. I had found out they were kids he knew from a place called the Helping Hands Center. He volunteered twice a week, tutoring kids, listening to them, and just being there for them. I recognized Olivia and some of the others from the photos. It made me smile to remember Olivia as the "best hugger."

Everyone who came received an Order of Service program and a Tootsie Pop with a message attached. Messages like, "Smile at someone who is rude to you today" or "Send a thank you to someone who helped you."

My message read: *Make a connection with someone you haven't seen in awhile or with whom you've had a falling out.*

Wrong. Today was a Strangle Reede day. *I'm not making any connection with Reede unless it's my fist to her face, do you hear me, Mr. F? Okay, maybe I wouldn't really hit her but you were totally wrong about her. She didn't need a friend like me and no way did I need someone like her in my life. I don't need people who abandon me and move away.*

I stuffed the Tootsie and message into my purse and followed my parents to a pew.

My mom sat on one side of me, with Jilly and her family on the other. Mark, Tyler, Carla, Steve, and Rosie were in the row behind me, along with tons of people from Molly Brown.

Jilly reached out and squeezed my hand. The service began and I cried through the whole thing. People kept getting up and saying how great Mr. F was and talking about all the stuff he did. Not only did he tutor at Helping Hands, Mr. F also bowled on Friday nights and his team had shown up in their Nicky's Pizzeria shirts. He was also involved in his church and he and Mrs. F liked to fish. The more I listened, the more I realized how little I knew about him. In all our conversations, I'd rarely asked him about his life.

My heart was heavy and I felt a desperate desire to run. But as much as I wanted to, I knew I couldn't. This was Mr. F's service. I had to stay.

After it was over, we went to a reception in a big room off the chapel. We stood in line, waiting our turn to talk to Mrs. F. There were five grandkids standing next to each other. I saw one boy pinch the girl beside him. She smacked him. I looked at Chris.

"Brother and sister," we said at the same time, smiling. Then we frowned because the smiles felt like a betrayal.

A few minutes later, Mark walked over. Carla hovered nearby, looking uncomfortable, with Steve just behind her. Mark gave me a hug. I held on tight, sinking into his arms, smelling his familiar Mark smell. I didn't care what Carla thought; I just wanted him to hold me. "I'll call you later," he said, squeezing my shoulders as he slipped out of my grasp.

As we got closer to Mrs. F, my stomach clenched and I felt lightheaded. "I can't face her," I said to my mom.

"You need to," my mom said, squeezing my elbow.

When it was our turn with the family I hung back, but then Mrs. F opened her arms and I stepped into them before bursting into tears.

"I should have come that night," I whispered over her head, not sure she could hear me. "I'm sorry."

"Not to worry, Erin," she said, brushing a strand of hair from my face. "No one could have known." *Don't be nice to me,* I wanted to scream. *You don't know what I did. If you knew, your eyes would turn dark like my mom's and you'd hate me.*

Mrs. F smiled, unaware of the emotions rolling around inside me. "You were a special friend to Jacob."

"He was *my* friend," I said, my voice clogged with tears. "But I never did anything for *him.*" Saying it relieved some of the pressure in my chest. Mrs. F pulled back so she could look at me. She handed me a tissue and I blew my nose. "Oh, Erin. That's not true at all. You gave him such a gift." Her eyes glistened, but she held my gaze steadily. "Our grandchildren," she said, nodding toward the five kids now in line at the food table, "live in New Jersey so we don't get to see them as often as we'd like. Jacob loved talking to you and feeling like he was making a difference in your life." She squeezed my shoulder. "He was so proud of you. He always talked about how smart you were, how capable. He was so impressed at the way you handled things last year, and this year you were doing even better."

I hung my head. "But I —"

"People are waiting," my mom whispered in my ear.

"No matter what," Mrs. F said, looking me right in the eye, "he loved you and I love you." She reached into her pocket. "And he wanted you to have this." She held out a small white envelope. On the front was my name, written in shaky handwriting. I bit my lip, willing myself not to cry. Had he written this the night I was at the party and hadn't visited? Oh, God, I was suffocating again.

I hugged Mrs. F and hurried outside, sucking in big gulps of air.

A few minutes later my parents came out. We all climbed into the car for the ride home. I rolled the window down and shoved my head out like a dog catching a scent. But I still felt claustrophobic.

"Can you pull over?"

My mom turned around, concern on her face. "Are you sick?"

I shook my head. "I need to get out. I need to walk."

"But it's almost two miles to our house," my dad said.

"Please," I whispered, my hand on the door handle.

My parents exchanged looks.

"Let her walk," Chris said. Then he held out his cell. "Call us if you need a ride."

I gripped the phone like a life raft, mouthing "thank you" to Chris.

My mom nodded to my dad, who pulled the car over to the corner. "Don't forget to call if you need us," my dad said. I raised a hand in response before putting one foot quickly in front of the other. It felt so good to move, to feel my muscles working, my breath pulling in and pushing out as my heart pumped. I started to run. Maybe if I ran I would be able to fly, and maybe if I could fly, I would finally get away from the weight of the guilt.

I ran, but I couldn't fly. By the time I reached my house, my legs were rubbery and I was exhausted. I could barely climb the stairs to my room but when I got there I collapsed on my bed, begging sleep to give me a brief escape.

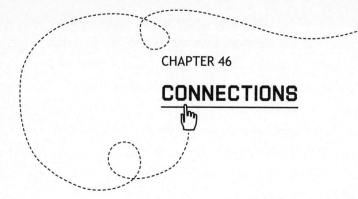

CHAPTER 46

CONNECTIONS

MR. F'S FUNERAL ON FRIDAY was the start of spring break. On Saturday I walked into the family room where my parents were reading. They looked up at the same time, concern and questions in their eyes.

"Is everything okay?" my dad asked.

"I just wanted to talk to you," I said. "Is this a good time?"

"Of course." My mom put her book down and sat up. I perched on the edge of the chair opposite them and gripped my knees.

I took a deep breath. "I'm sorry I yelled at you. I'm sorry for everything. I know I went a little crazy and did some really stupid things." I shook my head. "Sometimes I can't believe it was *me.*"

My mom nodded.

"And I know it will take a long time to earn back your trust but I hope I can." I took a breath and let it out. "I'm just really sorry."

"Thanks, Erin," my dad said.

My mom stood up and knelt next to my chair, her hand on my knee. "I'm sorry, too, honey," she said. "Sometimes I forget what it was like; wanting to fit in, try new things, grow up overnight. Parents get scared. There are so many things we can't protect you from, we try to at least protect you from the things we can." She sighed. "We've always been so close, Erin, and then to see you pushing me away, treating me like

I'd seen other daughters treat their mothers—it was more than I could stand." She sighed. "And then Mr. Foslowski—"

"I know."

"There are a lot of things your dad and I have been discussing," Mom said, "and I think you were right to an extent. I was still treating you the way I had since you were about ten, not really changing the rules to account for how you'd grown and matured." She sighed, smiling ruefully. "And maybe I didn't want to face it, you growing up, not needing me as much anymore."

I knelt on the floor next to her and wrapped my arms around her. "I'll always need you, Mom." She hugged me tight and I sunk into her. It had been a long time since we'd hugged. I had no idea how much I'd missed it.

"Hey," my dad said. "What am I, chopped liver?"

I laughed as I got up to give him a hug. "I'd say you're at least hamburger. Maybe even steak."

"Thanks a lot," he grumbled, but his smile gave him away. "You're making me hungry with all this talk of meat," he said. "How about a cookout?"

"That would be great," I said. Dad stood up and squeezed my shoulder before heading out.

Mom put her arm around me. "I'm glad you came to talk to us. I know it wasn't easy."

"Part of the whole maturity, getting trust back thing."

Mom smiled and we sat for a moment in silence. I looked down at my hands. "Mom?"

"Yes?"

"I had my period," I said quietly. "Back in September."

"I know."

I looked up. "You do?"

She nodded. "I saw the signs. Laundry, trash, you know."

That explained why there were always supplies around when I needed them.

"Why didn't you say anything?"

Mom shrugged. "I figured you had a good reason for keeping it to yourself and you'd tell me when you were ready."

I glanced away. "I'm sorry I didn't tell you."

"Me, too." Her eyes were bright. "But you know something? We're in sync now."

I smiled. I knew she wasn't just talking about our cycles.

"So, I was wondering," I said. "Is it too late for lunch and chocolate?"

Mom smiled. "It's never too late for lunch and chocolate."

Monday, March 29

I'm back to writing in my blog. I'm not sure I'll keep it up but we'll see.

& yes, it's official. The Hot-o-Meter is out of service. Possibly permanently but never say never. It just seemed so middle school 2 keep a list of guys I think r hot when I'm so close 2 going 2 high school.

THINGS THAT CONFUSE ME

✱ Mark's being nice but also keeping some distance . . . (I think he's close 2 announcing that Carla is his girlfriend but isn't sure how 2 tell me).

✱ I feel sad when I think abt that.

THINGS THAT ARE VERY INTERESTING 👁

✱ Kara & Tyler made out in the custodian closet.

✱ They didn't get caught—except by me—& I think Mr. F would be okay w/ that.

✱ Jilly, who always had 2 like some1 or have a bf, is now totally happy just hanging out w/ me & her other friends.

✱ Jilly hasn't mentioned any guy since she & Bus Boy split & hasn't done any GF/BF quizzes in her mags.

OTHER STUFF

✱ I've been going over 2 c Mrs. F, helping her around the house & just talking about Mr. F. It makes me feel closer 2 him 2 be w/ her.

✱ I've got Rosie, Tyler, Carla, Mark, Jilly, & even Serena going 2 the Helping Hands Center w/ me once a week. It's really fun.

Olivia runs out 2 meet me every time, giving me the best hugs in the entire world. I live 4 those hugs & I can't wait 2 go every week.

I would like 2 have gone there w/ Mr. F. I wonder if he ever would have invited me or if I ever would have asked 2 go.

I like 2 think he would have or I would have.

(sigh)

CHAPTER 47

UNDERCURRENTS AND OVERFLOWS

TYLER CALLED MARK AND ASKED him if it was okay if he went out with Kara. Mark called me right after.

"I started laughing," Mark said to me. "I mean, it was so weird."

"What did you tell him?"

"That he didn't need my permission and it had been a zillion weeks since we broke up."

"Good answer," I said, thinking about how broken up Kara had been; how I'd caught her kissing Tyler. I'd never told anyone. I figured it was their business.

"Well, I guess this means I'm definitely free to ask out other girls." Ah ha. He had just been waiting for Kara to be with someone else so he could go out with Carla.

"Definitely," I said, surprised at how easily Mature Erin came out, almost like it was natural.

"Really?" Did he have to sound so excited to ask Carla to go out with him? But what right did I have to be bummed? I should be happy we were back to being good friends. We were proving that Harry and Sally thing wrong. That was a good thing, right?

"Sure." I rolled my basketball on the floor with my foot.

"What about you?" he asked. "You got your eye on anyone?"

"Maybe," I said, lying through my teeth.

"But not the guy with the car? The one you went to see at the party?"

"No," I said. "It's someone else." *Someone I used to like, then didn't anymore, but now I think I do again. An undercurrent of liking.*

There was a pause. I could hear him breathing through the phone. I had a memory of his Goldfish breath. I wondered if he had eaten any today.

"Will you tell me first?" he asked finally. "Before you start, you know, going out in public?"

"Sure. Will you tell me about yours?" *Even though I already know?*

"Deal."

My Mature Erin Smile couldn't have been any bigger, even though he couldn't see it.

And my heart couldn't have felt any heavier.

Monday, April 5

ONE THING THAT FREAKED ME OUT BUT I GOT OVER IT ⚡

I ran in2 Jeff Massey. My mom & I were in the store buying toothpaste & shampoo (thank goodness there were no feminine hygiene products in the cart). He was w/ 1 of the girls from the party—not Parrot Head. They had their arms around each other. I tried 2 sneak down another aisle but he saw me. They both smiled @ me. Please. But I did apologize again abt spitting on him & he goes no worries & WINKS @ me. Can I puke now? I am not 2 be winked @—I'm almost 14! He goes c u next year . . . yikes . . . forgot we'll be @ the same school . . . & not just him but a lot of people from that party. Hope they all have short memories.

I got rid of the heart undies . . . maybe that will help.

So life goes on. I don't know how, but it does. Mr. F is dead but people r crushing on other people & making out in closets & not getting caught & I'm actually paying attn 2 it again. Not like I used 2. It just doesn't seem 2 matter as much now. But it makes me laugh & it's something 2 talk about.

ONE THING THAT BUMS ME OUT WHEN I KNOW IT SHOULDN'T 💔

✱ Mark seems really happy abt being able 2 go out w/ Carla . . . didn't seem bummed @ all that I might like some1 else . . . need 2 get over him—AGAIN—& be happy that he's happy.

Okay, visualization time, like Jilly taught me. If I'm ready for it, it won't hurt so much when I c it in real life . . . I'm picturing Mark & Carla holding hands in the hallway. Mark w/ his arm around Carla. Mark kissing —

> **In Memory of Jacob Foslowski**
>
> ---
>
> Excellent cleaner, great listener, dispenser of good advice & delicious Tootsie Pops. Friend extraordinaire.
>
> I love you & I miss you.

Not helping. Hurting. & I've had enough of that 4 awhile. Maybe I'd be better off living right here, right now . . . not preparing 4 things that might never happen, like Mr. F said . . . you can never really be prepared.

4 anything.

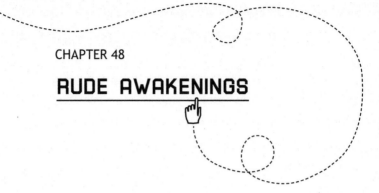

CHAPTER 48

RUDE AWAKENINGS

MAKE A CONNECTION WITH SOMEONE you haven't seen in awhile or with whom you've had a falling out.

I stared at the crumpled Tootsie Pop message from Mr. F's service.

"Fine," I said aloud. "But don't blame me if it doesn't go well."

Reede had always been sort of vague about where she lived and every time I suggested we go to her house, she always had an excuse.

Now I knew why.

I sat in our car on Wednesday, staring up at an apartment complex, the brick cracking in spots, the paint peeling. This wasn't the big house I'd pictured her living in with her genius computer dad and perfect, beautiful mother. The bus stop was across the parking lot and I saw why she knew the bus system so well. That's how she got around. To school, to the mall, to my house—everywhere.

"Do you want me to go up with you?" my mom asked, but I shook my head. She patted my arm. "Well, then wave to me so I know she's home," she said. "I'll run across to the grocery store for a few things and come back for you."

I walked up the two flights of stairs to Apartment 340 and stood in front of a door in need of paint as badly as the rest of the building. I reached out and pulled off a piece of paint, staring at the faded blue in my fingers before dropping it. Then I took a deep breath and rang the bell.

One Mississippi, two Mississippi, three Mississippi. Nothing. They must be out. If their phone hadn't been disconnected, I could have called first. But now I'd wasted time coming here and —

Footsteps behind the door — fast, angry. The door swung open and a tired, annoyed woman stared at me. She was wearing black pants and a stained white shirt with a "Hi! My name is Cammie!" nametag pinned to it. Her hair was pulled back in a messy bun and her makeup was heavy. I could see hints of Reede in her, though, and knew this was her mother.

"Yeah?" Mrs. Harper narrowed her eyes and clutched the door tightly against her side, as if I might barge in at any moment. She smelled like the party had — stale beer, cigarettes, and leftover pizza — with a heavy dose of perfume to try to cover it up.

"Is Reede here?" I asked. "I'm Erin Swift. A friend from school."

Mrs. Harper raised an eyebrow. "She's around here somewhere, except when she isn't." She looked over her shoulder. "Reede!"

I cringed. Part of me wanted to vault over the side wall, falling the three stories down and taking my chances with broken bones so I could be back in our safe, familiar car. But I didn't. I turned to wave over the wall at my mom, then faced Mrs. Harper.

"You a friend from last year's school, this year's first school or this year's second school?"

I frowned. "This year's first school, I guess." I looked past her. "So, you're not moving back to San Jose?"

Mrs. Harper snorted. "I don't know why she keeps telling people that every time she screws up and has to change schools. We haven't lived there for years. Not since I divorced her sorry excuse for a dad when she was six." She cocked her head. "She also told you he worked with Bill Gates, right?"

I shifted uncomfortably. "Not exactly."

"He fixed computers," she said. "Repaired them. Swapped out parts, replaced hard drives, that kind of thing. That was the extent of his computer knowledge." She jerked her head over her shoulder. "Reede!" Mrs. Harper didn't move to let me in so I stood on the landing, my arms wrapped around me against the cool April afternoon.

"What!" Reede's voice rose from somewhere behind Mrs. Harper, sharp with annoyance.

Mrs. Harper opened the door just wide enough to show Reede that I was standing outside. I was struck by how pale she looked. Her face seemed sunken and bland without her makeup, though her eyes blazed at me.

"Get out of here!" she shouted, before turning on her heel, practically running from the room.

I stared after her, shocked. "I'm s-s-sorry," I stammered to Mrs. Harper. "I would have called first but —" I looked away, embarrassed. "— your phone is disconnected."

"That would be because her sorry excuse for a dad is behind on child support," Mrs. Harper said. She cocked her head at me, rubbing her red lips together.

"Maybe I should come back another time."

"Whatever you want," Mrs. Harper said. "I've got to get to work." She strode back toward the hallway. "Reede! I'm going to work!" she shouted. "Do whatever for dinner. I'll be late." As she returned to the door, she patted my shoulder. "If you try to talk to her again, you'll need more than that jacket to protect you."

I looked down at my thin jean jacket as she slipped past me, the heavy scent of her perfume lingering behind. Then I looked through the open doorway into the apartment. The easy thing would be to reach out, close the door, and run down the stairs to my mom. Reede didn't want me here. I didn't want to be here. The whole place gave me the creeps.

But something kept my feet planted on the cracked cement.

Taking a deep breath, I stepped inside, closing the door behind me. The carpet was bare in spots, the couch sagging in the middle, with coffee stains and cigarette burns on one side. I saw a stack of Internet and web design books from the library on the floor next to the couch. No computer. Maybe it was in her room. But somehow, I doubted it.

Music blared from behind the closed door. I knocked twice. Then louder. I was about to knock again when the door flew open.

"Leave me alone!"

I caught sight of the room behind Reede — clothes all over the floor, makeup scattered across a dresser. There were no posters or pictures on the wall, just peeling paint.

Her gaze wavered when she saw it was me, then her face hardened again. "I told you to go away." She slammed the door.

"Reede," I said, knocking. "I just want to talk."

The door flew open again. "You want to talk?" Her face screwed up in an ugly sneer. "About what? What a horrible person I am like you said in your e-mail? Or maybe you'd like to move on to something different like the fact that I live in a dump. That I lied to you. That my dad isn't a bigwig Internet guy and the only thing I know about web design is what I learned in books and when I can get online at the library. That my whole life is a lie." Her eyes were bright, her fists tight at her sides. "Is that what you want to talk about?"

I shook my head. "I'm sorry I said what I said. I don't think you're a horrible person. I just —"

She flipped her hair over her shoulder and I caught sight of something familiar.

"Omigod!" I said. "My mom's earrings!" The Celtic knots dangled from Reede's ears. "I can't believe it. Give those back!" I reached for them but Reede turned her head away, elbowing me in the cheek.

"Ow!"

She took the earrings out of her ears and threw them at me before slamming the door in my face. I stood frozen for a moment, heart bouncing crazily in my chest. Then I bent down and picked up the earrings, gripping them in my fist. "I could call the police, you know!" My breath came fast, tears of anger and frustration pricking my eyes. "I could tell them you stole them!"

"Go ahead!" Reede shouted through the door. "I dare you!"

I pounded on the door. "Mr. Foslowski died!" I screamed. "He died and I was supposed to visit him but instead I was on a bus going to a stupid party that YOU MADE ME GO TO. Then you abandoned me and he died! I hate you, Reede Harper! I hate you!" I banged the palm of my hand against the door, hardly aware of the sting shooting through it.

Bolting out of the apartment and down the stairs, I wiped my hand across my nose before pulling the Tootsie Pop message out of my pocket. I ripped it up into tiny pieces, letting them flutter behind me as I hurried across the parking lot. When I slid into the front seat of our car, I pulled the door shut and yanked at my seatbelt. I was shaking so much, my fingers fumbled to click the buckle into place. I sucked in a quivery breath before dropping the earrings on the console between us.

"Happy?"

My mom picked up the earrings gently; they glinted in the sunlight. She sighed deeply. "No," she said. "I'm not."

I leaned my head against the window, my anger seeping out of me. "Let's just go home."

It wasn't until we had turned down our familiar street that I noticed my mom's hand wrapped around my own. She pulled it away to steer into the garage.

"Sometimes what you see on the outside is trying to hide what's on the inside," she said as we got out. "I'm proud of you for trying."

"Please, Mom," I said, opening my car door. "I've had enough fortune cookie sayings for a while."

But her words stayed with me as I lay in bed that night. I kept picturing Reede in that apartment with her mother, without her dad, without a lot of things. Thinking of her trying to be cool, to have fun, to be someone, anyone, and maybe not being herself.

Of being someone on the outside who hid someone else on the inside.

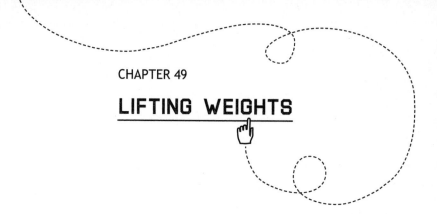

CHAPTER 49

LIFTING WEIGHTS

THURSDAY I SAT AT MY desk in my room, staring at the jar of Tootsie Pops. Sun streamed through my window, illuminating the jar, making the wrappers look brighter. I traced my finger across the glass, images of Mr. F at school flashing through my mind: Tipping his Windex bottle at me, handing me a dustrag, knocking fists, the messages at his memorial service —

— the lies I'd told, the party I'd gone to, my parents waking me up in the middle of the night. I stood up, shaking my hands, like I could shake the guilt right off my fingers.

But I couldn't.

I sighed and stood up, pacing around my room. I'd thought trying to talk to Reede would help. Of course, that ended in a shouting match so instead of feeling good, I felt horrible. Then I had sent her an invitation to my birthday party with a note saying I was sorry for getting so mad. I thought sending the invitation and the note would make me feel better. It did, but only part way. There was still more yucky feelings down inside me.

And I knew there was probably only one way to get rid of them.

*   *   *

A cool breeze blew at the cemetery Saturday morning. Mrs. F and I stood in front of Mr. F's gravestone, which read: *Beloved father, devoted husband, friend of many.*

"Mrs. F?"

"Yes, Erin?"

I shifted on the uneven grass. "That Friday, when we were supposed to come visit him? The day before he —" I stopped. I still couldn't say the D word around Mrs. F.

She didn't say anything, just rearranged the flowers at the base of the gravestone.

"I—I lied to you." My shoulders sagged. "Instead of visiting him that night, I —"

Mrs. F held her hand up, silencing me. "Don't tell me," she said. "Tell him." She pointed to the mound of dirt in front of us. I bit my lip as she stood up. She reached over and squeezed my arm, her eyes full of warmth. "Tell *him*."

I watched her walk slowly down the road away from me, her yellow shirt bright against the green grass rolling out all around us. Kneeling down next to the dirt mound, I pressed my fist into the hard soil, blinking back a tear. Then I pulled Mr. F's envelope out of my back pocket. Two weeks had passed since the funeral and I still hadn't been able to open it. I stared at the wobbly writing: *Erin P Swift.*

Slowly, I slid my finger under the flap, tugging it open.

> *Dear Erin,*
>
> *You have been a bright red Tootsie Pop in my life. I have enjoyed our talks at school and our friendship. Like Margo probably told you, our grandkids are far away and you have been kind enough to make an old man feel needed.*
>
> *You are meant to do great things, Erin. I look forward to seeing what those great things are going to be. I feel privileged*

to be part of your journey, wherever it takes you and wherever
I am.

    Fondly, your friend,
    Mr. F

My shoulders shook as I cried. Did he know? Is that why he wrote the note? Did he know he wouldn't see me again?

"Why didn't you tell me?" I said out loud. "You should have called me."

But that was wrong. And I knew it. The truth had a way of wiggling out from under excuses and blame, waving at you like a little kid begging for attention.

"So I went to this party," I whispered. "I was supposed to visit you and I would have if you hadn't had to have that test and we couldn't come till later. But see, I was supposed to meet Reede at eight which meant catching the bus at six forty-five which I couldn't have done if we'd come to see you." I paused, sucking in a breath. I let out a long, ragged sigh. "I'm sorry I didn't come. I should have come. The party was stupid and horrible but even if it wasn't I should have come. I can't stand that I didn't come. Please don't hate me for not coming. I'm so sorry."

I drew my knees up and sobbed into them, wrapping my arms tightly around myself. I wasn't meant to do great things. I was just meant to screw things up, then apologize for them afterward. That was the story of my life.

I don't know how long I sat there, rocking and sobbing, wiping my arm across my nose, but then there was a shadow and a hand holding a tissue and Mrs. F kneeling next to me with her arms around me, saying, "It's okay, everything's okay, everything will be okay." I couldn't tell if she was comforting me or herself or both of us and it didn't matter. It just felt good to be in her arms.

Before we left, I stuck a cherry Tootsie Pop in the dirt. "Remember the wisdom of the Pop," I said, my voice hoarse but stronger. "I know I will, thanks to you." I patted the dirt before standing up.

I walked slowly across the grass beside Mrs. F, the blue sky stretching endlessly beyond the trees, a few wispy clouds brushing across like a painter's afterthought. I breathed in deeply, aware of the freshness of the air, the soft beat of my heart and how the weight around my shoulders had slipped a little.

I turned and knocked my fist toward Mr F.

I'm pretty sure he knocked back.

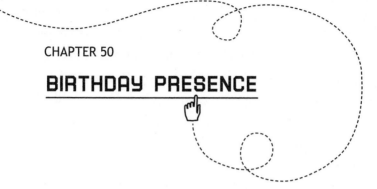

CHAPTER 50

BIRTHDAY PRESENCE

REEDE CAME TO MY BIRTHDAY party. I was stunned. I really hadn't expected her to. She showed up about half an hour into it, with some of us playing badminton and my parents and Mrs. F flipping burgers and dogs.

"Reede!" I ran to meet her, throwing my arms around her. The hug took her by surprise and she stood stiffly for a moment, before hugging me back awkwardly. "I'm so glad you came," I said.

"Hey, Erin." She pulled back and smiled shyly. "I figured you could use my cool factor."

I laughed. "You look great." And she did. Younger, fresher . . . happier. Her hair was a light brown—no evidence of bottled blond anywhere—and her makeup was light, summery. She wore jeans and a loose shirt.

"It's been awhile since I've been to this kind of a party," she said, nodding toward the badminton net, where my friends were trying to pretend they weren't watching us. She waved tentatively and they all waved back. "So, thanks for the invitation. I didn't expect it after . . ."

". . . you slammed the door in my face and I told you I hated you?"

Reede smiled ruefully. "Yeah. That." She looked away. "Sorry I freaked when you came to the apartment. It was like—I don't know. Like you didn't belong in that picture. You're such a nice person with a perfect family and a great house and —" She shrugged. "That apartment was a dump." Her shoulders slumped slightly, but then she straightened them. "But we're in a really nice place now. Across town. Sorry Excuse Dad finally came through. Big time. I'm going to West Highland." She gave me a shove. "More middle school babies. You know."

I smiled.

She looked out across the yard for a moment, then turned back to me, eyes bright. "And I'm sorry about dissing you at the party. That guy I was with? He went to my old school and I was afraid he would blow my cover." She looked me right in the eye. "You figured out that I'm a year older than you and that I didn't just move here from Silicon Valley, right?"

I shrugged.

"I got held back," Reede said. "Not applying myself and all that. Hated seeing all my buds ahead of me. It sucks but that's the way it is."

"Who cares?" I said. "I know I don't."

"You're all right, Erin P. Swift," she said, cocking her head. "By the way, what does the P stand for? Perfect? Pretty? Popular?"

"Pariah," I said. "Didn't you hear about the whole underwear thing at the party?"

She laughed. "If anyone can survive that, you can."

I pointed toward the deck. "Want some food?"

"After I talk to your mom about her earrings." Without waiting for a response, she strode right over to my mom, who was helping my dad get burgers and dogs onto plates. My mom stepped away and Reede started talking, dropping her head a few times. Then my mom said something, and Reede looked right at her. Mom reached out and squeezed Reede's arm and she grinned. She practically bounced over to me, something I would not have expected from the sophisticated Reede Harper.

"Your mom's cool," Reede said. "You're really lucky."

"Yeah," I said, smiling over at my mom, who waved at me. "I am lucky." We stood for a moment, listening to the drone of a lawn mower in the distance.

"I'm really sorry about Mr. Foslowski," Reede said quietly. "I really liked talking to him, you know? Poor guy heard a lot about me and the stuff I didn't tell him, he figured out on his own." She smiled ruefully. "He was on to me from the beginning but he never said anything to anyone. Just let me screw up and eventually find my way."

I smiled. "Yeah, he was good at that." We started toward the steps of the deck.

"Hey, did I tell you I quit smoking?" Reede said. "Our apartment is brand new and I told my mom I didn't want to stink it up, you know? So she's trying to quit, too. It's pretty sad. We stand around chewing gum, snapping at each other all day."

I laughed. "Well, that's good. I think." I motioned her up on the deck. We leaned against the railing, watching the badminton game.

"So," Reede said finally, "Serena is now officially a part of your posse?"

"Serena has turned out to be a good friend," I said, thinking about how she'd defended me in the bathroom against her so-called friends. "I never thought I'd say that, but it's true." I looked at her. "My mom always says people can surprise you."

"Your mom's a smart lady." Reede cocked her head, her eyes still on the players. "And I'm glad to see you finally hooked up with the Hottie with the Hair. It took you long enough."

I shook my head. "He's with her," I said, nodding to Carla.

Reede laughed. "You know, for someone named Swift, you aren't very."

I narrowed my eyes at her.

"Open your eyes, Erin. She's with him —" She nodded toward Steve, who was trying to toss the birdie at Carla's head. "And he —" she said, nodding to Mark, "— is still crazy about *you*."

"Right," I said. But inside my stomach did a little skip.

Everyone left around eight, except Jilly, Mark, and Mrs. F, who all insisted on cleaning up.

Reede promised to keep in touch. "We've even got a computer and slower than a turtle dial-up, thanks to Sorry Excuse," she said before she left.

I sat at the table on the deck, watching Mark talking to Jilly as they picked up trash.

Mrs. F sat down next to me. "Remember that boy you liked last year who didn't like you and then he liked you this year but you didn't like him?"

I looked at her and burst out laughing. "Where's your Windex bottle?" I asked.

Mrs. F laughed, then nodded toward Mark. "Why don't you ask that nice young man to go for a walk with you."

"I can't," I said.

"Of course you can," Mrs. F said. "Just open your mouth and say the words."

"I've already had my chance—more than one chance actually— and I blew it. Besides," I said, looking down at my hands, "it wouldn't be right."

"Erin Penelope Swift! Don't talk nonsense. You know Jacob would be absolutely exasperated with you right now."

I sighed deeply. "He said I was meant to do great things."

"And you have," she said. "Look at Reede. And Serena. And the kids at the Helping Hands Center."

"Those are different," I said. "What's so great about going on a walk with Mark?"

"Only you can answer that," Mrs. F said. "But you won't be able to if you don't do it."

"You sound just like Mr. F," I said, and we both laughed again, before tears pricked my eyes. "I miss him so much." The words tightened my throat.

"Me, too," Mrs. F said, squeezing my hand.

We sat for a few moments, crying and sniffling, and then we were quiet, watching as a breeze fluttered the leaves on the aspens next to the deck.

"You know," I said, breaking the silence, "last year he said a good friend can be better than a boyfriend."

"Mr. F said a lot of wise things," Mrs. F said. "But he always left it up to us to make the choices, didn't he?"

I nodded.

"People change," Mrs. F said, looking out on the lawn at Mark again. "Circumstances change." She reached into her pocket and pulled out a Tootsie Pop. "I'm sure you'll handle these circumstances with your usual good sense, Erin P. Swift."

I spun the basketball on my finger as Mark and I headed down the street toward the court at our neighborhood park. We walked in silence, the only sound the basketball's steady rhythm against the sidewalk as we bounce-passed it back and forth to each other in the yellow glow of the streetlights.

He nudged me before snatching the ball and twirling it high, out of my reach. We got to the park and started shooting to warm up. Then we played a game of one-on-one. He won the first game easily, reaching above me to get just about every rebound. When had he gotten so much taller than me?

"No fair," I muttered, but he just laughed.

We took a break after the second game, hands on our knees, breathing hard. I glanced at him, then away, swallowing.

"Hey, Mark?"

"Yeah?"

"Remember on the phone, when we promised each other we'd tell the other person if we were going to start going out with someone?"

Mark's expression was unreadable. "Yeah."

"I think you've been wanting to tell me something, but haven't because of Mr. F and all."

Mark dropped his eyes.

"Carla's great, Mark. Really. I think —"

"Carla?" He laughed. "You think I want to go out with Carla?" He shook his head. "She likes Steve."

"But you've been with her so much," I said. "I thought . . ."

"I did ask her to play basketball that one time to make you jealous," Mark admitted. "But then I told her and we laughed about it. We're friends. She wanted me to help her get with Steve."

Geez, Reede was like psychic.

"Oh." It did explain why it was taking so long for them to go public.

I snatched the ball and went around him for a layup. He went up for the block and when we came down, our arms tangled and we fell behind the basket into the grass. I landed on top of him, my face inches from his.

"Haven't we been here before?" I said.

"Yeah," he said, a question in his eyes.

"This time," I said, "it ends differently." And then I kissed Mark Sacks. *Really* kissed him. His lips were soft and warm and it was like we'd always been kissing, it was so comfortable and familiar.

When we pulled apart, we looked at each other and smiled.

"Hi, Harry," I said.

"Hi, Sally."

I sighed. "So much for proving that theory wrong."

"Who cares?" Mark said, squeezing my hand. I squeezed back and we sat in the grass, enjoying the night air.

"So," I said, breaking the silence. "You aren't afraid this will ruin our friendship?"

Mark shook his head. "I've been waiting a long time for this. I'm willing to risk it."

I smiled before pulling my hand out from under his and jumping to my feet. "That block you made was such a foul."

"What?" Mark leapt to his feet. "No way."

"Totally."

"Not even."

I grinned and lined up on the free throw line. "It's my birthday, remember?"

"Only because it's your birthday," he grumbled, trying to hide his smile.

I bounced the ball twice, bent my knees, then bounced again before shooting the ball. It arced into the sky, then dropped neatly through the metal net with a satisfying clang.

"Yes!" I pumped my fist in the air and Mark laughed and grabbed me and we kissed again.

When we came up for air, Mark raised an eyebrow at me. "You're not going to put all this in your blog, are you?"

His question made me pause. I realized how little I'd been on the computer, except for I-Club. Between school and sports, and going to the Helping Hands Center and hanging out with Mrs. F, I really hadn't had time to be online or even write in my blog.

Funny, but I hadn't really missed it.

"No," I said to Mark, smiling.

Some things just weren't meant to be written down, to be catalogued and listed, to be analyzed and quizzed about.

I took Mark's hand.

Some things were just meant to be.

And that was pretty great.